A TASTE OF HONEY
DeWanna Pace

Toya and Betina have been friends forever. But can their friendship survive when Toya is promised to a man Betina secretly loves?

WHERE THE HEART IS
Sheridon Smythe

Orphans Natalie and Marla were like sisters. And now as adults, when the orphanage was destined to be sold under Natalie, Marla had plans—to match her up with the orphanage owner!

LONG WAY HOME
Wendy Corsi Staub
(July 1999)

Cira Valentino and her best friend, Lucia, are desperate to reach America. But when disaster strikes, can a handsome American heir save Cira, and make her and Lucia's dreams come true?

Where the Heart Is

Sheridon Smythe

JOVE BOOKS, NEW YORK

FRIENDS is a trademark of Berkley Publishing Corporation.

WHERE THE HEART IS

A Jove Book / published by arrangement with
the author

PRINTING HISTORY
Jove edition / June 1999

The Penguin Putnam Inc. World Wide Web site address is
http://www.penguinputnam.com

ISBN: 0-515-12412-5

A JOVE BOOK®
Jove Books are published by The Berkley Publishing Group,
a division of Penguin Putnam Inc.,
375 Hudson Street, New York, New York 10014.
JOVE and the "J" design are trademarks
belonging to Penguin Putnam Inc.

PRINTED IN THE UNITED STATES OF AMERICA

10 9 8 7 6 5 4 3 2 1

Friends are as valuable and irreplaceable as your great-grandmother's china. I know, because I have a best friend. (I don't, however, have my great-grandmother's china.) And because I'm one of the lucky people who have a long-lasting friendship, writing my portion of this book came as naturally as breathing.

Donna, here's to another twenty-something years of friendship, and God bless you for putting up with me.

Sherrie Eddington

I'd like to dedicate this book to real-life potential hero material. A heartbreaker from day one, easygoing, lovable, intelligent, gorgeous, and ever so charming—my second-born son, Marcus Bryan McGuirk. This one's for you, Markie. Someday you'll read about yourself because you've got all the right stuff. I love you.

Donna McGuirk

Where the Heart Is

Prologue

1875, Chattanooga, Tennessee

"Your new ma and pa are here," Natalie Polk announced from the doorway of the room she shared with her best friend, Marla, and several other orphaned girls. "I told them you'd be right down."

"Okay."

Holding on to a brave smile, Natalie clasped a handful of her homespun dress and twisted the rough material, watching as Marla carefully wrapped an old garment around her most precious possession, a music box. It played a timeless tune, popular since 1823, "Home Sweet Home." The music box had been salvaged from the rock slide that had killed Marla's parents and younger sister. Marla often gathered her orphaned brothers and sisters around and played the music box, lifting everyone's spirits and reminding them in a voice old beyond her ten years that someday they would be taken into a loving home. Marla had never given up hope, and now her adoptive parents were waiting proudly in the parlor for their new daughter. The event was both inspiring and traumatic to them all.

Natalie swiped at her wet cheeks with a grubby hand and said with as much dignity as an independent seven-year-old could muster, "The Masons seem nice." She meant it, even if Mr. Mason's beard needed trimming, and Mrs. Mason smelled of sweet peach brandy. They had given each child a peppermint stick and a nice smile—a rare treat for the orphans of Ivy House.

When Marla finished wrapping the music box and faced her, Natalie saw that Marla was about to cry, too. She was happy that Marla was being adopted but sad to lose her best friend. What would she do without her? What would they *all* do without Marla? Marla never let them give up hope and was always there to wipe a tear or lift a chin.

"I'm going to miss you." Marla's voice wobbled endearingly. "Everybody, in fact. But . . . I'll be back to visit. Mrs. Mason said I could. She promised." Patting the bed beside her, she urged Natalie to sit. When Natalie had climbed onto the bed, Marla said earnestly, "Now, remember, if you ever need me—for *anything*—just holler. I'll find a way, even if I have to walk! You and me are like sisters, Natty, and we'll never let anything come between us." She spat into her palm and held it out. "Let's make the spit promise."

Natalie spat into her palm and clasped her hand firmly against Marla's, sealing the promise. She nodded vehemently. "Nothing," she whispered. "I swear it."

"And when I grow up and get married, I'm gonna adopt a child from this place," Marla declared. "All of them, if I can." It was a wild, passionate promise, but at the moment, Natalie believed that Marla meant it with all her heart.

"Your husband might not like that," Natalie said. She'd watched couples come and go, saw them avoid the hopeful gazes of the older children and eye the younger ones far too critically.

Marla tossed her black curls. "Then I won't marry

him, if he don't like it. You'll do the same, won't you, Natalie?"

Natalie flushed, pulling her hand free and wiping it on her dress. "Mrs. Boone says no man will want to marry me because I don't know who my pa is. She says my mama was a who—"

Aghast, Marla clamped her hand over Natalie's mouth before she could finish the ugly word. "Bite your tongue! And don't listen to Nelda Boone. She was probably corned on that cheap whisky she buys with *our* money. Mrs. Mason told me that your ma was a fine schoolteacher—"

"She *knew* my mama?" Natalie bounced on the bed in her excitement, jiggling the cloth-wrapped music box. Marla grabbed it and held it against her chest in a protective gesture. Chastened, Natalie grew still, her lips parted expectantly.

"Yep. She said your mama was a good person, but she fell in love with a scoundrel."

"What's a scoundrel?"

"A man who makes promises he don't intend to keep just so's he can get a woman to show him her bosom."

"Oh." Natalie plucked at the covers in thought. "You mean, like he promised to marry her, but then he didn't . . . after she . . . showed it to him?" She didn't have a bosom yet, but if she did, she couldn't imagine wanting to show it to anyone. And now she was *positive* she wouldn't, after hearing what had happened to her mother.

Marla nodded. "Exactly."

Both girls fell silent, aware that time was running out. Soon, Miss Nelda would lumber up the stairs in search of Marla, and Natalie might never see her again. Natalie couldn't bear the thought.

With a sob, she flung herself at Marla, her words muffled against Marla's thin shoulder. "Please stay, Marla! We'll be your family, even better than before. I'll watch my mouth and do more of the chores and give you my bread pudding every single night and mind the young ones and—and *anything,* if only you'll stay!''

Gently, Marla patted her back, then pulled away. Just as she had done a hundred times, she wiped at Natalie's tears. ''Be brave, Natty. You have to be the big sister now. Take care of the others. And don't forget, I'll just be down the road a piece. We can visit as much as we like.''

''You'll forget me,'' Natalie sobbed. She just *knew* it.

''No, no, I won't. I made the spit promise, didn't I? If you ever need me, just holler. I'll be here faster than Miss Nelda can stumble to the outhouse.''

They both giggled through their tears. Marla lifted the music box from her lap, and with a determined smile, she held it out to Natalie. ''I want you to keep this as a reminder. Someday you'll have a new ma and pa, too.''

Eyes wide with shock, Natalie took the box. ''You mean it? I can have it?''

''Yes. You can keep it until you get married.'' When Natalie frowned, she hastily added, ''Or until you have a home of your own. Then I want it back.''

''Are you sure?'' Natalie couldn't believe Marla was giving up the only thing left to remind her of her parents. It was the greatest gift she could think of. Bravely, she swiped at her tears and thrust her chin forward. ''I *am* happy for you, Marla.''

''I know.''

Bonded by friendship and love, the two girls embraced. They both knew that from this day forward, their lives would be forever changed, but they knew in their hearts they would always have each other.

They'd made the spit promise.

1

"*What* does it say? Natalie, I'm going to die from curiosity if you don't read it out loud! Who's it from? What's it *say*? Is it bad news? Good news? Are they going to increase the yearly allowance for the orphanage?"

Marriage had not dulled Marla's optimism, Natalie thought, wishing with all her heart that Marla could be right. Unfortunately, she feared the opposite was true.

Needing a moment to gather herself, Natalie ignored her well-meaning friend and read the letter again, gripping the expensive stationery until her knuckles turned white. Maybe she was mistaken. . . .

When Marla jiggled her hand, she scowled and batted it away. "Hold your horses, Marla. I want to read it to myself first." In truth, Natalie hadn't wanted to read it at all. When Marla had handed her the letter a moment ago and Natalie saw that it was addressed to Nelda Boone, she had known it was going to be bad news.

It turned out to be worse than bad; it was the very thing she had dreaded since Nelda Boone's disappearance six months ago. Like the coward she was, Mrs.

Boone, housemother for the orphanage for over twenty
years, had deserted a sinking ship without telling a soul
there was a leak in the hull.

Heaving a long-suffering sigh, Marla folded her arms
over her protruding stomach and began tapping her foot
on the worn boards of the mercantile. "I'm waiting."

Natalie glanced up, then back to the letter, wishing
she could hide the devastating news from Marla a bit
longer, say five more months. In her delicate condition,
Marla didn't need the added worry.

And she *would* worry, Natalie knew. When Marla left
Ivy House twelve years ago, she'd kept her promise. She
hadn't forgotten them, returning often with gifts and
sweets for the children, and continuing their friendship.

Marla would not only worry, but she would also be
very angry when she found out that Natalie hadn't revealed everything she knew. Nelda Boone's leaving was
a mere drop in the bucket compared to everything else
that had happened.

Licking her dry lips, Natalie knew she couldn't put it
off any longer. She looked around to assure herself that
the store was temporarily empty and took a deep breath
before she began. "It's from Elliot Montgomery in
Nashville. He's coming to inspect the orphanage, and
he's arriving by steamship tomorrow."

Her mouth forming a perfect circle, Marla leaned
heavily against the counter. "Montgomery? Isn't he—
why, he's the founder, isn't he? Why would he come
all the way from Nashville to look at Ivy House? He
never has before!"

This was the moment Natalie dreaded. "Elliot's not
the founder. *His* name was Gill Montgomery. Elliot's
his grandson."

"Was? *Was?*" Marla squeaked. "What do you mean?
You don't mean that the founder's . . . dead?" Her
friend quickly put the facts together, as Natalie knew
she would.

She braced herself for the storm. Marla didn't disappoint her.

"You knew, didn't you? How long have you known? Why didn't you tell me? That's the reason that old sot ran off, isn't it? Mrs. Boone thought with Gill Montgomery dead, Ivy House would be history."

Natalie hung her head in shame. She deserved a tongue lashing for keeping secrets from her best friend. "I think you're right about Mrs. Boone, and yes, I knew. But, Marla, I didn't want to—"

"Upset me?" Marla straightened from the counter, her dark blue eyes glittering with either unshed tears or anger.

Natalie hoped it was the latter, because she couldn't bear it if Marla cried.

"You didn't tell me because I'm going to have a baby?"

The storm was going to be a bad one, Natalie thought. "Noah said—"

"Noah?" Again, Marla squeaked her amazement. "Since when do you listen to my crazy husband? You said yourself that he's been acting foolish since I told him about the baby. He won't let me do a *lick* of housework, and I had to pout for three days just to get him to agree to let me work in the store for a few hours a day! The man's off his rocker, and you're *listening* to him?"

When Marla said it, it did sound foolish. And of course Natalie knew Marla didn't mean what she said about Noah. She knew Marla loved her husband to distraction. "I'm sorry, Marla. I was just trying to protect you." Wrong choice of words, Natalie realized the moment she said them. She bit her lip.

"What else have you protected me from, Natalie Polk? Come on, I can tell by the look on your face that there's more."

Natalie winced. It seemed she had fumbled in trying

to protect her friend and had wound up hurting her feelings instead. Poking a strand of light blond hair behind her ear, Natalie sought to make amends. "I found out about Mr. Montgomery's death by accident. It was after I discovered Mrs. Boone gone, and I was going through her desk looking for the yearly allowance I knew she had received at the first of the year."

"You didn't find it because she took it with her." Marla was still fuming, but her eyes had lost that angry glitter.

"Yes, but I told you about that." The reminder earned a tiny smile of forgiveness from Marla. Encouraged, Natalie continued. "What I did find was a page from a letter Nelda received from the late Mr. Montgomery, written a few years before his death. He was informing her that when he died, he would be leaving the orphanage to his grandson, Elliot, to do with as he wished. Mr. Montgomery strongly hinted that his grandson wasn't interested in keeping the orphanage open."

All traces of anger gone now, Marla's brow puckered in thought. "So, when Nelda heard of his death, she got the letter out and read it again, deciding she wouldn't wait around for the ax to fall."

"I came to the same conclusion." Natalie did her best to look unconcerned, but she suspected she hadn't fooled Marla for a moment.

Marla confirmed this. "And all this time, you've been worried sick about what would happen to you and the children."

"Not me, just the children. I could take care of myself, but they wouldn't have a home." Natalie swallowed a lump in her throat. "Jo, Lori, Brett, and Cole are too old for adoption and still too young to make it on their own. Thank God you and Noah adopted Hickory." Natalie smiled at the thought of the five-year-old boy she had raised and nurtured since infancy. She never understood how someone could give up such a beautiful baby.

Marla grimaced and placed a hand on her stomach. "Noah loves Hickory, and so do I. I just wish the little fella would believe it when we tell him that just because we're having a baby, doesn't mean we don't want him anymore. Noah's gettin' tired of running to Ivy House to fetch him back."

Natalie refrained from commenting, knowing it troubled Marla when Hickory returned to the orphanage. Marla felt as if she had failed the little boy in some way. Natalie knew this wasn't true, but she couldn't convince Marla or Noah.

Making a mental note to sit Hickory down and have *another* talk with him, Natalie said, "He's insecure, but he'll come around. Now, back to the problem at hand. . . ."

"What will you do? Mr. Montgomery's not going to be pleased when he discovers that a nineteen-year-old woman has been running the place for the last six months. In fact, I'd say he'll feel even more justified about closing the place, *if* that's his intention."

As usual, Marla was probably right. Natalie bit her lip, thinking hard. What could she do? Her pensive gaze wandered to the beautifully handcrafted dollhouse in the window of the store. "Any luck?" she asked hopefully.

Marla sighed. "No. The first four went fast, but this one has been sitting for three weeks. I've had a lot of admirers, but no buyers."

Natalie turned to her friend. "I've got a little saved from the first sales. If we could just stall him somehow, until we sell enough dollhouses to buy Ivy House from him—"

"That could take years, Natalie, unless you're lucky enough to find someone who's willing to invest and help you market the dollhouses in the bigger cities like New York and Chicago. Besides, you've been having to spend some of the money on supplies, and with winter coming, you'll also have to buy wood for heating, shoes for the children, and warm clothes.''

"What happened to your optimism?" Natalie asked with a lift of her brow and a hint of desperation. "Don't you believe in luck? Don't you believe that it's possible someone could walk in here and see the potential in our dollhouses?"

Marla had the grace to look ashamed. "I didn't mean to sound as if I don't believe it could happen, Natalie. The dollhouses are beautiful—I plan to buy one for this baby, if it's a girl—but you have to be realistic. If Mr. Montgomery has decided to close the orphanage and sell the house, how could you possibly change his mind or put him off? Maybe if Mrs. Boone were still around, she might convince him—"

Natalie gasped. That was it! She grabbed Marla by the shoulders and danced around her, forgetting her condition and laughing joyously. "You're a genius, Marla! A genius!"

"I am?" Marla blinked her bewilderment. "What did I say?"

"You said, 'Maybe if Mrs. Boone were still around'!"

Narrowing her eyes in suspicion, Marla demanded, "And just what are you up to, Natalie Polk? What have you got in mind?"

Oh, this would work—it had to! Natalie muttered a quick prayer for forgiveness and proceeded to tell Marla of her brilliant plan to fool Elliot Montgomery.

Tomorrow, when he arrived, he would find Ivy House professionally managed by a slimmer, younger Mrs. Nelda Boone, but someone considerably older and wiser than Natalie Polk.

It was love at first sight for Elliot Montgomery.

Standing at the ship's prow, he lost his heart to the

port of Chattanooga as the steamship rounded Moccasin Bend and chugged happily into the harbor. Surrounded almost completely by steep mountains and lush forests, he thought it looked exactly as he imagined a peaceful, magical kingdom would look.

"They say you can see seven states from Lookout Mountain," the captain said, coming to stand beside Elliot.

Elliot followed his pointing finger to the tallest mountain, hovering like a sentry over the town. He could well imagine the view from its steepest peak.

"Over yonder is Signal Mountain. From there you can see clear down into the gorge. It's where the river cuts through the mountain," he explained proudly. "During the war, there were battles on Chickamauga Mountain, Lookout, and Missionary Ridge."

He pointed to each mountain as he spoke, and Elliot dutifully looked; he'd heard the town's history from his grandfather long ago. To look at the peaceful view now, however, it was hard to imagine that twenty-two years ago, the city was an important Confederate communications point during the Civil War and the scene of many bloody battles.

Gill Montgomery had never recovered from his own losses during the war. He had lost not only his leg but his wife, as well. Elliot never got to meet his grandmother. "Chattanooga certainly has its share of history, doesn't it?"

The captain grinned as if he were the mayor himself. "Sure does! Too bad your sweetheart ain't up on deck to share your first glimpse of paradise."

"Yes. Too bad," Elliot said tersely, ignoring the captain's sly wink. Suetta had turned out to be a pain in the rear when it came to riding on a steamship. She hated the noise. She hated the smell. She hated the food. And when Elliot had urged her to join him when the captain had announced their approach, Suetta had informed him

she hated the fine spray of water that misted their clothes
when they stood on deck.

Lifting his face to that spray now, Elliot sighed. Was
there anything Suetta *didn't* hate? He was beginning to
wonder. He was also beginning to wonder if he
shouldn't try to back out gracefully from this arranged
engagement. His grandfather had wanted the marriage,
as did both of Suetta's parents. Friends since childhood,
they had all just assumed he and Suetta would marry.
Elliot couldn't even recall proposing to Suetta.

Now his grandfather was dead, and without his constant encouragement, Elliot found himself yearning to
be free of her. A slow, lopsided smile curved his mouth
as he thought of an excellent way to prompt Suetta into
breaking the engagement. He could simply tell her that
with the death of his grandfather, he was penniless with
an unpaid debt looming like doomsday in his future. He
could tell her that he had secured a loan to finance this
trip, and that once he sold Ivy House to pay the loan
and his grandfather's debts, he'd be lucky if anything
was left.

If none of those ominous revelations deterred her,
then he could tell her that Bo Carnagie could become
rather nasty when he didn't get his money. The man was
ruthless, which made it all the more difficult for Elliot
to understand why his grandfather had associated with
the shark at all. Several days ago, a man by the name
of Randal Evans had approached Elliot, demanding he
settle his grandfather's debts. Randal Evans worked for
Bo Carnagie.

Elliot recalled the unpleasant conversation with a
grimace. He'd managed to distract Evans long enough
to slip away, but he knew Evans would find him again.

Yes, selling Ivy House was the only choice.

Maybe there would be enough left to start a small
business of some kind. Perhaps he could make a few
wise investments with the money until he could decide

what to do with his life. As for the orphans of Ivy House—if there were any—he had already put aside money from the loan to use as an enticement for couples willing to adopt.

Money could be a powerful persuasion.

Uplifted by the possibility, Elliot made his way across the deck to tell his fiancée they were about to depart. For a while longer, he would keep his financial problems to himself. His luck could change any day now, saving him the embarrassment of having to tell everyone. The worst that could happen would be for Carnagie's men to find him before he sold Ivy House.

He jiggled his pockets, hoping the accommodations in town were not *too* expensive. The dwindling amount of coins wouldn't go far.

After those were gone, he was flat busted—until he sold Ivy House.

All was in readiness for Elliot Montgomery's arrival.

Hickory sat at Marla's feet, playing with a covered wagon Noah had whittled and sanded to a smooth shine. About every five seconds, he would lift his blond head and ask, "Now, Mama?" To which Marla would reply with a gentle smile, "Not yet, Hickory."

Each time he called her "Mama," she about swooned with joy. Yet it saddened her to know the reason he was so excited about his part in the plan: He would get to see his "real" family again. It didn't seem to matter to Hickory that he saw Natalie and the children several times a week.

For the last half hour as the clock slowly ticked, Marla jumped at the slightest sound. She fumbled with every purchase, spilling flour, snagging material. The air was still redolent with the scent of spiced peaches from the jar she had dropped and broken.

She counted at least ten apologies since opening that morning. Why, she hadn't been this nervous on her wedding day! But then, on her wedding day, she hadn't been about to participate in a deception.

When she finally heard the steam whistle announcing its arrival, she shrieked, startling Mrs. Newberry into dropping a basket of apples. They rolled across the floor in every direction.

Hickory looked up at her, his face eager. "Now, Mama?"

"No. Not now, dear."

"I ain't a deer, and I ain't a cow, and I ain't a pig," Hickory declared. "I'm Hickory!"

Marla giggled nervously. "I know." Keeping her gaze glued to the window overlooking Main Street, Marla reached down and ruffled his sun-bleached hair. "Soon, Hickory. Very soon. Why don't you help Mrs. Newberry pick up those apples?"

The clock continued to tick. Marla bagged Mrs. Newberry's purchases without fumbling once. She was so pleased with herself, she forgot to watch for Elliot Montgomery as she chatted with the customer. In fact, she didn't pay any attention to the warning bell over the door, either, because she was in a deep discussion with Mrs. Newberry about how to treat a colicky baby.

"Are you the postmistress?"

Mrs. Newberry stopped in midsentence at the sound of a man's deep, resonant voice. Despite the impressive population of Chattanooga, strangers were still regarded with healthy curiosity and a smidgen of suspicion.

It hit Marla at that moment just who *this* particular stranger probably was, and for a long moment, she stared rudely at the man standing behind Mrs. Newberry.

She had imagined a much older, portly man, for surely the late Mr. Montgomery was an old man when he died. Yet before her stood a handsome devil with amusement sparkling in his light blue eyes. He was at least a foot taller than herself, lean, yet broad-shouldered. His golden hair looked ruffled, as if he had stood at the prow of a ship and let the wind filter through the sun-kissed strands.

Judging by the water droplets splattering his slightly wrinkled clothes, maybe he had, Marla thought.

She swallowed and blinked in confusion. Could this be Elliot Montgomery? Why, the man didn't look much older than she, and she had just turned twenty-two last month!

"Marla?"

"Hmm?" Marla gave her head a slight shake and jerked her gaze back to the waiting Mrs. Newberry. "I'm sorry, what did you say?"

"The man asked if you were the postmistress here. Since you seem to be taking a nap, I told him you were." On that disapproving note, Mrs. Newberry gathered her packages together and with a nod at the stranger, left the store.

"Now, Mama?" Sensing something in the air, Hickory abandoned his favorite toy and stood. "Now, Mama? Can I go now?"

Absently, Marla shook her head. "Just a moment, Hickory." She forced herself to look at the man again. There was a chance she was wrong and this wasn't Elliot Montgomery, and she couldn't send Hickory off until she knew for certain. "May I help you?" she offered in her politest voice. It quivered slightly, much to her dismay.

He smiled, revealing a mile of white teeth, their only flaw a tiny chip on an upper front tooth.

And Marla, happily married woman that she was, found herself giving him a silly smile right back. Whoever he was, she decided right then and there, he would be perfect for Natalie. Saints above, if she wasn't a married woman . . .

"I'm Elliot Montgomery. The harbor master said there was a letter waiting for me at the Thompson Mercantile." He stuck his hands in his pockets and rocked

back on his heels, looking around as if searching for a
sign to confirm he'd found the right place.

Hickory tugged at her sleeve. "Now, Mama?" he
whispered loudly, watching the man curiously.

"Now, Hickory. Run like the wind, and *come right
back here.*"

Taking her words to heart, Hickory tore from the
store, banging the door hard enough to rattle the windows. Marla watched him go for a moment, taking the
time to master her thoughts. She didn't know how or
why—it was just a blaze of insight she was often prone
to—but she was absolutely certain that Elliot Montgomery and Natalie Polk *belonged* together. Just how she
was going to bring this about was another matter for
reflection.

Right now she had a job to do; she had to stall Mr.
Montgomery so that Hickory had time to warn Natalie
of his arrival and give Natalie time to prepare.

The man lowered his head and centered his sky-blue
eyes on Marla. "Hickory. An unusual name."

Marla moistened her lips. *Keep him talking,* she
thought. After that, she would think of something else.
"He was named after Andrew Jackson. Are you in town
for long, Mr. Montgomery?"

"The name suits him. He's a fine young boy."

He likes children! Marla could have danced on the
spot.

"As for how long I'm staying . . ." he began, then
paused and looked out the window.

Marla followed his gaze to the waiting carriage. She
could see the shadow of someone inside but couldn't tell
what gender. Oh, please God, don't let him be married!

"I'm not sure," he concluded, a tiny frown creasing
his tanned forehead.

"Is . . . did your wife accompany you?" Noah would
strangle her, she thought, if he overheard her ask such
an impertinent question! She was a little shocked herself.

To hide the certain flush on her face, Marla pretended to look beneath the counter for a letter that didn't exist.

"Not my wife, but my fiancée."

At his amused reply, Marla's flush of embarrassment deepened to crimson. Engaged! Frantically, she riffled through the mail, her heart sinking. Still, there was a slim chance—

"Did you find it?"

Marla straightened and gave him a blank look, suppressing the urge to fan her fiery face. "Find what?"

"The letter."

"Oh. Oh, the letter! Oh, that. Well, it seems I've misplaced it. . . ." He cocked a brow but didn't appear to be too bent out of shape.

He likes children, he's handsome, and he's a gentleman. The fiancée would have to go. This was Natalie's man!

"Well, I can return some other time. Can't imagine anyone knowing I was coming, to tell you the truth. Do you by any chance remember the addressee?"

Marla floundered. "I—I—"

"I understand." His teeth flashed in a smile of assurance. "Tell me, do you know of an orphanage nearby?"

"You mean Ivy House?" Marla blurted, then could have bitten her tongue. The plan was that she *wouldn't* know if he should ask, therefore causing more delay as he searched for directions.

"And could you give me directions?"

"Directions? Oh, it's down the road a piece." Ah, she was such a ninny! He must think her completely addle-brained. "Follow Main Street until it ends, then turn right. It's about a quarter of a mile after that." She prayed Hickory didn't get distracted along the way, because basically those were the right directions—with a small detour.

"Thank you. I'll come back another time for the letter."

Frustrated, Marla watched him walk to the door. But as he reached it, he paused, his gaze drawn to the doll-house in the window. She held her breath as he moved closer to study it with an intensity that made her feel dizzy.

Natalie desperately needed an investor, but surely it was too much to hope Elliot Montgomery himself would be interested.

He whirled around, his expression taut with excitement. Marla gasped and stepped back, holding a hand to her racing heart.

"The carpenter?" he demanded.

Good gracious, what next? Marla knew she couldn't possibly tell Elliot Montgomery that the orphans of Ivy House had made the dollhouse, not without Natalie's permission. She wasn't prepared to answer the questions that she was certain would arise.

So she stalled, something she was becoming very good at. "The dollhouse? Isn't it splendid? It's hand-crafted, of course, and constructed out of the finest wood—" Marla choked, gripping the counter. Heaven help them, she just remembered where Natalie had gotten the lumber for the making of the dollhouses. Now she *knew* she couldn't tell him.

It was Elliot Montgomery's house Natalie was taking apart!

Before she could think up a fictional name, they were interrupted by a sharp rap on the window fronting the store. Startled, they both turned to look.

Outside on the boardwalk, a woman stood waving a parasol vigorously at Elliot, motioning him outside. Dressed in a full-skirted burgundy dress with a matching short jacket, she looked hot, Marla thought. She also looked mighty angry about something.

Elliot turned from the window and shot Marla a weary look that filled her heart with pure joy. Aha! The man didn't appear very happy with his current sweetheart.

Perfect! Squinting, Marla saw that his sweetheart also couldn't hold a candle to her Natalie in face *or* form. And judging by the harsh twist of the woman's mouth, Natalie won the disposition contest as well. Last but not least, he appeared uncommonly interested in Natalie's project. Her instincts about the two of them belonging together had been right.

Perfect, perfect, perfect!

''I'll come back when I've gotten rid—when I have more time.'' With one last glance at the dollhouse, he slammed from the store.

Marla slumped against the counter, feeling weak with relief. What a morning! And what she wouldn't give in exchange for a glimpse of Natalie's face when she set eyes on Elliot Montgomery.

Chuckling, Marla began to tidy up the mess she'd made looking for the fabricated letter. In her mind's eye, she imagined the encounter between the young couple. Natalie would take one look at Elliot and fall in love. Elliot, in return, would take one look at Natalie, compare her to the pasty white miss with the tight mouth and fall *completely* in love.

''Lord!'' Marla groaned and covered her face with her hands as the most horrible realization hit her.

Elliot would be looking at a *different* Natalie, a made-up spinster who wouldn't attract a blind man.

She had to do something, and fast. If Natalie's plan worked, Elliot would leave on the next steamboat without having ever met the *real* Natalie. Her best friend would miss out on the opportunity of a lifetime to snag the man of her dreams. And, of course, there was the nice Mr. Montgomery, who might be saddled with a shrew the rest of his life if she didn't do him this favor.

As to confirm her plan, the baby kicked her soundly. Marla gave the top of her stomach a loving pat and looked at the clock. Noah would come to relieve her in

fifteen minutes, and if Hickory minded her, he should
be back any second.

Hickory didn't know about Natalie's disguise or the
reason, but he would recognize *his* Natty instantly and
demand to know what was going on.

Natalie was about to have unexpected company, and
Elliot Montgomery was about to meet the woman of his
dreams.

2

"**N**atty! Natty!''

Heart pounding, Natalie stepped away from the upstairs window before the little boy barreling up the walk could see her. She drew a deep, calming breath.

Hickory's appearance meant that Elliot Montgomery had arrived.

Could she go through with the farce? Could she fool Elliot Montgomery? Convince him to keep Ivy House open? Natalie grabbed her throat and swallowed hard. She had to succeed . . . for the children . . . for herself.

Natalie frowned, remembering how she'd prayed as a child for a loving couple to take her away to a home of her own. When had Ivy House become a haven she fiercely defended instead of the temporary shelter she despised?

Footsteps pounded up the stairs, interrupting her thoughts. Natalie gasped and stepped behind the bathing screen, fearing that Hickory had managed to slip by Jo or the boys. She couldn't let Hickory see her like this; he wouldn't understand.

Jo's freckled, gamine face appeared around the door

frame. A hank of her short, dark hair had fallen over
one long-lashed brown eye, but the bashful young girl
made no move to push it away. "Hickory—"

"I heard." Natalie smiled in reassurance, hoping Jo
hadn't noticed her trembling hands. She casually put
them behind her in the pretense of adjusting the ridicu-
lously large bustle she'd donned for her disguise. "Did
you convince him to go back to the store?"

Jo nodded, her mouth quirking in a half smile. "I had
to give him one of those fancy cakes I made this morning. That boy's got a nose like a bloodhound! I also had
to promise to take him fishin' Saturday."

Natalie laughed. "He misses you—*and* your cooking.
Are you sure you won't wear a dress, Jo? Something of
mine, perhaps?"

The girl's smile vanished instantly. She glanced down
at the boy's clothing she wore and shook her head, just
as Natalie knew she would. Still, it didn't hurt to try.
Someday she hoped to restore Jo's confidence and make
her realize becoming a woman was nothing to be *afraid*
of or ashamed of.

"I won't. I told ya, I don't care what that highfalutin
man thinks about me. I ain't wearin' no sissy clothes for
nobody."

"They're not *sissy* clothes, Jo. It's what young
women your age are supposed to wear." Natalie's lecture fell on deaf ears. Jo was as determined as ever to
deny her sex, despite Natalie's constant reassurances.
Whatever had happened to Jo in her childhood remained
locked away.

Jo began to back away in the direction of the stairs
and escape, mumbling, "Gotta make sure the others
keep their grubby paws off the cakes. Done chased Brett
clear to town and back over eatin' more than his share.
He thought it was funny. Well, he didn't think it was
funny when I caught . . ."

Her voice drifted away downstairs. Natalie moved to

the mirror beside her bed to check her appearance one last time, praying the children behaved themselves during Mr. Montgomery's visit. Mrs. Boone hadn't been much on discipline these past few years, and without it the children had grown a little wild. The housemother had kept to herself, preferring a bottle of cheap whiskey to the rowdy antics of the orphans and Natalie's disapproving stare.

Natalie had gradually taken over Mrs. Boone's duties until she felt quite competent in the role of housemother. Well, most of the time. It hadn't been easy.

Now all she had to do was to convince Mr. Elliot of her ability to run Ivy House. Natalie wasn't particularly fond of duping people, but she thought God might forgive her this one small deception. If she succeeded, she might consider telling Mr. Montgomery the truth and throwing herself at his mercy.

Perhaps he was a kind and understanding man like his grandfather had been. Natalie bit her lip as she made her way downstairs, bustle swaying unsteadily with each careful step she took in the cumbersome shoes she'd found among the things Mrs. Boone had left behind. She couldn't forget Gill Montgomery's letter and his ominous hint that his grandson might not share his sentiment for Ivy House.

Laughter exploded as she reached the foyer adjacent to the spacious parlor. A wide, arched doorway separated the two rooms, giving the children a clear view of Natalie. At the sound of their laughter, she attempted to look haughty, but her lips twitched in response. She'd studied her reflection in the mirror; she knew how ridiculous she looked. But that was because they—and she—knew how she *really* looked.

Moving to the doorway, Natalie scrutinized each one, skipping Jo, the oldest of the orphans Nelda Boone had left behind. As rehearsed, Cole, a gangly thirteen-year-old with thick black hair and eyes to match, sat on a stool by the cold fireplace, surrounded by gardening tools he intended to sharpen or repair during Mr. Montgomery's visit. Natalie hoped their new benefactor would be impressed by how self-sufficient Ivy House was.

Brett, Cole's brother by a scant year, knelt on a rug at the opposite end of the fireplace. He held a carving knife and a piece of wood; the beginnings of the fourth leg that would complete the chair at his side. Mr. Montgomery would have to be a blind fool not to be impressed, Natalie thought. She took a moment to admire his amazing craftsmanship before moving on.

At only eight years of age, Lori was the youngest of the orphans, now that Hickory lived with Marla and Noah. A year ago, Natalie had given the young girl a shirt to mend and discovered that Lori possessed an amazing skill with the needle. Her thin face framed by a mass of red curls, Lori sat on the sofa, poised with needle in hand. In her lap was a nearly completed cushion for the chair Brett was making, a beautiful piece of work the pickiest of homemakers would covet.

Marla's mother-in-law, Mrs. Thompson, had already agreed to make an even exchange: the chair for a bolt of material she had purchased and never used so that Lori and Natalie could make shirts for the boys and Jo for the coming winter.

Finally, Natalie's proud gaze landed on Jo as she fussed with the small table filled with dainty iced cakes, two glasses, and a jug of cold apple cider. Delicate lace napkins, compliments of Lori's skillful needlework, graced the small chipped plates.

As far back as Natalie could remember, Jo had managed the meals. The tomboy looked incorrigible standing beside the fancy table dressed in breeches and a man's shirt, arranging and rearranging the items, but no one knew more than Natalie how creative she could be in the kitchen. When Jo shot an anxious glance at Natalie,

Natalie softened her smile, hiding her trembling hands in the folds of the stiff black taffeta. The heavy dress was hot and scratchy, and she couldn't wait to get out of it.

"The table looks wonderful, Jo. I'm sure Mr. Montgomery will be impressed." She wasn't sure at all, knowing Mr. Montgomery to be a city man, but she saw no need to increase Jo's anxiety by sharing the thought.

Jo restacked the plates and inspected the glasses for spots, groaning when she found one. She rubbed vigorously at the spot with her shirttail. For a breathtaking moment, she juggled the glass in her hands. "A-are you sure? What if—"

"Everything is fine, Jo. Mr. Montgomery will love the cakes, and I'm sure he'll recognize those glasses are real crystal. Mrs. Boone was *so* kind to leave them behind, although it's strange that she did. They came from her wedding chest."

"*If* the old cow was ever really married," Cole muttered, picking up on Natalie's faint sarcasm in reference to Mrs. Boone's kindness. "We just got her word, and we all know what *that's* worth."

Lori glanced up from the sewing material in her lap, her brows drawn together in a pensive frown. "Mrs. Boone'll be fired up if she comes back and finds out we used her glasses."

"I don't think she's coming back," Natalie announced softly. She hated to tell them the news, but the hopeful light in their eyes tore at her heart. She couldn't allow them to keep believing Nelda would come back. Nelda hadn't been the best example to her orphans, but she had represented stability. From the moment the children realized the housemother had deserted them, they'd talked of nothing else. Each time they mentioned her now, it was in a disparaging way, but Natalie sensed an underlying hurt she didn't know how to assuage.

Drunk, indifferent . . . Mrs. Boone had been their only anchor in a cold world.

Now Natalie was their anchor, and she was fiercely determined not to let them down as Nelda had done. So much depended on this impending visit from Mr. Montgomery.

A distinct rap at the door interrupted her thoughts and sent her nerves skittering.

Jo whirled around, nearly upsetting the refreshment table with her hip. "Lord, he's here!"

Natalie calmly quieted the sudden babble of voices. "Everyone take their places and *please* be on your best behavior." She nodded at Jo and moved to stand before the staircase that faced the door. "Get the door."

Jo tripped to the door, stopped, hastily stuffed her shirttails into her trousers, then reached for the knob.

Natalie gripped her hands primly together and stood tall and straight. *The moment of truth has come.*

Cole and Brett bent to their tasks, but their identical black eyes remained locked on the door.

As if she couldn't stand the suspense, Lori began plying the needle, her red hair covering her face so that the sharp point of her reddened nose—due to a summer cold she couldn't seem to shake—remained the only thing visible. She began humming a happy tune that made Natalie want to laugh hysterically.

It was *too* perfect.

Jo pulled the door open, and Natalie stepped forward, a polite smile literally plastered onto her face. Her first sight of Mr. Montgomery shattered the image in her mind of the older, distinguished gentleman she'd been expecting.

The man's broad shoulders filled the doorway. He held a dark gray overcoat casually over one arm. Natalie quickly assessed his rumpled white shirt and gray vest and noticed the way the dark gray trousers fit snugly over his taut thighs. He had tucked the trousers into knee-high boots that might have once gleamed with shine but were now covered with dust.

He looked travel weary, she thought.

Early afternoon sunlight highlighted his wavy blond hair as he stood poised, waiting for an invitation. Natalie lifted a hand to shield her eyes from the sun's unexpected glare and cleared her throat. She wanted to see his face, to know if her prayers had been answered. Was there a kind face to match his impressive form? She dearly hoped so.

"Please come in, Mr. Montgomery. We've been expecting you." She swallowed hard, her nerves stretched taut. She was hardly aware of the hushed silence that had descended on the room.

Stepping over the threshold and out of the blinding light, Mr. Montgomery slipped the coat from his arm and handed it to Jo, turning his head to smile at the awestruck girl.

Natalie reached behind her and caught the edge of the stair rail, her breath suddenly tight and hot in her lungs, her gaze drawn to the brilliance of his smile. *This* was Elliot Montgomery?

"You must be Mrs. Boone. My grandfather spoke highly of you."

Guilty heat scorched Natalie's face as Mr. Montgomery came forward and shook her limp hand. His low, rumbling voice contained no surprise, no suspicion. Exactly as she'd hoped.

Wasn't it?

Suddenly, Natalie regretted posing as a matronly woman, and it had nothing to do with her guilty conscience and everything to do with the handsome man standing before her. Yet, even had she known, how could she have changed things? Above all, Ivy House must be saved. Besides, she wasn't fool enough to think for a moment that someone of Mr. Montgomery's wealth and social standing would show the slightest interest in an orphan of questionable paternity like herself, a little miss nobody.

With this stern reminder, Natalie met his bright blue eyes with what she hoped was a proper, matronly look. Later, when she was alone with her daydreams, she could think about what might have been. "Nice to meet you, and welcome to Ivy House."

Elliot dropped the older woman's surprisingly soft hand, hiding his confusion behind a steadfast smile. The woman standing before him was younger than he'd imagined, although her gray-streaked hair, pallid skin, and outdated apparel suggested an older woman, as he knew Nelda Boone to be.

Yet . . . her voice was that of a much younger woman, and the slim, young-looking hands seemed out of place on her bulky, heavy-set frame.

But it was her eyes that held Elliot captive. A deep, indigo blue with a sparkle of youth and innocence totally in contrast to her age, they hinted at secrets and mystery, passion and promise. Uncomfortable with his thoughts, Elliot steered his mind in a different direction, embarrassed to be thinking of Mrs. Boone in such a way. Why, she was old enough to be his mother!

"I was sorry to hear about your grandfather, Mr. Montgomery."

There it was again. That soft, melodious voice. It couldn't possibly belong to the matronly woman before him, yet it did. Elliot gave his head a slight shake. Of course this was Nelda Boone. It was ridiculous to imagine otherwise. "Thank you." His voice dropped an octave. "He'll be sorely missed."

She nodded. "He was a generous man."

"That he was." Elliot sighed inwardly. So generous in fact, that he had died a pauper and left his grandson with the distasteful task of booting this widow and her orphans out in the cold. Elliot silently cursed the guilty wave of heat that crept up his neck. On the boat, his plan had seemed so simple, so necessary. Now that he was here, the words stuck in his throat.

How would they take the news? How would this kind, gentle matron react to losing her home? He suspected she'd be shocked and outraged at the turn of events. Horrified, in fact. According to his grandfather, Nelda Boone had dedicated her life to the running of Ivy House and caring for its orphans.

She startled him from his thoughts by waving a hand in the direction of a wide, arched doorway. The parlor, he presumed, glancing inside the room. He could see several more children seated about and recognized the girl who had answered the door as she hovered near a table.

"Won't you have some refreshments? Jo's fixed—er—prepared cakes and apple cider. She does all the cooking."

"I—"

"Please," she suddenly whispered as if she sensed his reluctance. "Jo's feelings will be hurt if you don't." More loudly, she said, "I'll introduce you to the children. They're anxious to meet their new benefactor."

Had she deliberately placed an emphasis on the word *benefactor*? Elliot ran a finger beneath his collar as guilt returned. He felt a sudden urge to take the coward's way out and leave. He could always send her a formal letter. "Well, I really should—"

"You shouldn't feel uncomfortable, Mr. Montgomery. Our home is your home."

Did she sound a little desperate? Elliot glanced into her intriguing blue eyes, then quickly looked away again. He had to tell her. Now. It wasn't fair to allow her to keep believing he was going to follow in his grandfather's footsteps and keep the orphanage going.

It was a financial impossibility. Surely she would understand.

"Mrs. Boone, I'm afraid I've got bad news." He flinched at her stricken look. Her face became even paler. Elliot felt several pairs of eyes boring into his skull from the parlor doorway. Children's eyes, waiting anxiously for him to continue.

He cleared his throat, searching his mind desperately for an alternative. There wasn't one, of course. "It concerns the orphanage." He was stalling, and he suspected she knew it. If only there was another way to break the news—

"Natty! Natty!"

They heard the high-pitched voice just seconds before the front door burst open and the little boy Elliot recognized from the mercantile came barreling over the threshold. Elliot heard Mrs. Boone gasp, but before he could question her reaction, Hickory slid to a halt before them. He looked from one to the other with huge, questioning eyes, then promptly placed his fists on his hips and glowered at Mrs. Boone.

Finally, he stood on tiptoe and smacked Mrs. Boone square in her generous bosom with a pudgy fist.

Stunned, Elliot held his breath, waiting to see what the good matron would do. Her eyes widened in shock, but to his further surprise, she did nothing.

"Natty, why you got that stuff in your hair? And what's that on your face? It makes you look old, and you ain't old!" Before she could respond, he darted behind her and gave a mighty tug on the bustle attached to her dress. "And you never wear one of these silly things!"

Elliot heard a ripping sound, followed by another gasp from the shocked Mrs. Boone.

"Hickory, stop that!" she squeaked in a high, girlish voice. "Don't you dare—oh!" She tried to whirl away from the determined little boy, but in doing so, she managed to help him tear the offending bustle completely from the dress, revealing to Elliot's continued shock a patch of her white bloomers visible through the gaping hole in the material.

She tripped over her own feet and lost her balance, teetering backward in his direction. Elliot automatically reached out to catch her, his arms slipping under her breasts. Something shifted to the left beneath his hands, startling him, just as the back of her head connected sharply with his jaw.

Elliot grunted, the force snapping his mouth shut. He tasted ashes. Bewildered, he stared over her head at the panting little boy gone mad. What in heaven's name was going on? He knew enough about a woman's body to know that something strange had just happened. And why in the world would her hair taste like ashes from an old fire?

"There you are, Hickory! Come along now."

Elliot turned with his burden, his gaze widening at the sight of the woman from the mercantile—the woman who had lost his letter and had given him the wrong directions—as she stepped through the open doorway. She gave him a pained smile, then beckoned to Hickory. Apparently, she didn't think it odd to find him holding Mrs. Boone in his arms, which Elliot found *very* odd.

"I'm sorry, Natalie. I tried to stop him, but you know how fast he can run."

Natalie? But Elliot was certain Mrs. Boone's first name was Nelda, unless his grandfather had been wrong all these years.

The woman in his arms slowly righted herself but avoided his puzzled eyes as she planted her hands over her exposed bottom and turned. Elliot politely averted his gaze, just as a precaution. He'd only gotten a glimpse, but it was enough to know that perky little bottom did not match the rest of her. In fact, it wasn't the only thing that didn't make sense.

Her bosom had moved!

"It's all right, Marla. This—this is probably for the best, anyway."

Elliot looked from one to the other, frowning. They both looked extremely guilty about something, and Marla looked not only guilty, but *smug,* which further mystified him.

"I'll just take Hickory and run along. You can explain to Mr. Montgomery. I'm sure he'll understand." With that hurried assurance, Marla and Hickory made haste to the door, shutting it firmly behind them.

Before Elliot could open his mouth to demand an explanation, the door burst open again. Marla threw her hands in the air. "Hickory won't leave until you give him a hug, Natalie."

The woman Elliot thought to be Mrs. Boone gave a wan smile and opened her arms. Hickory ran into them, his whisper loud enough for Elliot to overhear.

"I miss you, Natty."

"And I miss you, Hickory," she whispered back. She pulled away and looked at him sternly. "But you shouldn't make your mama run; she's gonna have a baby, you know. A little brother or sister for you to play with."

Hickory nodded vigorously. "I know. She's fat, so she can't keep up with me."

"Come on, Hickory," Marla called. "Papa's waiting on us."

Elliot saw the little boy's face light up at the mention of his papa, just before he twisted out of her embrace and raced to his mother. Finally, the door shut again, and silence descended. Elliot was very conscious of the other children watching from the parlor doorway.

Folding his arms over his chest, he faced her. Now he would get to the bottom of this nonsense. "You're not Nelda Boone," he said, stating the obvious.

3

"No, I'm not Nelda Boone." Natalie tried to recall to her dazed mind another time when she'd felt so thoroughly humiliated and couldn't. She lifted her chin a notch, knowing her face was on fire. Hopefully, the white powder she had applied would hide the worst of it. "Mrs. Boone left six months ago." Darting a glance behind Elliot to the children gathered in the doorway, she lowered her voice a notch. "She left in the middle of the night, taking with her the money and everything of value she could carry."

She watched his face as understanding dawned, bracing herself for his next question. In a few moments, it would be over. He would know the truth, and in knowing the truth, it would make his task easier. Tears burned the back of her eyes at the thought.

"Then *who* are *you?*"

A little miss nobody, Natalie thought in despair. But she'd never been accused of giving up hope, so she offered her hand, holding her back straight with what dignity she could muster. He knew, so there was nothing to hide. She felt a curious sense of calm. "My name is Natalie Polk. I've lived here all my life."

"You're an . . . orphan?" he asked incredulously, too much of a gentleman to ignore her outstretched hand. "You've been running Ivy House since Mrs. Boone left?"

"Deserted," Natalie corrected. His grip was warm and strong, and something about that feeling increased her urge to cry. But she couldn't. She had to show him how strong she was, how capable she was of managing Ivy House. "She deserted us. I'm the oldest, so . . ."

Elliot dropped her hand and resumed his stance with his arms folded ominously. "How old *are* you?"

"Nineteen." She gave his form a swift glance. "Not much younger than you."

A slight smile twitched his lips. Natalie gained courage from the sight. "As you can see for yourself, we've gotten along perfectly fine without Mrs. Boone. The children are healthy and well fed, the house is clean and up to standards, I—"

"If Mrs. Boone took the allowance with her, then how have you managed to run the household?"

Natalie refrained from biting her lip. Now she would have to embellish a little, because he would be furious if he knew the whole truth. "We . . . manage. The children work at odd jobs around town. I take in a little sewing"—a gross understatement—"and we have an excellent garden, a few chickens—"

"We used to have a cow, but we had to se—"

"Jo does the cooking," Natalie said in a rush, hastily interrupting Lori. "She can make a chicken stretch into four meals. Can't you, Jo?" Natalie smiled over her shoulder at the hovering children, beckoning Jo forward with a wave of her hand.

Jo tried to duck back into the parlor and out of sight, but Cole gave her a shove. She stumbled out into the foyer, head down, blushing furiously. "Yes, sir," she mumbled, jamming her hands into her pockets. "We don't need Mrs. Boone. She didn't do nuthin' but chug—''

"See? We manage just fine without her.'' Natalie sent Jo a warning look. She didn't see any need to talk bad about Mrs. Boone. He might think it a ploy to gain his sympathy.

"What about repairs?'' Mr. Montgomery still looked doubtful, staring around the house as if he expected it to fall down around his ears. "A house this size would need constant care.''

Natalie pounced eagerly, hoping beyond hope that his interest meant he was reconsidering. She wouldn't think about his reaction if he should see the second floor. "Brett, Cole, come here and introduce yourselves to Mr. Montgomery.'' When they reached her side, she put an arm around each shoulder. "These boys can fix anything. Brett is a fine carpenter, and Cole can repair just about anything he comes across, ain't that right, boys?''

Brett and Cole nodded. Cole was too bashful to look at Mr. Montgomery, but Brett held out a manly hand. When Mr. Montgomery took it, he gave it a hard shake that brought a smile to the man's face.

"Nice to meet you, Mr. Montgomery.'' He jabbed his thumb at Natalie. "Miss Natalie, she takes care of things around here. You can trust her.''

Natalie gave Cole a subtle poke with her elbow. Cole took the hint and reluctantly shook hands with Mr. Montgomery. Lori joined them and gave him a darling curtsey, surprising Natalie. *When had she learned to do that?* she wondered.

"This is Lori, the youngest.'' With everyone gathered around, they presented a united front before the man who held their future in the palm of his hand.

"We're all just one big, happy family, aren't we, children?'' Natalie forced a big smile to her face. Inwardly, she quaked with anticipation and fear. *Please God, let it work.*

"I'm not a child," Cole muttered beneath his breath, trying to shrug out of her embrace.

"Neither am I."

"Me neither," Lori added.

"Yes, you are!" Brett sneered.

"Am not!"

"You're a baby, *baby*!" Brett reached across Natalie's dubious bosom and made a grab for Lori's hair.

"Please!" At her sharp reprimand, the children quickly remembered themselves and became quiet. Feeling flustered and a little out of control, Natalie sent Jo to fetch an apron from the kitchen. She urged the others to wait in the parlor.

Jo returned and helped Natalie position the apron so that her backside was covered before she, too, scurried away. Blushing crimson, Natalie avoided Mr. Montgomery's amused gaze and turned away to adjust the false bosom. At least Mr. Montgomery appeared to have a sense of humor!

When she turned back around, she found Mr. Montgomery laughing silently. Instead of being relieved as common sense dictated, Natalie found herself becoming irritated. Their lives were at stake, and this man was laughing!

"I am glad you find this amusing, Mr. Montgomery. You have to know how frantic we were that you wouldn't approve of me running Ivy House."

He made a serious effort to control his laughter. Finally, he cleared his throat, his eyes sparkling with suppressed humor. "I apologize, Miss Polk. Believe me, I find myself admiring your spunk and . . . ingenuity." His mirthful gaze dropped to her large, makeshift bosom, which was still askew, despite her efforts to right it. "If that young boy hadn't come along, it might have worked."

Natalie clutched her stomach, dread clouding her eyes. "You mean . . . it *didn't* work?"

"Well, of course it didn't. I know who you *really* are."

"Oh." She laughed a little breathlessly, feeling foolish. "Oh, you mean *that*. I thought you were talking about—" Deciding it wasn't wise to voice her thoughts, Natalie clamped her lips shut. There was a slim chance she was wrong about his reason for being here, and Lord knew she didn't want to put any ideas into his head.

Elliot's mirth subsided abruptly. Natalie's stomach began to flip-flop all over again. She didn't like that serious look, not at all. And she didn't think she was imagining the flash of guilt in his eyes; she'd noticed it earlier.

"What did you think I was referring to?" he queried softly.

"Nothing, nothing at all." Natalie backed away, clutching the stair post for support. He would tell her now. He would tell her that he didn't intend to keep Ivy House open.

Where would she go?

More importantly, where would the children go?

What was she to do?

Reading the fear in her eyes, Elliot suddenly wished the floor would open up and swallow him. He wasn't angry about the way she tried to fool him—not at all. Anyone who would go to such extremes for a good cause showed spirit and courage, something he admired. To be honest with himself, he was more than a little relieved she wasn't *really* a widowed matron, not with the thoughts he was having when he first held her soft-as-silk hand.

Now he could admire her eyes and the sweet curve of her mouth without feeling strange. Now he could wonder what she looked like without the ugly, bulky trappings of her dress and the ash-covered hair.

Now he could get on with it and tell her about Ivy House, his lost fortune, his grandfather's unwise investments, his reason for being here. He would sit them all down and explain every last detail, no matter how humiliating.

After meeting Natalie Polk and the other orphans, he knew he could not send a letter or just bluntly tell them the truth. His honor wouldn't allow it. His *admiration* for Natalie Polk and her concern for her fellow orphans wouldn't allow it.

If his grandfather were still alive, *he* wouldn't allow it, either.

Gazing into her deep blue, anxious eyes, Elliot gathered himself together. "Miss Polk, I'm sorry to say—"

Someone rapped on the door, but before Elliot could sigh in relief at yet another interruption, a familiar voice called out.

"Yoo-hoo! Anybody home? Elliot!"

His gut twisted in response, and he groaned.

Missing the sound, Natalie moved to answer the door. She, too, looked relieved about the interruption.

As well she *should,* Elliot thought in sympathy, turning to face his fiancée. But instead, his gaze drifted to the white apron covering Natalie's behind. That tiny glimpse he'd gotten when Hickory had ripped the bustle away remained emblazoned on his mind.

Natalie Polk possessed a nice derriere, he thought.

"Elliot! There you are! I'm sorry I stayed away so long, but I found the most *wonderful* material for our parlor curtains." Suetta ignored Natalie and swept across the threshold, snapping her parasol closed. She continued to sweep in Elliot's direction, offering her cheek for his kiss.

Elliot automatically landed one in the air near her forehead, seeing Natalie's quirked eyebrow as she closed the door.

"Well," Suetta announced, looking around her with a faint frown. "Not too shabby, although I daresay it could use a little decorating. It might make a decent summer—''

''Suetta, I'd like you to meet Miss Natalie Polk. Natalie, Miss Suetta Riverstake . . . my—'' The word stuck in his throat. He forced it out. ''My fiancée.''

''Shame on you for interrupting, Elliot.'' Suetta tapped him with her parasol and twirled around to stare at the children who had once again gathered in the parlor doorway. ''Why, these must be the little orphans!'' Dismissing them just as quickly as she had Natalie, she craned her neck at the curving staircase and squinted her eyes. ''Did you meet with Mrs. Boone, dear? Have you told her yet?''

Elliot met Natalie's gaze across the room, his expression somber. ''Yes, I've met her. She's a fine lady and does a beautiful job running the orphanage. Now, let's get back to the hotel, Suetta. I'm as hungry as a bear in the spring.'' He didn't think he could force a bite of food between his lips, but he was desperate to get Suetta out of the house before she blurted the ugly news.

''Oh, but—''

''I can't wait to hear more about the curtains for the parlor. You can describe the pattern to me in the carriage.'' Elliot skillfully distracted Suetta as he grasped her elbow and urged her along. To his relief, Natalie stepped forward and opened the door.

Pushing Suetta gently in the direction of the waiting carriage, he paused, staring at Natalie's pale, upturned face. She looked fragile. *She knew,* he realized in that moment as he watched worry darken her eyes to the color of storm clouds. Somehow, she knew what he had come to Chattanooga to do.

''I'll be back tomorrow,'' he said, wishing he could ease her mind. There were other things he wished for, but one glance at Suetta climbing into the carriage reminded him that he had no business wishing them.

But as the door closed behind him, he found himself

wondering what lay beneath her disguise and anticipating the morrow. He already liked the Natalie he *could* see. How would he react to the *real* Natalie Polk?

"Are you 'wake, Natty?"

Natalie mumbled an indistinguishable reply and snuggled deeper beneath the covers. Whoever it was, she hoped they would go away. It had taken her hours to get to sleep, but once she had, she'd begun dreaming about Elliot Montgomery. In her dream, he didn't have a fancy fiancée, and he wasn't rich.

He was *hers*.

"Natty, I wanna sleep wiff you!"

The loud whisper intruded again. Natalie felt a small, chilled body slide under the covers and snuggle against her.

Cold feet touched her knees.

She yelped and sat up, fully awake now. Weak moonlight shone through her open bedroom window, illuminating Hickory's pale features as he snuggled into the mattress. "What on *earth* are you doing here, Hickory?"

He pulled the quilt to his chin, his voice matter-of-fact. "I wanna sleep wiff *you*! They won't let me sleep wiff them." His bottom lip quivered; his eyes were wide and staring.

Natalie shoved her freshly washed hair out of her eyes and blew out an exasperated breath. "It's the middle of the night! And of course Marla and Noah wouldn't let you sleep with them. You're five years old. You should be sleeping in your own bed, Hickory." She threw back her side of the covers, groaning because she knew what she would have to do. "I have to take you home."

"Don't wanna go." Hickory stretched the quilt over his head. "Ain't goin' home."

"But Marla will be frantic if she wakes up to find you gone!"

No answer.

With another groan, Natalie crawled over Hickory and struggled into her dressing gown. Although faded and patched, it was heavy and warm, swirling around her feet and covering her from head to toe. At this hour of the night, she shouldn't encounter a soul on the way.

When she had dressed, she jerked the covers back and folded her arms. "I'm gonna count to three, then I'm gonna go downstairs and get a bucket of water—"

"*No!*" Quick as lightning, Hickory slid from the bed, looking lost and adorable in his sleeping gown.

Natalie's heart softened. She knelt before him, ignoring the hard wooden floor. "Hickory, do you know how much this hurts Marla?" When his face screwed into a confused frown, Natalie tried again. "Her *feelings*, Hickory. Right here." She placed her hand on her heart and spoke softly. "You hurt Marla's *and* Noah's heart when you run away. They think you don't love them."

Hickory slowly shook his head. "No. I just miss you, Natty, and Jo and Brett and Cole and Lori."

"But your home is with Marla and Noah—and the new baby, remember? You've got your own room and a pony. Besides, you can see me any time you want, and you do, don't you?" Hickory nodded. Natalie took his hand and led him quietly downstairs. When they reached the door, she knelt before him again. "If you promise not to sneak away in the middle of the night again, I won't tell Marla about *this* time."

Hickory chewed on his finger, then popped it out to ask, "So it won't hurt her heart?"

"So it won't hurt her heart," Natalie agreed, hugging him so hard he grunted.

Elliot couldn't sleep. With a muttered oath, he rose and pulled on his dressing gown for the third time. His hotel room faced Main Street, and he went to the window now, staring out at the peaceful town of Chattanooga, huddled in the crook of majestic mountains, still and

quiet beneath a slice of bright moon and a sky full of
stars.

He knew why sleep eluded him. He couldn't stop
thinking about Natalie, Jo, Brett, Cole, and . . . Elliot
frowned in thought as he searched his memory. Lori—
Natalie had called the little one Lori. A frail, delicate
child.

His conscience pricked him at the memory, although
he knew he had no choice in the matter. He couldn't
continue to fund Ivy House, and if he didn't sell Ivy
House, then he'd be living on the streets, sleeping in
alleys and doorways, dodging creditors, and wondering
where his next meal would come from.

But wasn't that exactly what he was planning for
them? To put them out into the streets? Elliot slapped
his palm on the windowsill. No, he wasn't, by God. He
had money put aside, money for each of the orphans to
use to find a new home, money the creditors didn't know
about because they had yet to learn of Ivy House.

But it was only a matter of time before Bo Carnagie's
men *did* find out. Then they would hunt him down and
demand their money.

Elliot grimaced, his thoughts returning to the orphans
and the pending adoptions. What kind of people would
be tempted to take on a child just for the money? What
would stop them from taking the money, then ignoring
the child? That was something he hadn't thought of before.

A shadow on the street below snatched his interest.
Elliot leaned closer to the window and peered out, his
brows lifting in surprise. Who would be out at this hour
of the morning? Someone definitely was, he realized, as
the figure moved into a patch of moonlight.

Squinting through the predawn light, he noticed a second figure moving beside the first: smaller, tiny, in fact.
A child? Intrigued, Elliot quietly lifted the window,

watching the odd pair draw closer. Suddenly, the smaller figure bolted forward.

"Hickory, you come back here!" a frantic, hushed voice called after the running figure.

It was Natalie's voice, Elliot realized with a jolt. Natalie and Hickory . . . walking the streets before daylight when everyone else was abed. Why on earth? Elliot shook his head in bemusement. They certainly were an odd bunch.

He watched their progress, straining to get a good glimpse of Natalie now that she wasn't wearing that god-awful disguise. It was no use; the moonlight wasn't sufficient. Hesitating, Elliot waited until they had passed his window. Curiosity ate at him.

He shouldn't . . . but he was going to. He scrambled into his clothes and made his way silently to the street below, knowing he wouldn't sleep until he found out what was going on.

Shock thrummed to her toes as Natalie eyed the knarled old tree Hickory had used to make his way down from his second-story bedroom. She glanced at the open window, then to the branch a scant foot away. A long, shaky-looking branch . . .

"Hickory, tell me you didn't *really* climb down from way up there." Dismayed, Natalie glowered at the small boy. "You could have fallen."

Undaunted as usual, Hickory nodded proudly. "Na. I done it before. Watch me!" Agile as a monkey, he scampered onto a low branch and quickly climbed the tree. When he reached the shaky limb leading to his window, Natalie about swooned.

"Wait!" she whispered fiercely. "Don't move a muscle until I get there." Trembling at the thought, she quickly shed the cumbersome dressing gown and hiked her long cotton nightgown up to her knees, tying it securely. If Hickory started to fall crossing that limb, then maybe she could grab him in time. She shuddered at the thought of Marla finding out about this latest escapade.

Marla wouldn't be too pleased with *her* participation, either, she added gloomily. Taking a deep breath, she began to climb the tree, reminding herself that it hadn't been so very long ago when she'd been a tree-climbing child herself.

Within moments, she reached Hickory. "Now you can go ahead," she whispered. She held her breath as Hickory crawled along the limb to his window. Only when he was safely over the ledge did she breathe a sigh of relief.

Now for the climb down. Trying not to think about how far away the ground seemed, Natalie began her descent. She'd made it about halfway when Hickory's loud whisper made her pause.

"Natty!"

"Shhh! Hickory, are you trying to wake your ma and pa?"

"No. I was just gonna tell you good night, Natty."

Natalie searched the branch below with her foot, found it, and balanced herself. She prayed desperately that Hickory wouldn't remember the hug he always demanded. "Good night, Hickory."

"Good night, Natty. Good night, Mr. 'Gomry."

She heard the window slam shut just seconds before his words sank in. *Good night Mr. 'Gomry? As in Mr. Montgomery?* Natalie froze, closed her eyes, and prayed that Hickory only teased her. Elliot Montgomery was *not* standing below, watching her climb down from a tree in the middle of the night . . . *in her nightclothes!*

"Good night, Hickory."

The sound of Elliot's quiet reply startled a shriek from her throat. Her foot slipped from the limb. Her fingers slipped from their stranglehold on the tree. She clawed at the wood in desperation, but to no avail.

She began to fall.

$\mathcal{S}$he landed in his arms, but the momentum carried them both to the ground in a tangle of limbs, wildly curling hair, and what seemed like yards of cotton nightgown.

"Ooof!" Elliot exclaimed, trying to take the brunt of the fall. The possibility of this little warrior coming to harm alarmed him more than it should. "Are you okay?"

Breathlessly, Natalie struggled to a sitting position, prudently pulling her nightgown down over her bare legs. "I'm okay. Are *you* all right? Did I hurt you?"

Her anxious voice pleased Elliot for some reason he couldn't fathom. "No, you're light as a feather." He tightened his arms around her, inhaling the fresh, clean scent of her hair before leaning back. He wanted a better look at Natalie Polk.

By the light of the moon, his gaze soaked in the sight of the angel in his arms. Elliot smiled at his thoughts; she did indeed look like an angel with her long, wild hair cascading around her face and shoulders, dressed in a long, flowing white night trail. He couldn't be sure, but in the moonlight, the color of her hair appeared to be a pale gold—perhaps the color of summer wheat. Now that she had discarded the bulky baggage she'd used for her disguise, Elliot was extremely conscious of her slim form molded against his thighs and outlined by his hands at her waist. Yes, her body now matched the small, oval-shaped face watching him, he decided. The dimensions now so plainly apparent made his groin tighten in response.

Oh, and he couldn't forget her perky little bottom, which at the moment was pressed warmly against a very sensitive area of his body, an area rapidly changing. Through the thin nightgown, he could feel each contour, every quiver, and he could imagine how close her womanhood was to his—

"Can you stand?" he asked abruptly, cursing the huskiness in his voice and hoping she wouldn't guess the cause.

As if suddenly noticing their intimate position, Natalie gasped and leaped from his lap. She arranged her gown again and extended a hand to help him to his feet. "I'm—I'm *so* sorry! When I heard your voice, it startled me, and I lost my balance."

Elliot kept hold of her hand and slowly drew her closer, enchanted by the vision before him. She looked so wild and sensuous. He felt magic vibrate in the air between them, praying she felt it, too. How could she not?

To confirm his hopes, Natalie pressed a hand to her cheek, as if to feel the heat of her skin. She seemed agitated, and he felt her hand tremble in his.

Elliot understood entirely. His body trembled inside, and his blood felt thick in his veins. Mesmerized by her parted lips, he drew her closer still and lowered his mouth. The gentleman in him was outraged by his impulsive action; the man in him urged him shamelessly on.

Her hands came up to hold his shoulders, and Elliot felt his chest expand at her tentative touch. She didn't resist him but leaned forward as if to meet his mouth. Could she possibly be as eager as he for this wonderful contact?

He touched her mouth lightly with his lips, pausing to slip his hands to her slender waist and draw her gently closer. Not too much too soon, he cautioned himself. She was an innocent, an angel, a breathtakingly lovely woman in the moonlight.

Feeling heady with desire, Elliot tasted her lips and tenderly coaxed them open. He slipped his tongue inside, inhaling her spontaneous moan.

Still, she didn't resist.

He held her tightly now, tracing the curve of her waist, sweeping his hands upward to test the swell of her breasts, all the while deepening the kiss by slow degrees. He didn't want to shock her . . . didn't want to startle her. He wanted the kiss to go on forever. Natalie Polk . . . little orphan . . . felt so *right* in his arms.

She tasted sweet and hot, and when her questing little tongue brushed against his, he groaned, his control slipping.

He pulled her lower body flush against his so there would be no mistaking his hardened arousal. For a delicious moment, he could feel her heat against him. But his loss of control was his downfall. With a gasp of shock, Natalie pulled away and turned her back to him, lifting her hands to cover her face.

Elliot breathed heavily, watching her try to regain control.

"The moonlight," she whispered.

"Causes madness," Elliot concluded softly. He understood that she was attempting to explain her behavior. The realization made him want to drag her back into his arms and make her believe in magic instead of madness, but he had no right. Not only was he affianced, he was also penniless. He had nothing to offer someone like Natalie, someone who had never had the finer things in life.

She deserved better.

"I shouldn't have—"

"I didn't—" Elliot sighed in frustration and turned her around, staring into her huge, shocked eyes. He felt remorse slice through him like a saber. "You did nothing wrong, Natalie. It was my fault. Place the blame on *me*. I shouldn't have taken advantage of you after the fall. You were knocked silly." He was giving her the perfect out.

"Silly," she repeated faintly. Suddenly her voice grew stronger. She nodded, causing a riotous mass of curls to swirl around her shoulders.

Elliot had to physically resist the urge to reach out and grasp a fistful and bring it to his nose.

"Yes, I was knocked silly, dazed by the fall. I—I wasn't myself. You—you have a fiancée."

"Yes," Elliot agreed, unable to hide the bitterness in his voice. When she frowned, he ran a hand through his own hair to keep from touching hers. *If* he didn't have a fiancée, and *if* he wasn't a pauper, he wouldn't be apologizing for his actions. "Shall we start over?"

She shivered but nodded, rubbing her arms in the sudden chill. "Forget it ever happened," she whispered so softly he nearly missed her words.

Mourning the loss of the heat that had kept them warm moments before, Elliot retrieved her dressing gown where it hung from a lower limb and helped her into it. His hands hovered around the buttons right below the neckline, then abruptly fell away. Too tempting.

Forget it ever happened? He didn't think that was a possibility, and he hated to think *she* would be able to forget such a magical moment, either. *Pretend* it never happened? Maybe.

Forget? Never.

• • •

"I'll walk you home."

Home. Still light-headed from the kiss, Natalie fell into step beside him, thankful for the reminder. Ivy House was home, and that was what she needed to concentrate on. Saving it, saving the children, saving herself.

How could she have lost her head that way? How was she ever to convince Elliot how reliable and mature she was after tonight? And not just the incident with Hickory, but falling into his arms afterward.

She shuddered and drew the neck of her dressing gown together with her hand. What was he thinking about her this very moment? Only women of question-able morals participated in intimacies before marriage. Yes, they'd only kissed . . . and touched, but she wasn't altogether certain it was right.

Natalie blinked at sudden tears. She'd been told by Mrs. Boone that her *own* mother had been a loose woman, although Marla had later argued with the house-mother's story. Who was right and who was wrong? she wondered.

They came to the end of the lane and headed down Main Street. Elliot casually took her hand, and when she glanced sharply at him in question, he said gruffly, "For safety."

She started to assure him that Chattanooga was a safe town, but she refrained. She liked the comforting feel of her hand in his, despite the alarming tingles it caused. Her mother had supposedly been seduced by a scoun-drel. Could Elliot possibly be from the same mold? *No, no,* Natalie thought, shaking her head. *He had apolo-gized for his behavior and was the perfect gentleman now.*

They passed houses that were dark and silent, and as they reached the town common, businesses closed up tight for the night. It was dark, but the moonlight con-tinued to light their way along the street. Natalie didn't think she would ever think of moonlight in the same, absent way again. The moonlight would remind her of her first kiss . . . with Elliot Montgomery.

"Would you mind telling me about tonight? With Hickory?" He kept his voice low, and the timbre of it made her tremble in reaction.

How could the simple sound of a man's voice cause such an eager reaction? Not just any voice, Elliot Montgomery's voice. Natalie steadfastly ignored the slight squeeze he gave her hand. She especially ignored the way her heart leaped in response. "Marla and Noah adopted Hickory from Ivy House last year," she began quietly. "He hasn't adjusted well, and then, with the new baby coming, he's grown even more insecure."

"That's understandable."

"He keeps running away and returning to Ivy House. I raised him from a tiny baby—"

"Where was Mrs. Boone?" he interrupted sharply.

Natalie kept her eyes on the road and kept her voice neutral. No matter what her personal opinion of the housemother, she didn't believe in maligning a person who couldn't defend herself. "Mrs. Boone had her hands full with the other children, and I"—she shrugged—"took over caring for him."

"A noble thing for a fourteen-year-old to do."

Flushing with pleasure at his compliment, Natalie said, "He was a beautiful baby, sweet and lovable. It wasn't difficult to get attached to him."

"And he to you," came his deep reply. "I can understand."

Although his words sent weakness to her knees, Natalie strove to ignore his remark. "I think I fancied myself as his big sister, and *he* fancied *me* as his mother. Marla tries to be patient, but it hurts her feelings when he comes home—back to Ivy House."

"Poor Marla." He sounded sincere. "And poor little

Hickory. He must be confused. So that's what happened tonight? He came to you?''

Natalie let out a soft laugh and blurted out before she could consider how provocative her statement might sound, ''He slipped into my bed and planted his cold feet on my knees!''

Elliot stopped in the middle of the road. Since he held her hand, Natalie had no choice but to stop with him. She waited expectantly, tense to the bone. What had she said to cause that frown?

''How did he get into the house?'' he demanded. ''Don't tell me you don't bolt the door at night.''

''I have no choice. In March when there was still snow on the ground, I found him asleep on the porch. He was nearly frozen to death. I decided then and there that it was worth the risk.'' She pulled at his hand and continued walking. Reluctantly, he followed. ''I think you'll find Chattanooga a peaceful town, Mr. Montgomery.''

''Elliot. After what we shared—''

''Which is forgotten, remember?'' When he continued to frown at her, she relented, secretly pleased. She already thought of him as Elliot in her mind. ''Oh, all right, Elliot, then. Although I don't know what people will think—''

''They'll think we're friends. We *are* friends, aren't we?'' he asked softly, lifting her hand to his lips. His eyelids drooped as he gave her a slow, thorough look that made her feel warm all over. His look said he'd like to be *more* than just friends.

Natalie drew in a sharp breath. ''Don't . . .'' Desperately, she scrambled for something to distract him. ''Suetta—''

''Ah, yes, Suetta,'' he said harshly. ''The woman my grandfather picked out for me.''

''Regardless of the reason, you *are* engaged.'' The words felt thick in her throat. She hated to remind him, but to do otherwise was wrong. She tugged gently, and he relented, dropping her hand. Natalie stuffed both hands into the pockets of her dressing gown. Although she felt his hot gaze on her, he continued walking.

"Hickory's parents?" he resumed, as if nothing had happened.

Nothing *had* happened, Natalie sternly reminded herself. And nothing would. Gathering her thoughts, she said, "We didn't see who left him."

"And the others?"

"Marla—"

"Marla was once an orphan at Ivy House?" he asked in surprise.

Natalie lifted her chin, her tone both defensive and challenging. "Does it surprise you that she turned out so well?"

"Not at all. I just didn't know."

"As I was saying, Marla's parents died in a rock slide not far from here. She was adopted by the Masons when she was ten years old. We were very close—still are. I was next in age, and then there's Jo. Jo is . . . well, she came to us when she was about eight. We have never found out who her parents are or *were,* or why she came to Ivy House."

"Do you think she remembers?" He grabbed her shoulder and steered her around the dark shadow of a manure pile in the road that she hadn't noticed.

Natalie mumbled a thank you. "I think she does, but I don't think she'll ever talk about it." God knew she had tried to get Jo to open the festering wound and let the poison out, but Jo refused to discuss her past. Natalie had to respect her decision; she had little choice. "Cole and Brett are brothers."

"Easy to figure out."

"Yes, they do look a lot alike. We think there's about a year's difference in their ages. Cole, the oldest, was about two years old and Brett was barely walking when a traveler brought them to the orphanage. He found them in the mountains in an abandoned shack. No sign of their parents.''

''And Lori?'' Elliot's voice had grown curiously deep.

Natalie dared to hope that he was beginning to care about the children. Hearing their tragic history would move a stone, and she suspected Elliot was far from heartless. ''Her mother died in childbirth. Her father deserted her. She had no living relatives to take her in, so a neighbor brought her to Ivy House.''

''I feel for her—my own mother died having me. Did you care for Lori as you did Hickory?''

''We all pitched in.'' She didn't add that Mrs. Boone would have nothing to do with Lori, and the other children had no choice but to care for the infant. Each time a baby was left at Ivy House, Nelda Boone would disappear into her room for days. Sometimes, Natalie thought she heard the housemother crying.

Since Nelda's desertion, Natalie had decided it must have been her young imagination.

They had reached Ivy House. Natalie glanced at the dark, two-story house in the little hollow, surrounded by mountains and forests.

Home.

She knew very little about the history of the house, other than what Mrs. Boone had grudgingly told her. Making a mental note to ask Elliot at a more appropriate time, she mumbled awkwardly, ''Well, thank you for walking me home.''

Elliot grasped her arm as she started to walk away.

''Don't go yet.'' His voice was low and husky, his grip firm and exciting. ''You haven't told me about the other orphan.''

Natalie frowned at him, trying to still the quaking in her belly. She really *had* to get away from this man! ''What other orphan?''

"You."

No! was her silent, instinctive response. She could not tell Elliot about her mother and the circumstances surrounding her mother's death. He would be appalled, disgusted. "I—I need to go inside. Some other time, perhaps." She hoped that time would not materialize.

After a heart-stopping hesitation, he let her go. She felt his eyes watching her as she let herself in. With a sigh, she bolted the door, confident that Hickory would not return tonight.

He'd *better* not. The little scamp had caused her enough trouble for one night, not to mention the beginnings of a heartache.

"Elliot seems wonderful," she whispered regretfully as she slipped beneath the quilt. *But he's engaged,* her conscience added.

Defiantly, Natalie closed her eyes and conjured an image of Elliot as he had looked in the moonlight, just before he kissed her.

Dreams were harmless.

Weren't they?

Marla opened the door early the next morning to find Natalie on her doorstep. She rubbed sleep from her eyes and blinked. "Natalie? What on earth are you doing here this early? Is something wrong?"

Natalie shook her head and moved inside, craning her neck around. "Noah home?" she whispered.

"No. He's already gone to the mercantile."

"Hickory?"

"Still abed, the little sleepyhead. I don't know what's gotten into him. He usually doesn't sleep this late." With a worried frown, Marla urged her into the kitchen. "I'll make coffee. Sit down." Rubbing her stomach, she set about making a fire in the stove. Something was up, but she knew Natalie would get around to telling her in her own good time. It couldn't possibly be about Mr.

Montgomery, she decided, because she had spoken to Natalie after his visit yesterday.

"I need to borrow a dress," Natalie blurted out.

Ah. Marla hid a satisfied smile. "Which one? Lord knows I can't wear anything decent these days." She gave her stomach an affectionate pat and turned to look at Natalie. *Really* look at her. Marla's critical gaze skimmed her anxious features, noting the subtle changes in her friend this morning. She had drawn her naturally curly white-blond hair into a smooth bun at the nape of her neck, but a few unruly curls had already escaped, framing her face. The style emphasized Natalie's delicate, oval face and made her deep blue eyes look huge.

They *were* huge, Marla silently corrected. Huge and shadowed, as if she hid secrets.

"What are you hiding?" she demanded, suddenly certain something had happened she should know about. Maybe she was wrong and it *did* involve Mr. Montgomery. What else would cause this flush?

Natalie's blush deepened. "Nothing."

She squirmed in the chair, avoiding Marla's direct gaze. *Another* sign that Marla recognized. Natalie was definitely keeping something from her. Sniffing, Marla pumped water into the kettle and measured the grounds. She was growing mighty tired of everyone mollycoddling her just because she was going to have a baby. Slamming the kettle down on the hot plate, she finally turned to face Natalie. If everyone insisted on treating her like an invalid, then she was going to use it to her own advantage. Served them right!

Schooling her features into a look of extreme anxiety, Marla twisted her hands together and suddenly wailed, "Is it so terrible you can't tell me?"

Her ploy worked. Natalie jumped from the chair as if she'd sat on something hot. "No! No, nothing like that." She rushed to Marla and grabbed her twisting hands to still them, her own expression mirroring Marla's.

Marla felt a tiny flash of guilt. She quickly squashed it. If she didn't work at stopping this ridiculous nonsense of treating her like she was made of glass, then she'd be screaming long before this baby was born.

"I promised not to tell," Natalie said in a voice so miserable, Marla instantly knew what she meant. "But I can't tell you *what* happened without telling you *why* it happened."

"Hickory."

Natalie nodded and began to chew on her nails. From a habit formed long ago, Marla gently pried her fingers away. "Tell me. I promise I won't break."

They both sat at the table as the kettle ticked and steamed on the stovetop. Marla braced herself for bad news. Outwardly, she forced herself to appear calm and *strong*. Whatever it was, she could handle it. She had to show them that she was stronger than they believed her to be.

Reluctantly Natalie told her the story—all of it. When she was finished, she plucked at the tablecloth, obviously in an unusual state of agitation. A fierce blush added a wonderful color to her cheeks.

Marla thought she'd never seen Natalie look lovelier, and she couldn't have been more pleased. Hickory's part in the adventure hurt a little, but she was coming to terms with his love for his Natty.

"Do you think I'm just awful?" Natalie asked in a strangled whisper. Her huge eyes beseeched Marla.

Covering her laughter with a cough, Marla shook her head. "Of course not, silly! In fact, I envy you. A romantic interlude in the moonlight with a handsome man like Elliot Montgomery—"

"But he's *engaged*," Natalie said, sounding shocked.

Marla shrugged, her smile mischievous. "Engaged, Natalie, *not* married. Engagements can be broken, and if ever I've seen one that needs to be broken, this one does. He and Suetta are *not* suited, mark my words, and Elliot seems so unhappy."

Natalie quieted, her expression growing thoughtful. "He *did* make a remark that led me to believe he wasn't exactly overjoyed with the arrangement."

Remembering his pained expression yesterday when his fiancée had banged on the window of the store, Marla silently agreed.

Getting to her feet, Natalie began pacing the kitchen. Her faded gingham dress swirled around her feet as she walked. The hem was worn, but the figure-flattering style suited Natalie. It hugged her slim waist and outlined her small, firm breasts to perfection before flaring out at the hips.

"I can't get involved with Elliot Montgomery!" Natalie suddenly cried out.

"Why?"

"Because . . . well, because we know why he's here, for one thing. He's planning to close the orphanage. I could never be interested in a man who would turn helpless children out into the street."

"You're not certain that's why he's here," Marla argued. "Besides, even if that was his *first* intention, maybe after meeting you, he's changed his mind."

With a hopeful look, Natalie halted her restless pacing. "Oh, if only that were true!" Her expression crashed. "But, Marla, he said he had bad news. He's coming back today to tell me. I don't think a little kiss in the moonlight's going to change his mind."

She began her furious pacing again. Marla was beginning to feel dizzy watching her. "A *little* kiss?" Marla shook her head. "Doesn't sound like a *little* kiss to me."

"But he's engaged! And I'm a little miss nobody. An illegitimate *orphan*."

Narrowing her eyes, Marla demanded, "What's wrong with being an orphan?"

"Nothing," Natalie corrected hastily. "But what

about the rest of it? What will he think when he hears about my mother?''

Marla continued to glower. ''Maybe he'll hear it from someone who knows the facts and not from a drunken old bag who doesn't know beans.''

Suddenly Natalie dropped to her knees in front of Marla. ''You've got to help me.''

''Anything. Just ask.'' Marla was *dying* to get these two together. They were a perfect match, and no matter the obstacle, she and Natalie would overcome it together as they always had. They'd made the spit promise.

''I like Elliot.''

''I know.'' Ah, she'd called him *Elliot*. Marla kept her pleased smile to herself.

''But I can't. I shouldn't.''

''Why not?''

''We're too different.'' When Marla opened her mouth to protest, Natalie rushed on. ''He's wealthy and smart, and he knows exactly who his parents were. As if that's not enough, I could never consider giving up the children. You know that.''

Knowing Natalie as she did, Marla understood her feelings of loyalty to the orphans of Ivy House. Gently, she reached out and smoothed Natalie's hair. Just as gently, she said, ''Natalie, you've got your own life to live. The children will grow up. They're practically grown now. Don't miss this opportunity.''

Jumping to her feet, Natalie said with fierce passion, ''I'll *never* desert them as Nelda has done. Never. I can't believe you're suggesting it.''

Unperturbed, Marla shook her head. ''I wasn't suggesting you desert them, silly. You're probably not the only person capable of running Ivy House in Mrs. Boone's stead, however.'' She could tell by Natalie's surprised expression that her friend hadn't thought of the possibility of getting a replacement.

The hopeful light in her eyes quickly dimmed. ''No.''

She shook her head sadly. "No, you're wrong. Think about it, Marla. You know the children; they'd never take to a stranger, and someone else might not have the understanding and patience that I have with them.

"No, it won't work. Look at Jo: She dresses like a boy and refuses to let her hair grow. And Lori, poor sick mite, and Cole, with his bashful ways, and Brett with his bold ones." She sank slowly into the chair, much to Marla's relief. "They'd never get over my deserting them. Oh, what am I talking about? Elliot isn't really interested in little ol' me. It's just a—a temporary attraction, that's all."

With a sinking heart, Marla watched Natalie's mouth firm in that old, familiar way. It meant she was setting her mind on something, and heaven help them all when she did.

"I had a foolish moment, but now I'm thinking straight. Mr. Montgomery was merely carried away by the circumstances and the . . . moonlight, as I was. He's promised to another, a sophisticated, beautiful woman who will do him proud."

Marla winced at the glitter of unshed tears in Natalie's eyes. She doubted Natalie was aware of them.

"And . . . and he's here to ruin our lives. That fact alone should make me ashamed to be thinking such silly, useless fancies." Her chin tilted to a stubborn angle. "Well, whatever it takes, I've got to stop him, somehow, some way, for the children. I'm all they've got."

Marla couldn't argue that point. Natalie *was* all the children had, and a fierce warrior she was, too. *Did Elliot Montgomery know what he reckoned with?* Marla wondered with an inward swell of pride. If there was a way, Natalie would save Ivy House. But Marla feared it would be at the expense of Natalie's own happiness.

Natalie rose and pasted a brave smile on her face that didn't fool Marla. "Well, that settles it. If Mr. Montgomery is determined to save money he probably doesn't need by closing us down, then I'm equally de-termined to change his mind. Now,'' Natalie said as she helped Marla to her feet, ''about the dress.''

Marla felt as if the sun had suddenly appeared after a rainy day on hearing Natalie's request. Her smile was genuine. ''Which dress?''

''The blue one with the tiny white dots,'' Natalie said without hesitation. Then, as if sensing the direction of Marla's thoughts, she added firmly, ''Looking my best will give me confidence and show Mr. Montgomery that we are fully capable of taking care of ourselves. We don't need his ol' money! I still have faith that someone will see the potential in our beautiful dollhouses and make us rich. Then I'll *buy* Ivy house from him.''

''By that time, there won't *be* an Ivy House to buy,'' Marla reminded her dryly.

Natalie looked startled, as if she had forgotten the vital fact that they were taking Ivy House apart for the lumber. Marla nearly laughed at her horrified expression.

''I can't let him go upstairs,'' Natalie whispered faintly.

''No, I don't think that would be wise.''

''I've got to replace the lumber as soon as possible—before he *does* see what we've done to his house!''

''I think that *would* be wise.''

Natalie put her hands to her burning cheeks. ''Oh, Lord help us.''

''Amen,'' Marla said fervently.

5

"*D*oes it really work?" Natalie asked, peering at the tiny mechanical elevator Cole had fashioned from pewter. He'd found an old vase in the attic among the rubble pile and, melting it down, had devised a remarkable elevator for the dollhouse currently under construction. Natalie was amazed at his ingenuity and entranced by the device. She'd known they existed, but she'd never seen a real working elevator.

Blushing at her admiring tone, Cole cranked a tiny handle attached to the outside wall of the house. To Natalie's delight, the elevator began to rise with a squeak. Natalie watched it pass through the tiny windows of the doll house until it reached the third floor.

"It's amazing, Cole," she whispered sincerely. This dollhouse would certainly sell. It had to. "Is it nearly finished?"

Absently Cole nodded. "Yep. It'll be ready to paint by Sunday."

It was Thursday. Three more days, and Natalie could put the finishing touches on the dollhouse and display it alongside the one already in the store. Flushed with pride, Natalie glanced at the others gathered in the attic around the project. It was obvious they all enjoyed their work. Her gaze landed on Lori.

With her lip caught between her teeth, Lori sniffled as she glued tiny cushions onto the furniture Brett had fashioned. Natalie sighed, wishing Lori didn't have to suffer such a nasty cold for so long. But Lori had always been a sickly child.

Sitting in front of the attic window to catch the light, Brett put the finishing touches on a miniature, delicately carved, four-poster bed. Jo stood nearby, gathering empty plates left from the lunch she had served them.

Cole placed a drop of oil in the winding mechanism to remove the squeak, his black hair falling into his eyes as he bent his head.

"You are all so talented!" Natalie praised, her eyes misting. She couldn't bear the thought of failing them; they were her family. They *needed* her.

"Yeah," Brett muttered, staring morosely at the doll-house. "Too bad Old Lady Boone didn't stay around long enough to see her birthday present."

Natalie winced, remembering the very first dollhouse and how hard they had all worked. Secreted in the attic with candles, bundled against the cold, they had worked late into the night on the surprise. Without actual words being spoken, Natalie knew they had all been hoping the gift would soften Mrs. Boone and bring a smile to her sad face.

But Nelda Boone had skipped out before learning of their efforts, and Natalie, intent on getting rid of the reminder, had coaxed Marla into displaying the doll-house for sale in the store window. They could certainly use the money.

To everyone's surprise and delight, it had sold the very first week to a wealthy couple visiting relatives in town. The couple had been unable to resist their little daughter's pleas, which, according to Marla, had soon escalated into screeching demands. Natalie grinned at the memory.

Jo tapped her on the shoulder. "*He's* here," she said anxiously. "From the window, I saw him coming up the lane."

Natalie's smile faded, but her traitorous heart leaped at the thought of seeing Elliot again. Brushing imaginary wrinkles from the pretty blue dress she'd borrowed from Marla, Natalie straightened her spine and went to answer the door.

By the time she descended the two flights of stairs from the attic, she was fully prepared for battle. Head erect, lips pursed, eyes glittering, shoulders back, she pulled open the door.

Her first glimpse of Elliot brought memories of their moonlight tryst rushing through her mind like a strong wind, flooding her face with heat and color. Staunchly, she ignored the telltale blush she could feel. "Mr. Montgomery." She nodded primly, just as she'd watched Nelda Boone do countless times when greeting visitors.

"Natalie." Elliot removed his hat, his eyes dancing with amusement at her rigid formality. He smiled so wickedly that Natalie gasped. "I thought we'd gotten formalities out of the way last night."

Natalie gasped again. The last thing she needed was a reminder! Her dreams after she'd finally fallen asleep had been filled with shameless, sensual visions of Elliot, so intimate she'd blushed in the privacy of her own room.

He was a—a monster for teasing her about her wanton behavior.

After several quick breaths, Natalie summoned her fighting spirit. If Elliot Montgomery thought to soften the blow with his charm, he would fail. She might be young, but she was old at heart. Precious lives were at stake, and he'd soon discover that using such underhanded tactics would get him absolutely nowhere with Natalie Polk. She wasn't like her mother.

"Would you like to come in? We can talk in the parlor."

He hesitated, then stood aside so that she could see the horses tethered to the porch. Natalie stared without comprehension.

"I was hoping you'd go for a ride with me. I'd like to see a little of the countryside where my grandfather grew up."

Natalie stuttered. "But—but isn't that Marla's mare? And Noah's stallion?" She loved to ride but seldom found the time.

"Yes, it is. I was in the store this morning, and your friend Marla mentioned that you loved to ride. She offered the loan of the horses."

She would, Natalie thought darkly. She and her matchmaking friend were going to have to have another long talk. Hadn't she explained very plainly to Marla that there was no future with Elliot Montgomery?

Natalie frowned, looking in the direction of town less than half a mile away, then shifting her doubtful gaze back to Elliot. He certainly looked fine this morning dressed in buckskin riding breeches and a black shirt. Too handsome. Too wicked. Too dangerous. Too hopeless.

"Scared?" he taunted softly, watching her face.

She stiffened. "Of you? Hardly. I was thinking of my reputation—"

"It's safe with me."

What an excellent liar he was! Natalie thought. Her body might be safe, but what about her heart?

"What about Suetta?" She nearly grinned as his wicked smile suddenly floundered. "What would your fiancée think of you dashing around the mountainside with an unattached young female?"

His expression suddenly grew serious. Natalie marveled at how quickly his mood could change. She found that she much preferred his teasing smile. When he smiled, she could almost imagine that he *wasn't* here to close Ivy House.

"Suetta doesn't concern herself with business matters. She's much too busy matching tassels to the curtain material she purchased yesterday."

Business matters. Natalie swallowed hard. Yes, he was here on business, and she'd do well to remember. Feeling chilled, she said, "I'll have to tell the children where I'm going."

"I'll wait here with the horses."

A few moments later, Natalie led the way along a mountain trail that would gradually lead them to a small creek where she and the children sometimes swam in hot weather. The mare responded well to her commands, having recognized Natalie from the previous times she had borrowed her.

When the trail widened, Elliot drew abreast. For a few moments they were silent, each gazing with appreciation at the lush forests surrounding them on both sides. Squirrels chattered and fought among the branches; above their heads, the sky was filled with beautiful, fluffy white clouds. It was a perfect day: a day for love, a day for romance. *For someone else,* Natalie sternly reminded herself.

Finally, she realized that Elliot had taken his fill of nature and was now watching her as if he found her much more interesting. She tensed and darted a quick glance his way.

Beneath the brim of his hat, he slid his gaze over her in bold appraisal. "You were lovely in the moonlight, but you're even more beautiful in the light of day," he said huskily. "Your eyes remind me of dark storm clouds just before dusk."

Natalie managed a careless laugh, though her heart warmed from the compliment. Flirting was something she knew nothing about, but the woman in her recognized it instinctively. "Shouldn't you be spouting such nonsense to Suetta?" She laughed again, this time spontaneously at his chagrined expression.

Quickly, before he could continue in the same vein, Natalie steered the conversation into safer waters. "Tell me the history of Ivy House."

"Mrs. Boone never told you?"

She shook her head, staring straight ahead. Looking at the handsome picture Elliot Montgomery made sitting astride Noah's stallion made her feel reckless and wonderful, without a care in the world.

And she had plenty of cares: four, to be exact.

So she just wouldn't look at him. She *wouldn't*.

"My grandfather named the house after my grandmother, Ivy."

Natalie forgot herself for a moment and glanced at him in surprise. She hadn't known. "How romantic," she blurted out. Blushing, she focused once again on the path ahead. What would it be like to be so loved as Ivy must have been?

"My grandfather loved his wife very much," Elliot agreed, his tone dropping. A hint of sadness removed the last trace of teasing from his voice. "He built the house for her, then went off to war. While he was away, my grandmother contracted a fever while tending the wounded soldiers, and she died. Thank God she died before she found out my father had been killed in battle."

Tears pricked Natalie's eyes. She blinked. How awful it must have been for Gill Montgomery to lose first his son and then his wife!

Elliot continued. "Grief-stricken over my father's death, he returned to Ivy House to find my grandmother dead and buried. He couldn't bear to stay in Chattanooga without her, so in her honor, he turned Ivy House into an orphanage and moved to Nashville, taking me with him. He never returned.''

Remembering his mother's tragic death, her heart went out to Gill Montgomery for his double loss. Through a throat clogged with tears, Natalie sniffled and asked in a wobbly voice, ''Why an orphanage?''

Elliot muttered a soft oath and pulled their horses to a halt on the trail. He offered her his handkerchief. ''It wasn't my intention to make you cry.''

Wiping her eyes, Natalie returned the damp hanky. She felt foolish. ''I'm fine. It's just such a sad, tragic story. How could anyone not be moved? Please, tell me the rest. Why an orphanage? Why not just sell the house?'' She pulled the reins from his grasp and nudged the mare forward, embarrassed by her weakness.

After a moment, Elliot said, ''My grandmother always wanted a big family, but Father was her only child.'' He shrugged. ''I guess that's why my grandfather decided to turn Ivy House into an orphanage. He put his heart and soul into building that house, and this way, I suppose he thought it would benefit many but never be completely out of his hands.''

Reflecting on his words, Natalie had to agree. Ivy House *had* benefited many. It was home to those who had no home, people like herself. Sadly, it had taken her a long time to realize how fortunate she was. ''I always wondered. The house is so beautiful, majestic. It doesn't seem—''

''Like an orphanage?'' he finished, slanting a surprised glance at her.

Flustered because she wasn't certain *what* she had meant, Natalie said, ''Well, Ivy House is probably worth a lot of money. I guess I can't imagine anyone so selfless as your grandfather. Most people would have sold the house.'' She stared pointedly at him, gratified when he flushed. Yes, Elliot understood her meaning all right.

She had also given him the perfect opening, she realized belatedly. Her clammy hands tightened on the reins as she waited for him to speak, to tell her the devastating news.

He met her steadfast gaze, his expression unreadable. "Ivy House would bring a tidy sum, I suppose. My grandfather imported the lumber by steamship." He looked away at the surrounding trees, missing Natalie's startled look. "You won't find cypress trees around here, and he wanted only the best for my grandmother. Cypress wood can withstand any weather."

Natalie felt faint. "Imported? You—you can't find it around here?" she repeated. *No, he can't be right.* She fully intended to replace the missing lumber before he saw what she had done! How on earth could she manage if there wasn't any cypress to be found? The expense of importing it . . . Natalie's mind boggled at the amount, which probably wasn't anything close to the actual cost.

Elliot Montgomery was going to be *furious* with her!

"Yes, imported from Louisiana, I believe. The price of cypress lumber has escalated since my grandfather's day, and I can't imagine what it would cost to build a home like Ivy House these days." Suddenly, he caught sight of her sickened expression. "Are you all right, Natalie?" He leaned close and steadied her with a hand at her shoulder as if he feared she'd topple from the horse. "You look as white as a ghost!"

A ghost. Natalie licked her dry lips. Oh, yes, she would *be* a ghost when he got through with her.

"Maybe we should turn back," he growled in concern. Without waiting for a reply, he turned the horses around and began to head back.

Natalie clutched the pommel as he urged the horses into a bone-jarring trot down the trail. His words kept echoing inside her head, hindering her attempts to think straight. *I can't imagine what it would cost to build a home like Ivy House these days,* he'd said.

What had she done?

• • •

"I'm telling you, Elliot, I can walk! Put me down this instant!"

Her demands fell on deaf ears. Elliot wasn't about to put her down. In fact, he planned to carry her all the way upstairs and make sure she went straight to bed. Back on the trail, she had given him a fright when he noticed how pale she'd become. He never wanted to feel that gut-clenching panic again.

Maybe he should call the doctor out to have a look at her, to ease his mind. Damn it, it was his fault for telling her that tragic story about his grandparents. He should have been more sensitive.

"Elliot! Let me walk!"

"No. I'm carrying you, so you might as well stop struggling." In fact, he wished she *would* be still. Every time she jiggled, her bottom bumped against his arm. Gripping her tighter in his arms, he stepped onto the porch with his burden.

The door opened before he reached it. Jo stood there, her mouth open in shock. "What the he—heck happened to Natty?"

Cole and Brett shouldered Jo aside. Identical faces glowered at him. "Did you hurt her?" Cole demanded, clenching his fists.

"You'd better not have," Brett added, mimicking his brother.

Simultaneously, they lifted their fists. Jo rucked her sleeves back and joined them. Ready to defend Natalie, they blocked the open doorway.

Natalie buried her face in Elliot's neck. Her warm breath sent shivers down his spine. He could feel her firm breast pressed against his hammering heart.

"They're really harmless," she whispered.

"They don't *look* harmless," he whispered back, his mouth inches from hers. Her lips looked moist and tempting. He wanted to kiss her. Desperately. "What shall I do?"

"Put me down, for starters."

He shook his head. He liked having her in his arms. She belonged there. "I'm not putting you down until I get you upstairs. To rest," he added hastily.

Her reaction totally surprised him. With a screech, she struggled out of his arms, landing on her rump before he could catch her. She jumped to her feet, her face the opposite of pale. Beet red, in fact. Elliot stared.

"You—you can't take me upstairs."

"Well, then, I'll just follow you to make sure you get there safely. You nearly fainted out there on the trail—"

"No, I didn't." Natalie brushed herself down, her eyes not quite meeting his. "I'm perfectly well, thank you."

Elliot narrowed his eyes. His amusement faded. "No, you're not."

"Yes, I am."

"Would *someone* tell us what's going on?" Jo demanded. She placed her fists on her boyish hips and looked from one to the other. The boys were equally curious.

"She almost fainted," Elliot snapped.

"I did not!" Natalie denied. She turned to the children. "I—I didn't eat much this morning—"

"But, Natty, you—" The young girl broke off at a meaningful look from Natalie.

Elliot caught the look, and a suspicion began to grow.

Natalie continued, still looking beautifully flustered. "And I felt a little *dizzy* for a moment. Elliot overreacted, brought us back, and now he insists on taking me *upstairs*."

Her eyebrows lifted for emphasis. Elliot clearly understood she was sending a silent message to the youngsters, but he couldn't imagine what that message was.

Baffled and even more suspicious, Elliot moved into the foyer and closed the door.

He wasn't leaving until he got to the bottom of this. With his instincts his only ammunition, he said firmly, "You *are* going upstairs to lie down, and I'm not leaving until I see you safely to your bed. Look at you— you're shaking."

"You—you can't go upstairs with me! It isn't proper—"

"We have our pick of chaperones," Elliot argued dryly. He doubted they would get two feet without all three children on their heels anyway. Crossing his arms, he stood firm. He couldn't forget the memory of her pale face on the trail.

Jo stepped forward to stand beside Natalie. "I guess we'll have to tell him about Lori, Natty."

"Lori? Oh, Lori. Well, we don't want to worry Mr. Montgomery."

Elliot frowned. For a moment there, he could have sworn Natalie didn't have the slightest idea what Jo was talking about. Taking the bait simply because he was curious to see what developed, he asked, "What about Lori?"

Natalie and Jo exchanged a glance that was not missed by Elliot. Natalie opened her mouth, but Jo hurriedly answered his question. "She's sick, so you can't go upstairs."

"Oh? What's wrong with her? She looked fine yesterday." With yesterday's deception fresh in his mind, Elliot didn't consider for a moment that she told the truth. For some reason, it appeared they didn't want him to go upstairs, and he would discover a reason, or he wasn't a pauper.

"Fever."

"Malaria."

Jo and Natalie spoke at once, then glanced at each other in surprise. Elliot suspected it was because they hadn't known their answers would be so similar.

Taking the initiative, Jo explained, "She's suffering from a strange fever. We think it's malaria because of the way it comes and goes."

Elliot looked straight into Natalie's guilty eyes, daring her to lie. "The only cases I've heard of are those abroad. Has the doctor looked at her?"

Natalie's eyes flickered, then brightened as if she'd just remembered something. "Yes. He has. He said she should be well in a few weeks."

Elliot searched for a lie and saw nothing but honesty in her direct gaze. Still not convinced he wasn't being played for a fool, he stepped by Natalie and sauntered to the stairs. "I think I'll check on her myself."

"I'd feel just awful if you got sick, Elliot."

He halted with his hand on the stair rail at Natalie's urgent, sincere voice. Yes, she sounded sincere, but what about his earlier suspicions? What about the trick they had pulled on him yesterday?

"Natalie! I don't feel well."

He glanced up at the sound of Lori's weak call followed by a bout of pitiful coughing. Before he could recover from the realization that they'd been telling him the truth all along, Natalie sped past him, skirts held aloft as she raced upstairs. One glance at her alarmed face in passing swept the last of his doubts away and left him feeling like a fool.

Jo came to stand at his elbow, her brown eyes bright with triumph. She stuck her hands in her pockets. "Would you like a bite of something to eat, Mr. Montgomery?"

Elliot thought about Natalie's comment of yesterday when she'd proudly exclaimed that Jo could make four meals out of one chicken. The thought of taking a single bite of food from these youngsters made him feel ill.

His gaze wandered back to the stairway landing

above. He could barely hear Natalie's soothing voice as she talked to the sick child.

His dismay increased tenfold. If he thought the task of telling them was going to be difficult before, how could he possibly tell them now?

Nobody would want to adopt a sick child.

6

"What do you mean, you haven't told them you're going to close the orphanage yet?" Suetta's mouth was pinched in anger as she faced him in his hotel room. "Elliot, we talked about this. Your grandfather was a softhearted fool. This is a prosperous town. Let them build their *own* orphanage!"

"And meanwhile?" Elliot stared at his fiancée as if seeing her for the first time. He'd known she possessed faults, but he hadn't realized how completely selfish she was until now. Still, for the sake of their lifelong friendship and in memory of his grandfather, he felt honor-bound to try to make her understand. "Even if the town *would* build another orphanage, where would the children stay until it's finished?" Where would Natalie go?

"That's not your concern," Suetta snapped. "Look at all the money your grandfather wasted on that—those—" Unable to think of a proper word, Suetta stamped her foot in frustration. Finally she drew a deep breath, as if to contain her anger. "Elliot, if you must, build them another house. Something smaller, cheaper. I want *that* one. It will make a perfect summer retreat for us."

"I can't." Obviously this trip had not strengthened their relationship as he'd hoped when he invited her to come along.

He'd put off telling her the truth long enough. The time was now. His expression grim, he looked at the woman he might have married. Slowly and distinctly, he announced, "I'm broke."

"Broke?" she repeated stupidly. *"Broke?"* She began to shake her head, her face a mask of disbelief. "No, no, you're lying, Elliot. Everyone knows that Gill Montgomery was a rich man. He left everything to you."

"He left *Ivy House* to me," Elliot explained in a soft voice threaded with impatience. "After the debtors got their share, there wasn't a penny left." He wasn't about to sour his grandfather's memory by telling Suetta the rest. She didn't have to know about the money from the loan tucked away in his jewelry case or how he intended to use it to help the orphans find a home.

Digging deep into the pockets of his trousers, he grabbed the bottom edges and turned them inside out. They were empty. As empty as Suetta's eyes had suddenly become, he thought, mildly surprised. Had his money been the attraction all along? Was there no love at all between them? To think he had never given it much consideration.

Feeling irrationally uncertain now, Elliot hesitated. He suspected it was mostly his bruised pride talking, but he had to know. He couldn't let her walk away without finding out. Closing the distance, he tilted her face to his, searching, searching for a single trace of affection in the translucent clarity of her face.

For an unsettling instant, another, softer face clouded his vision: Natalie Polk, her beauty illuminated by the moonlight.

Elliot firmly thrust it away. Just as there was no future for him and Suetta, there was no future with the spirited orphan who occupied his thoughts, not for many years to come, not until he could build a business and regain lost ground.

He was a man without money, a pauper with no future to promise to anyone.

Suetta's mouth remained pinched with anger and shock, but her eyes glittered. Tears? Elliot doubted it. Frustration, maybe. And why shouldn't *he* feel betrayed, as well? Yes, he had lied to her—or omitted the truth—but, apparently, she had lied to him too.

Harshly, he growled, "Have you never loved me, then?"

"I'll just look him straight in the eye and tell him the truth," Natalie mumbled, searching along the hall for Elliot's room number. The clerk downstairs had given her the information reluctantly, obviously wondering what an unattached female wanted with the very *attached* Elliot Montgomery. Steeped in guilt, she had nearly blurted the answer to the clerk's silent question, just to see someone else's reaction before she must witness Elliot's.

She could just see the clerk's face now as she told him, "I'm here to tell Elliot Montgomery that I've been taking his house apart and using the lumber to make silly dollhouses." Thank goodness she managed to stop herself in time.

Natalie continued to mutter about the dire consequences as she paused at each room. 206, 208, 210. Her steps lagged as she drew closer to room 212.

He could put her in jail.

He could throw them out today.

He could strangle her, *then* have her thrown in jail.

Her mouth went dry at the thought. Suddenly, she wasn't certain she would have the courage.

"Of *course* I loved you—I *do* love you, Elliot!"

Natalie ground to a halt outside a partially open door at the sound of Suetta's shrill declaration. Quickly, she read the number on the door, her heart sinking when she saw that it was indeed Elliot's room. An amorous sigh from within painted an unwanted picture in her mind, that of Suetta in Elliot's arms being thoroughly kissed.

Natalie *knew* that sound, because she had heard it from her own lips when Elliot had kissed *her*.

She stuffed a fist in her mouth and whirled for the stairs, admonishing herself along the way even as she fought tears. Of course they were kissing. They were going to be married.

The kiss she and Elliot had shared in the moonlight had meant nothing, just as she suspected. Elliot was in love with Suetta, and Suetta had just reassured Elliot that *she* loved him—loudly and clearly.

What a silly, naive fool she had been!

Natalie rushed downstairs and past the astonished clerk behind the desk. His expression reminded her that ladies did not run. She forced herself to finish the last few feet to the door at a hurried but dignified walk. As she pushed through the doors, bright sunshine mocked her with its promise and warmth.

If her heart ached, then it was nothing more than she deserved for thinking for a single instant that Elliot was sincere when he hinted he wasn't happy with Suetta. She should have listened to the strong voice of reason inside her when it firmly warned her about his actions.

Natalie walked briskly in the direction of Ivy House, ignoring her burning eyes. She'd been right all along; Elliot Montgomery had merely been wooing her to soften the blow.

That scoundrel! That rogue! That—that *devil*!

Well, he wouldn't win this game, Natalie vowed, turning onto the grass-grown lane to Ivy House. She would fight him till the bitter end, and if she lost anyway, then she'd have the knowledge that she'd done her best. *If* she lost, it wouldn't be because Elliot Montgomery had made a fool out of her.

Stomping onto the porch, Natalie surprised the children with her forceful entry. The heavy door crashed open.

Three pairs of eyes turned to look at her expectantly. Although her fever had broken during the night, Lori was still abed—Natalie's orders.

Natalie plastered a brave smile on her face.

"You look mad," Jo said.

Brett nodded in agreement. "Your cheeks are all red. Did you and Mr. Montgomery have a fight?"

"Is he runnin' us off?" Cole's voice cracked endearingly as he asked the question.

So the smile didn't work. Natalie should have known she couldn't fool them. They knew her too well. Avoiding a direct answer because she couldn't possibly explain to them what *did* happen, she said, "We've got work to do if we're going to save Ivy House." She glanced at Cole. "Is the house ready to paint? Do we have another in the making? I'll take them to Nashville by steamboat and beg the stores there to display them, if I have to."

If she could hold Elliot off for a few weeks, then maybe they would have enough money saved to offer a small down payment. Surely Elliot wouldn't turn them out without giving them a chance.

She couldn't be *that* wrong about him, could she?

Marla could hardly contain her joy as she accepted Suetta's money for the steamboat ticket.

Suetta was leaving Chattanooga!

With difficulty, Marla kept the happy smile from her face as she counted out the correct change. "Leaving us so soon?" she asked guilelessly.

Suetta's mouth tightened, and for a moment Marla thought the woman was not going to answer, but years of practice in the art of proper etiquette finally won.

"Yes, I am. Although Chattanooga is a *quaint* little town, I'm more accustomed to the city."

When Suetta offered no further information, Marla boldly persisted. "Just one ticket?"

Again, Suetta looked as if she'd bitten into a sour apple. "Yes. Mr. Montgomery is remaining behind for the time being. I may rejoin him at a later date."

This time, Marla sensed Suetta wanted to add more to the statement, but to her frustration, the woman clamped her lips shut. Marla placed the change in her gloved hand. "Well, we'll look forward to your next visit, then. Although I don't blame you for leaving." She paused deliberately before dropping her voice to a hushed whisper. "What with the danger and all."

"What do you mean?" Suetta demanded, her attention caught.

Marla feigned surprise. "You mean you don't know? I thought someone would have warned you."

Suetta's patience slipped. "Speak plainly, woman!"

Eying the fat sausage curl lying against Suetta's scrawny neck, Marla fought the urge to wrap her fingers around it and give it a good yank to remind the woman of her manners. Instead, she crossed her fingers out of sight and lied blatantly, "I'm talking about the Indians who live in the mountains."

"Indians?" Suetta squeaked, clutching her throat. "There are Indians around these parts?"

Marla nodded solemnly. "Yes, ma'am. Indians. They ain't too friendly, either. We call them renegades, and sometimes they slip into town in the dead of night—"

"That's enough! I've heard quite enough." Suetta glanced wildly around her, as if she expected an Indian to jump out from behind a ten-pound sack of flour. "I've got a boat to catch. Good day."

Pleased with herself and just a tad ashamed, Marla watched Suetta flounce from the store with more haste than grace. Her smile faded, though, when she saw the identity of the man Suetta literally barreled into just outside the door.

With growing anxiety, she watched Elliot and Suetta converse. She couldn't hear what they were saying, but the sight of Suetta's wildly waving hands and bobbing head gave her some indication of what the conversation was about: Indians.

When Elliot produced a handkerchief for Suetta, Marla winced. She hadn't meant to make the woman weep with fear, for goodness' sake! Finally, to her great relief, Elliot helped Suetta into the waiting carriage.

Then he climbed in after her.

Marla sucked in a dismayed breath. What if Suetta had convinced Elliot of her preposterous story and he, too, was leaving? But no, she assured herself, he hadn't purchased a ticket. She gave a guilty start at the gruff sound of Noah's voice behind her.

"Are you responsible for upsetting that poor woman, Marla?"

Slowly, she turned to face her husband. Apparently, he had emerged from the small storage room in the back of the store and had witnessed the scene on the boardwalk. How much had he overheard? "I—I didn't mean to—" To her mystification, she burst into tears.

Concerned, Noah gathered her in his arms and patted her back as she soaked his shirt. "There, there, Marla. I'm not angry with you, but this should teach you a lesson. No good can come from you meddling in other people's affairs, you know."

"I know," she sniffled. Noah was right. Poor Suetta, hysterical because of her meddling. And yes, she *had* learned her lesson—because now Elliot was consoling his fiancée, and she most definitely had not meant for *that* to happen!

Noah gently took her shoulders and forced her to look at him. "No more meddling?"

"No more meddling."

"Promise?" Noah persisted gently.

Marla stared into his loving brown eyes and nodded. "I promise. If it was meant to be for Elliot . . . and Natalie, then it will work out."

She prayed that it *would* work out. Elliot was Natalie's man!

The steamboat chugged out of sight around Moccasin Bend, the departing whistle a forlorn sound that echoed around him like a coyote's mournful cry. Elliot stood for a moment, feeling sad yet relieved that this part of his life was finally behind him. Although in the end it was a mutual agreement to end the engagement, Elliot still believed that Suetta had not loved him at all but had only loved his money.

What was his excuse? Why had he let things just drift along when he knew they weren't suited?

At the hotel, he'd kissed her one last time to be sure about his nonexistent feelings. She'd moaned and kissed him back with more passion than she'd ever shown him, but Elliot had instinctively known it wasn't sincere. Gazing into each other's eyes and sad for the time they had wasted together, they had finally admitted the truth; yes, they were friends, but no, they were not meant to be life mates.

It was over. She was gone and wouldn't be returning.

Elliot turned from the river and began to walk in the direction of town. He had sent the carriage on not only because he needed this time alone with his thoughts but because he was aware of how little money he had left. Even that small amount for the driver would be money taken from one of the orphans.

What was he going to do about Ivy House? He shook his head and sighed, wishing there was *something* he could do besides closing the orphanage and selling the house to settle his grandfather's debts.

His own dismal future no longer seemed important,

compared to four young lives—five, including Natalie.

A cool breeze stirred his hair, and the sun beat warmly upon his head. Summer was fading, but the lush greenery around him mocked the season's changing. In the distance, he heard the musical laughter of a child.

The sound increased the despondency in his heart, because it reminded him of four helpless orphans and one very determined, spirited, loyal young woman. As if he could ever forget!

Elliot came to the edge of town and moved onto the boardwalk. Head down, he pondered the future. How would he live with himself if he did what he knew he must do? Was he really so callous he could evict a young woman and four orphans into the streets for his own gain?

No, he couldn't, but there was no alternative.

As he passed before the mercantile, the dollhouse in the window caught his attention. Stopping abruptly, Elliot stared at the unusual creation. Suetta was gone. There was nothing to keep him from satisfying his curiosity, no pressing engagements other than delivering bad news, no fiancée waiting impatiently.

He went inside and, seeing that Marla was busy behind the counter, knelt to get a closer look. His first impression had been right; this was remarkable craftsmanship, right down to the yellow-and-white-checked curtains in the windows. Dollhouses could be bought in Nashville and the larger cities, Elliot knew, but he'd never seen any to compare to this. He couldn't see what manner of lumber was used because of the paint, but he suspected it was high quality. Someone was very talented indeed.

"Interested in buying the dollhouse, Mr. Montgomery?"

Elliot straightened at the sound of Marla's voice, but his gaze remained on the dollhouse. The design reminded him of something, but he couldn't quite place it. "No, I don't have anyone—" He stopped abruptly, thinking of Lori, sick in bed. A child so deprived would appreciate a gift such as this, if only he could purchase it.

His hands went to his empty pockets, belatedly remembering he'd left what money he had in the hotel room. He let them fall slowly away, a flush staining his cheeks because Marla was staring at him strangely, as if she knew.

"I don't have any children," he said softly. "If I did, I would definitely buy one. They're exceptional. In fact, I've never seen anything to compare."

"I agree." Marla darted a quick glance to the back of the store, then focused her gaze on Elliot again. "We've sold four already."

When she began twisting her hands together in front of her, Elliot narrowed his eyes in suspicion. "And?"

"Well, I was just thinking . . . about how well something like this would sell in, let's say, Chicago or New York. Even Nashville. Don't you think?" Before Elliot could respond, she rushed on. "It's a shame Mr.—Mr.—Smith, yes, *Mr. Smith,* has declared himself a hermit. He lives in the mountains and rarely ventures into town. Yes, it's a shame. He could market these dollhouses and make a fortune."

Elliot looked at the majestic little dollhouse, then back to Marla. Excitement flooded his bloodstream, sending his heart on a mad gallop fueled by hope. Marla was right; they would almost assuredly sell fast in the bigger cities. It was a gamble, but what did he have to lose? If the dollhouses *did* sell, it would buy time—for himself and for Natalie and her orphans.

As if she sensed his interest, Marla prompted, "Whoever acted as middleman for Mr. Smith would reap a tidy profit as well, wouldn't he?"

Dazed by the whirlwind of ideas and possibilities, Elliot nodded absently. Would his gold pocket watch—he

grimaced at the thought of parting with it—bring enough
to buy the dollhouse? If it did, then he could send the
dollhouse to Warren Pemberton, an old school friend of
his who now lived in New York. Warren owed him a
favor. Warren had valuable connections. Warren would
help.

With sudden urgency, he rasped, "How long does it
take Mr. Smith to make one of these?"

Catching his excitement, Marla grinned. "A week at
the most. Maybe less."

"Hold this one for me. I'll be back in less than an
hour."

"Yes, sir!" When he made to leave, Marla stopped
him. "Mr. Montgomery, can we keep this to ourselves?
At least until we see how things will work out? I don't
want to get Mr. Smith's hopes up, you understand?"

"Of course. It's our secret for now." Elliot didn't
mind her request; he wasn't ready to reveal his sad financial state to the world, and if people knew he was
about to embark on such a desperate venture, well, they
might make a shrewd guess.

He couldn't risk Carnagie finding out about Ivy House
before he had a chance to save it.

Everyone would find out soon enough.

Flushed with victory, Marla followed Elliot to the door,
peering after him to see which direction he would take.
Hmmm. His destination appeared to be the jewelry shop
two doors down from the mercantile. Just as she suspected when she'd seen him pat his empty pockets, Elliot Montgomery was not all he appeared to be. With a
satisfied nod, she closed the door and began to hum a
happy tune on her way back to the counter.

She spent the next half hour thinking about her discovery. It was a shame Mr. Montgomery appeared to
have empty pockets, but it was not a total loss. To
Marla's thinking, Mr. Montgomery's lack of money re-

moved another obstacle from Natalie's path. Natalie couldn't complain about him being rich, *if* she decided it was wise to tell Natalie what she knew. Lord, if Noah found out—

A noise behind her stole her breath from her lungs.

Slowly, she turned, certain she would find Noah standing with his arms folded, giving her that exasperated, patient look that always made her feel miserable.

It was Hickory, rubbing his sleepy eyes and yawning. One strap of his overalls hung down to his elbow; there were new holes in both knees.

Marla let out a relieved, guilty sigh and held out her arms. "Are you ready for a nap, darlin'?"

Hickory frowned. "I'm Hickory, Mama. Not dawlin'."

Laughing, Marla gathered him to her and squeezed him hard. Life was good! She couldn't *wait* to tell Natalie she had found an investor!

7

Natalie stared at her friend in open-mouthed shock. "You didn't!"

"I did!" Marla nodded happily, obviously pleased with herself. "I sure did."

"Tell me word for word how this came about." Shaking with excitement, Natalie grabbed Marla's hands and pulled her through the foyer and into the kitchen. She pushed her gently into a chair. If Marla teased her, she would pull every hair from her head! "Tell me," she demanded again, scared to hope, to believe that her dream had come true. This could be the answer to their prayers! Ivy House might be saved.

"Where are the children?"

Stifling her impatience, Natalie gritted her teeth. "Jo's outside in the garden, Cole and Brett are working in the attic, and Lori is taking a nap."

"How is she?"

"Better." Natalie gave Marla's hands a warning squeeze.

"Did you know you have paint on your nose?"

"Marla!"

Marla laughed and relented. "Okay, okay. Well, this man—"

"What did he look like?" Natalie didn't want Marla to leave out the slightest detail. "Old? Young? Rich?"

"Old." Marla looked away, frowning as if in thought. "Gray hair, with a paunch belly. Nicely dressed. He had on a checkered woolen suit—"

"Enough." Natalie could contain her patience no longer. She squirmed in the chair, then hopped to her feet to pour Marla a cup of water she didn't ask for from a pitcher on the counter. "Tell me what he said."

"Well, he saw the dollhouse and exclaimed over the craftsmanship, then asked who the carpenter was."

"You didn't tell him!" The thought made Natalie's mouth go dry. If the man in question happened to run into Elliot . . . She took a deep gulp of Marla's water, her teeth chattering against the tin cup. "Of course you didn't."

"No, I didn't," Marla echoed, her voice laced with amusement. "As I was saying, I told him a Mr. Smith was the carpenter, a hermit living in the mountains."

Natalie stifled a nervous laugh with her hand. "You didn't!"

"I did. And then he asked if I thought Mr. Smith would be interested in making more dollhouses. I told him I thought he would and asked him why. He said that he would like to buy the one in the window and take it to New York City—"

"New York City!" Natalie gasped. All the way to New York City! It was even more than she could hope for. "Go on."

"Well, he said that it might take a few weeks, even a month, but that he would let me know when he needed more. He seemed *certain* that he would be needing more." Marla was grinning hugely now.

"And we'll have them ready," Natalie vowed.

Marla's grin faltered. "What will you do for lumber?

You can't keep using the house, Natalie. If Mr. Montgomery finds out—''

"He won't find out." Natalie swallowed hard, remembering yesterday at the hotel and how close she had come to making a greater fool of herself. Elliot Montgomery and his underhanded ways didn't deserve her honesty. "Right now, we have no choice in the matter, but as soon as we start making a profit, I'm going to have Cole and Brett replace the lumber upstairs." *And pray he doesn't notice it's not his precious cypress!* But telling Marla *that* particular information would only make her worry, so Natalie kept quiet. Surely, Marla would forgive her for keeping this tiny little secret.

After a week of hard work, Natalie declared a day of rest at Ivy House, concerned at how pale the children looked. They needed fresh air, and the day promised to be warm enough for a swim at the creek—possibly their last opportunity of the season. Jo packed a lunch, and by eleven, they were gathered in the kitchen, ready to head out.

Natalie peered into the basket, masking her dismay on viewing the pitiful contents. "Potatoes? Does this mean I need to go to the market?" Come to think of it, she couldn't remember the last time she had gone to replenish the pantry.

Jo shrugged. "We have plenty of potatoes in the garden, and there's still a lot of apples to be picked. I'll gather the eggs later for supper. We're not starving, Natty."

Not starving. Natalie winced. No, they weren't starving, but the children needed something besides potatoes, apples, and eggs! She should have been more observant, more responsible. But right now, they were off for a swim; tomorrow, she would buy what they needed. Smiling brightly at the gloomy faces surrounding her, Natalie rubbed her tummy and attempted to bring a little sunshine into the house. "Roasted potatoes—my favorite."

"I *hate* roasted potatoes," Cole muttered.

"I hate potatoes of any kind," Brett added. He shot Jo a sour look as if she were responsible. "How come *she* gets to stay and we have to go with you?"

Natalie sighed, wishing she understood their reluctance to take a break from their work. Most children would be anxious to go for a picnic and a swim on such a beautiful day. "Jo is older. She doesn't want to go with us."

"Neither do I," Cole responded.

Lori poked at one of the crackling skins of the potatoes and made a face. "Can't we have something else? And I don't want to go with you. You said I couldn't swim anyway!"

Patience, Natalie. "No, you can't swim because you've been sick, but you need the fresh air and sunshine just like Cole and Brett do. Jo works in the garden, so she gets out of the house."

Despite their rumblings along the mountain trail, by the time they reached the creek, they were hot and thirsty, and the boys were eager to jump into the refreshing water for a swim. Natalie sat on the bank with Lori, making mud pies; she didn't have the heart to swim without her.

As children sometimes do, they soon forgot their worries. Cole and Brett made a game out of splashing the girls. Natalie and Lori squealed in pretend outrage, secretly enjoying the sprinkling of water.

No one seemed to be hungry.

When they headed for home, Natalie noted with satisfaction that they all looked refreshed and happy. She, on the other hand, felt like a limp rag. Her hair was damp, prompting the curls to spring into tiny ringlets from her thick single braid; her dress front was soaked through, and her bare feet were caked with mud.

They'd had fun.

She was very pleased with herself for *not* thinking about that rotten Elliot Montgomery. Not once in the last two hours had she wondered why he hadn't returned to Ivy House since early last week. He was still in town, Natalie knew. Marla kept her informed.

Natalie lifted her chin, her eyes narrowing on the trail ahead without seeing a thing. Maybe Elliot Montgomery was a coward and was spending his time gathering his nonexistent courage.

After all, it must take a *lot* of courage to close an orphanage and leave four helpless orphans homeless!

"Natty, I'm tired. Will you carry me? Just for a little bit while I rest?"

Jolted from her reflections about Elliot, Natalie blinked and gazed down at Lori's upturned face. Her heart melted. "Sure I will, honey." Before she could shift the basket and her shoes to her other arm and oblige the child, however, Cole volunteered to ride Lori piggyback.

The moment Lori was settled, he took off down the trail at a mad gallop, mimicking a horse with remarkable likeness. Natalie laughed as Lori held on for dear life and began to scream in mock terror. Brett jumped out from behind a tree and began to growl ferociously, stalking them like a wild bear.

She vowed to plan outings like this more often. The children needed serenity and happiness in their lives, not fear, lack of proper nourishment, and hours of hard work.

They should never have to worry about someone taking their home away.

Following the noisy children, Natalie vowed that someday they would never, ever have to suffer this agonizing suspense again.

When they reached Ivy House, she dropped her muddy shoes on the porch and entered the foyer. Her nose twitched. Something smelled wonderful! Not chicken, but . . . beef! How on earth?

"Jo? What are you cooking?" Natalie ventured into the kitchen, a keen feeling of foreboding skimming her nerve endings. Jo stood by the ancient stove, stirring something in the heavy iron pot they used to make soups and stews. With each stroke, the smell of beef wafted upward in the air, filling the kitchen with its rich aroma.

Not chicken, but *beef*. How long since they'd had the luxury of beef? Ages and ages. Last Christmas, if Natalie's memory served her right.

Jo removed the spoon and replaced the lid. "Supper should be ready in about a half hour. Did y'all enjoy yourselves?"

Natalie frowned, frozen in the doorway. Jo was avoiding not only her question, but her eyes as well. "Jo, where did you get the beef for the stew?" she asked quietly.

With a typical shrug, Jo tried to make light of her answer. "Someone gave it to us."

Natalie gripped the door frame. "Someone?"

Tilting her chin, Jo finally faced Natalie. "All right, Mr. Montgomery brought the beef."

"But, Jo—"

"And I invited him to dinner."

"What!" Natalie felt faint. Elliot was coming to dinner!

"He was nice enough to bring us the beef, so I asked him if he'd like to eat supper with us. He said he'd be delighted."

Natalie swayed. Mr. Montgomery apparently suffered a guilty conscience, but did he really believe an offering of food would soften the blow? No one could be that naive, she thought with angry amazement. Licking her dry lips, Natalie asked hoarsely, "When did he say he would be back?"

"He should be here any time now. Natty, you're not

mad at me, are you? Wasn't it the right thing to do, since he brought the beef?'' Jo brushed her hands nervously across her apron. It was the most feminine article of clothing she would allow herself to wear. ''He looked kinda lonely.''

Lord! It was worse than Natalie thought. He had managed to make Jo feel sorry for him. Her gaze went to the painting of the Last Supper hung on the wall above the kitchen table. Would *this* supper be any different? He'd eat with them, tease the children, make them laugh, pretend to be their friend, then calmly take their home. Yes, Elliot Montgomery was a Judas among them, smiling and seemingly innocent.

Natalie had never been so certain of anything in her life.

And this certainty filled her with incredible sadness for what might have been, had Elliot been anyone other than the man who controlled their very future.

''The stew is delicious,'' Elliot complimented as he dipped a second helping into his bowl. ''Best I've ever eaten.'' *Amazing that a girl so young could work such wonders in the kitchen,* he thought, savoring a spoonful of the rich broth and hearty pieces of carrots and onions. Strangely, there were no potatoes in the stew.

Jo gave him a shy smile, her youthful cheeks blooming with color. ''Thank you, Mr. Montgomery. It wasn't hard to fix.''

''Did your grandfather really build Ivy House with his own two hands?'' Brett asked.

Turning to answer his question, he caught Lori staring at him, her expression awed. He smiled gently at the pale, freckle-faced girl, remembering the dollhouse and how badly he'd wanted to purchase it for her.

Elliot transferred his gaze to Natalie, who sat across from him, seemingly engrossed with her meal. She hadn't spoken more than three words to him since they sat down to eat. He found himself looking forward to finding out why. To Brett, he said, "Well, I'm sure he didn't do it all alone. Perhaps the neighbors helped." His grandfather had often reminisced about the advantages of living in a small town. "Sort of like a barn raising," Elliot added, recalling the tale. "Do you have those in Chattanooga?"

Both boys nodded. Natalie didn't look up from her meal, as if she hadn't heard his question. Elliot frowned. What had he done to deserve such ill-mannered treatment? Deciding to test the waters, Elliot directed a question at her. "Natalie, have you ever participated in a barn raising?"

He nearly choked on a bite of stew as she suddenly lifted her blazing eyes to look at him. With little effort, he could imagine streaks of lightning shooting from the dark storm clouds of her eyes. Yes, she was furious. Because of the beef? Or was it because he'd wheedled an invitation to dinner from Jo? And why did she keep glancing at the painting on the wall of the Last Supper?

Her tone held the chill of an early-winter morning. "We are never invited to social functions, Mr. Montgomery. The townspeople aren't cruel to us, but neither are they overly friendly. Most fear that our parents were murderers or thieves, and that makes *us* their spawn."

Elliot reached for his water, suddenly noticing that he was the only one with a glass. Everyone else drank from a tin cup. Spurred by his own embarrassment and the pity her statement aroused, Elliot felt his own anger rising. She knew damned well he wasn't one of the townspeople. "Should I have left my valuables at the hotel, then?" he asked in mock alarm.

Natalie gasped in outrage, her face going pale.

Jo laughed, realizing his jest for what it was, despite the anger behind it. Soon Brett, Cole, and Lori joined her. The noise of their combined laughter nearly deafened Elliot, but their mirth was contagious. It was impossible to listen to their genuine, belly-hugging laughter and stay angry.

He smiled.

Natalie didn't. She rose from her seat, raked a scathing glance around the table—with no results—and stalked from the room.

Elliot stared in fascination at her rigid back and swaying hips until Jo gave his arm a good-natured punch.

"Go after her," she said with a gasp, wiping her streaming eyes. "You—you—" She couldn't finish, breaking into fresh laughter.

He found her on the porch, gripping the railing and staring out into the gathering dusk as if she weren't aware of his approach. But Elliot saw the telltale tightening of her shoulder blades and knew she was perfectly aware of his presence.

"I'm sorry," he said softly.

"It doesn't matter."

"Liar." From his position behind her, he could see her hands gripping the wood railing. Her fingers turned white. He moved closer, itching to touch the baby-fine curls at the nape of her neck or trail his finger lightly along the enticing curve of her spine.

Whenever he was near her, he wanted to *touch*.

She took a deep breath but didn't turn. Her words came out in a soft explosion. "Liar, thief, murderer. Maybe all three."

Elliot ignored the taunt, sensing the pain and heartache behind her bitter words. He longed to enfold her in his arms and soothe the hurt of a lifetime, yet he hesitated, fearing she would mistake his comfort for pity. "I don't care if your father was Jesse James, Natalie." Daringly, he turned her around and pulled her close. He looked directly into her widened eyes. "It doesn't matter to me at all."

"Why don't you just get it over with?" she whispered. "Why are you keeping us in suspense?"

His gut twisted at her words. She struggled to break free of his hold, but he held tight. If he let her go now, he feared he would lose her forever. "Natalie, I—"

"Is it some cruel game you enjoy playing? We know why you're here, so stop being a coward and just say it!"

Elliot stared at her trembling lips. He could hardly think with her mouth so close to his. The memory of that sweet, devastating kiss in the moonlight raddled his brain and made his blood hum in his veins. If he didn't kiss her now, he might never get the opportunity to taste her again.

A selfish reason.

He ignored his conscience and buried his fingers in her hair, pulling her mouth to his before she could think to resist. This kiss wasn't gentle. It wasn't sweet. It was a wild, passionate claiming that should have satisfied his craving.

It didn't. Instead, it made him hunger for more. With a primitive growl, Elliot drew her lower body against his, snuggling his hardened arousal into her soft haven. The intimate contact—even through layers of clothing— shot heated arrows of desire coursing through him, nearly buckling his knees.

She brought him closer by clutching his head, her tongue seeking his with a fevered urgency that exhilarated Elliot. Her hips moved against him, rocking against his hardness. Yes, Natalie wanted him as much as he wanted her.

With a sudden, shocking shove, she broke the kiss, dousing the inferno just seconds before it consumed him.

Chest heaving, mouth swollen and glistening, she glared at him. Pain darkened her eyes to black in the dusky light. "My mother was a schoolteacher," she rasped. "I don't know who my father was because he disappeared after he planted his seed in my mother's belly.

Only hours after I was born, she left me on this porch before hanging herself from the schoolhouse rafters.''

Stunned by the self-loathing in her eyes, Elliot stood frozen. She lifted her hand to her mouth as if to touch her swollen lips, then slowly dropped it.

"He refused to marry her. So, you see, Elliot, I'm not the spawn of a murderer or a thief or even a liar. I think it's pretty obvious that I'm the daughter of a who—"

"Don't say it," Elliot warned softly. "You don't know what you're saying." Natalie's soft, bitter laugh made him flinch.

"Don't I?" With a sad, mocking twist of her lips, she lifted her hands and touched her breasts, drawing his attention to the hardened peaks of her nipples visible through the straining material of her dress.

Elliot was disgusted by the sudden flare of heat in his groin. She was in pain, and he was getting aroused!

"I didn't know that I was like her until you kissed me in the moonlight." She cocked her head to one side, and Elliot wanted to throttle her and kiss her at the same time. "It seems Mrs. Boone was right all along."

If Mrs. Boone were here right now, Elliot vowed he would throttle *her* for causing Natalie this pain and confusion. But at the moment, convincing Natalie she was wrong took precedence. "Natalie, have you responded to other men as you respond to me?" He was certain she was innocent, but just the thought that he could be wrong made him clench his jaw until it ached.

She slapped him hard across that clenched jaw.

"No! You're the first man who's ever kissed me!"

With a rueful smile, Elliot said, "I guess I deserved that. I apologize, but I think I made my point. Has it occurred to you that maybe you *like* me, and this is the reason you enjoy . . . kissing me?"

It was obvious by her surprised expression that it *hadn't* occurred to her. Her brow puckered. "Of course

I like you, but that doesn't explain why I want to—want to—''

"Make love?" Elliot supplied huskily. He made an instinctive move in her direction, but she stepped out of reach, her huge eyes wary. He sighed. "Kissing doesn't necessarily lead to lovemaking."

She arched a disbelieving brow, then lifted her fingers to trace the hardened peaks again. Her gaze dropped deliberately to the swelling in his trousers.

"Stop that," he growled. "What I meant was, kissing doesn't *have* to lead to lovemaking. There are a lot of pleasant steps in between." Very pleasant. In fact, he was throbbing right now because he wanted to take that next step.

He wanted her to touch him where he ached the most. He wanted to touch *her* and thrill to the sounds of her moans of pleasure, feel her moist heat.

"Kissing won't help, you know. It won't make me hate you any less."

Elliot frowned in confusion. "I'm not following you."

Natalie braced her back against the porch post, her dark eyes boring into his with such intensity Elliot wanted to look away.

Solemnly, she said, "You came here to close the orphanage, didn't you?"

"What does that have to do with *kissing*?" Elliot asked, avoiding the question.

She began to fiddle with her braid, faltering uncertainly. "You thought—you thought to soften the blow by—by—"

"Flirting with you? Kissing you? Dreaming of you?" Elliot advanced, his voice growing harsh. "Thinking of you every moment of the day? Worrying myself sick about you and the children?" He didn't stop until his body touched hers, relishing the way her eyes fluttered closed at the contact. Reaching his hands up between them, he covered her breasts. Her nipples pebbled against his palms. Her lips parted in response.

He groaned. "Do you really believe I have to have an ulterior motive for wanting to touch you?" he whispered softly as he rubbed his thumbs across the sensitive peaks. He brushed his mouth lightly against her parted lips. "The truth is, Natalie, you make me lose my sanity. The urge to kiss you, to caress you"—he filled his hand with her softness—"comes over me, and whatever I was going to say becomes lost in a fog of desire . . . *for you.*"

Her lashes fluttered open to reveal passion-glazed eyes. But it was the naked shame he saw that gave him pause and brought him to his senses.

Natalie, ashamed. The realization washed over him like a sudden downpour of cold rain. His desire ebbed. He dropped his hands away and stepped back, holding her shadowed gaze.

"It's time I told you everything," he said. And this time, nothing would stop him.

8

"What's he doing now?" Cole whispered, trying to move Jo aside. For his efforts, he got a sharp elbow in the chest. "Ouch!"

"Shush! Do you want them to hear us?" Jo's heart beat a rapid tattoo as she watched the couple on the porch through the window. Natalie had moved to the porch post, and Elliot was standing before her—close, very close—with his back to Jo, blocking her view.

She'd seen people kiss before, but not the way Elliot and Natty had kissed. Were they kissing again? Jo wondered.

"Jo, if you won't tell us what's going on, we're gonna drag you away from the window and see for ourselves." It was Brett, his fierce whisper blowing hot air against her neck.

Jo relented, knowing Brett meant what he said. With Cole on one side, Brett on the other, and Lori behind her, she wouldn't stand a chance against the three of them. "I can't really tell what they're doing—it's so dark. Elliot's standing in front of Natalie, real close. I think he's talking." Or kissing her.

"Do you think he's telling her, Jo? Is he?" Lori tugged at Jo's shirtsleeve for emphasis. "Is he taking away our house?"

"I don't know! I'm not a mind reader." She frowned into the gloom. "But after that kiss, I'd say they like each other."

"A lot?" Cole asked.

"Yes, a lot."

"Maybe they're gonna get married," Brett suggested.

The thought sent a spear of fear through Jo's heart. "If they do, what will happen to us?" she wondered aloud.

"Yeah." Cole sounded gloomy. "What will happen to us?"

Lori tugged on Jo's shirt again, excited at the possibility. She completely missed Jo's low-voiced question. "I hope they *do* get married. Natty deserves a handsome man like Mr. Montgomery, doesn't she, Jo?"

A thick silence fell after her innocent statement. Jo looked at Cole, then Brett, reading the same expression of shame in their eyes that she knew was in her own. "I hope they get married, too, Lori. Natty *does* deserve it."

"She would probably tell him no if he asked her," Cole said.

Jo nodded, feeling miserable because she knew it was true.

"Why?" Lori prompted.

"Because," Brett began slowly, "Natalie would never leave *us*."

Winter had come to Ivy House. Natalie was convinced of it. Her fingers were icy cold, and her heart pounded with brittle precision, as if it would shatter any moment into a million tiny ice shards.

Standing beside Elliot in the parlor, she stared at the expectant faces of the children. The blatant apprehension in their eyes made her want to weep. "Mr. Montgomery has something to tell us." She tried to smile encouragingly, but her numb lips wouldn't cooperate. What was the use? They knew exactly what was going to happen; they had known all along. She hadn't kept it from them.

A quick glance in Elliot's direction showed her that he didn't look any happier about the news. Yet . . . she couldn't allow herself to feel sympathy for him, not when there were four anxious pairs of eyes trained in their direction to remind her of why he didn't deserve their sympathy.

Elliot remained standing, so Natalie gratefully sank into the only chair that wasn't occupied. Her legs had begun to tremble as if from a chill. It matched the cold numbness around her heart.

"I have some disturbing news," Elliot began solemnly, gripping his hands together in front of him. "Please be assured if there were some other way—"

"Will you please get to the point?" Natalie whispered. He glanced at her briefly, then nodded, his face now empty of expression. Her heart gave a painful squeeze. How could he calmly destroy their lives this way? What kind of man was he? What kind of woman was *she* that she could kiss a man such as he?

"I guess Natalie's right; there's no need to beat around the bush," Elliot agreed. "Before my grandfather died, he invested his entire fortune in the railroad. The deal fell through, and he lost everything."

"Why didn't you stop him?" Natalie blurted out, rising to her feet. A wild rush of anger made her reckless. "How could you let him do such a thing?"

Elliot eyed her evenly. "I was abroad. By the time I came home, it was too late."

Her fingers knotted in the folds of her dress. Her throat ached with unshed tears. They trembled in her voice as she said, "So that's it? You've marked Ivy House from your list?"

His jaw hardened, and a flush stained his cheeks. "There *isn't* any list because there isn't any money."

She didn't believe him. How could she, when she'd heard with her own ears Suetta planning to turn Ivy House into a summer home? Did he think she was a fool? She gave an inward snort. "Well, rest easy, Mr. Montgomery. We don't need your charity; all we need is Ivy House, and we intend to *buy* it from you." She was bluffing, stalling, hoping and praying, but he needn't know.

"How? How will you buy Ivy House?"

"That's none of your business!" she snapped. "You'll get your precious money—don't worry." *Please, God, let the dollhouses sell! And give this man patience.*

Elliot looked slowly around the room at each of the children. They stared back, silent and waiting. Finally, he faced Natalie again.

She stiffened at his resolute expression.

"With my grandfather dead and Mrs. Boone gone, the children are my responsibility. I have to do what's best for them."

His responsibility? Oh, the nerve! "And you think taking away the only home they've ever known is *best*?" Natalie cried.

"They need a loving home."

"They *have* a loving home—here, at Ivy House, with *me*!"

"You're only nineteen, too young to assume the responsibility of four children." His mouth firmed into a determined line.

Natalie tossed her head, every muscle rigid with anger. "I've assumed it for six months. Aren't you just making excuses, Mr. Montgomery? Why don't you tell the truth, that you really want no part of the orphanage?"

"That's not the truth. The truth is . . ." He broke off,

glaring at her. "The truth is these children would be better off in a loving home with *parents*. I intend to see them adopted."

Natalie felt the wind leave her sails. He sounded as if he meant it. "You mean, you won't give us a chance to buy Ivy House?" Oh, how she hated him for making her plead!

Elliot hesitated, his eyes shadowed with regret. He clearly didn't think she stood a chance of raising the money. "You've got about three months. In the meantime, we'll start interviewing couples looking to adopt. I don't think it's wise to wait until the last moment."

Natalie lifted her chin, fighting the tears that pressed painfully at the back of her throat. How could she have been so wrong about this man? Because she felt further argument useless at this point, Natalie said, "Very well. I'll see you to the door." The stony look she cast him left him in little doubt about her meaning. She wanted him out of Ivy House.

Now.

She gathered a lamp from the table and rudely turned her back on him as she made her way to the door. He followed her onto the porch, grabbing her arm and startling a gasp from her. "Do you honestly believe I'm enjoying this?" he grated out, his eyes boring into her bright ones.

Natalie jerked free from his touch, appalled at her body's instant reaction to the feel of his hand. "If you weren't enjoying it, then why do it? Why not just leave us alone?"

"Because I have no choice! Can't you get that through your pretty head?" He was nearly shouting now.

Natalie responded in kind. "You have a choice! I told you we don't need your charity! Just leave Ivy House to us, and you'll never hear from us again."

A muscle twitched in his jaw. He brought his face

closer, lowering his voice. His gaze fell to her trembling mouth. "You don't understand, Natalie."

"Then make me understand!" she challenged, ignoring the leap of her heart when he said her name. She couldn't possibly like this man after what he had done!

Elliot opened his mouth, then quickly snapped it closed, leaving Natalie with the impression that he had been about to tell her something important. Instead, he shook his head slightly. "I can't. Someday, you'll understand, but I can't explain it to you now."

Natalie managed a derisive snarl. "Can't, or won't? Need more time to think up a good lie?"

His smile chilled her blood. "I oughta bend you over my knee for that one."

"You wouldn't dare," she spat. For a moment, a dangerous light flared in his eyes. Natalie swallowed, fearing she'd pushed him too far.

The fierce glow in his eyes died. He relaxed visibly, allowing a small smile to play about his firm lips. Natalie tore her gaze away with an effort, ashamed of her weakness. She would not remember his mouth on hers. She *would not* think about it! When he left here, she would *never* think of him again!

"I want to spend some time with the children before we interview folks for the adoption," he announced softly.

Natalie was speechless. Her mouth worked. Finally, she forced the word past her frozen lips. "Why?" She couldn't allow it. It would mean she'd have to see him again, be around him, smell his masculine scent, feel his hot eyes on her.

No!

"To get to know them," he said. "I want to make certain they find the right family." His gaze squinted into the dark night for a moment, and for the first time, Natalie noticed the fine lines of weariness around his mouth.

She lifted the lamp a little higher as she reminded him, "You said we had three months."

"You do, but the least we can do is get them used to the idea and start the proceedings. When the time comes . . . *if* the time comes, they'll have a home to go to." He brushed a gentle finger across her cheek. "Where will *you* go, Natalie?"

She shivered and moved away from his disturbing touch, confused by the tangle of emotions Elliot aroused. How could she seethe with anger and shiver with desire at the same time?

"I'll be here," she stated with only the slightest quiver in her voice. "Right here at Ivy House."

Wishing she'd never met Elliot Montgomery!

Feeling like a thief—a very pregnant thief—Marla hurried across the yard to the barn behind her house. She pulled open the door and slipped inside, inhaling the smell of fresh hay and horse manure. Holding the lamp aloft, she crept forward, searching the shadowed interior. A noise to her left had her whirling around.

"Here we are."

"Oh!" Marla jumped, covering her mouth with her hand to muffle her shriek of surprise. She had known they were waiting for her, but Jo's voice had startled her, regardless. Raising the lamp high, she surveyed the group lounging on scattered bales of hay.

Jo, Cole, Brett, and Lori watched her in silence, looking serious enough to raise her heartbeat considerably.

"What's going on?" Marla demanded. She had never been one for patience, and since the beginning of her pregnancy, what little patience she *did* have seemed to have vanished. "Why do you all look so gloomy? Has something happened? Is it Natalie?"

They all nodded. Marla swallowed and lowered the lamp. Her voice sank to a terrified whisper as her vivid imagination took flight. "What's happened to Natalie? Is she ill?"

"No, she's not ill." Jo slid from the bale of hay and folded her arms. "We think she wants to get married."

"But she would never leave us," Cole added.

The terror that had nearly overwhelmed Marla slowly seeped away. She relaxed, leaning against the barn door. Natalie was all right, and from what she could gather, doing better than she could ever have hoped for. "What makes you think she wants to get married?"

"Because her and Mr. Montgomery were kissing on the porch," Jo said. Her gaze dipped to the barn floor. She began to shuffle her foot back and forth, stirring the loose straw.

Marla quirked a brow. "And how do you know this?"

"Because we watched them!" Lori admitted without a trace of shame.

Marla chuckled. "Well, so y'all were spying. That still doesn't explain why y'all look like you lost your best laying hen."

Brett and Jo exchanged a troubled glance before Brett said, "We're afraid she won't get married because of us. Her and Mr. Montgomery had a fight because he's gonna close Ivy House. He said he's gonna find us all a ma and pa because he thinks Natty's too young to look after us. So, me and Jo and Cole decided—"

"Hey, what about me!" Lori interrupted, smacking him on the arm.

"And Lori," Brett corrected, returning the smack. "We've decided we want to get adopted so she can get married, but we're afraid to tell her."

"Hmm." Marla pressed a thoughtful finger to her lips. The children had a valid point. She knew Natalie well enough to know that if she thought for a second that the children were doing this for her, she would never agree. In fact, she would pretend to hate Elliot and deny any chance of her own future.

"Natty's been good to us, staying with us when Old Lady Boone took off." Jo tucked her short hair behind her ear and stuffed her hands in her pants pockets. Her thin shoulders lifted inside the baggy shirt she wore as she shrugged. "It ain't right that she has to stay and watch us."

"I wouldn't mind having a ma and pa," Lori said.

Cole focused his dark eyes on her. "I guess I wouldn't, either."

Brett nodded his agreement, and Jo stared at the floor. Marla's heart went out to her, suspecting Jo was thinking about the future. At sixteen, it wasn't likely anyone would want to adopt her.

"I guess I could go to work at that fancy restaurant in town," Jo said. "I can cook and clean as well as the next person, I reckon."

Marla wiped tears from her eyes. Without a doubt, she was witnessing Natalie's loving influence. Although not much more than a child herself, Natalie had given to these children her unstinting love and support, without thought and without regret; now they were ready to give the same to her.

Through a shimmering wall of tears, Marla smiled at them. "Well, I guess we've got some planning to do. But first, who'd like a piece of fried apple pie and a glass of milk?"

"Who wouldn't?" Jo quipped, then blushed as everyone laughed.

Dawn trailed its glorious fingers across the sky, slowly sweeping away the blanket of night from the snow-capped mountain peaks. It crept over the mountains, and down, down, gathering speed until it burst upon the town of Chattanooga as if someone had suddenly shoved a curtain aside.

Elliot blinked against the blinding light, his eyes heavy and sensitive from his sleepless night. Noah's stallion shifted restlessly beneath him as they stood atop the hillside to watch the dawn. Finally, Elliot lowered his hat over his eyes and turned the horse away from the brightening sky in the east, heading into the still-shadowed valley below.

Rico's hooves pounded into the soft earth as Elliot gave him his head. They raced down the hill into a meadow of dying wildflowers with reckless abandon, streaking through the soft, cool breeze at top speed. It suited Elliot's mood, this recklessness.

He should have told Natalie the truth. Instead, he'd left her thinking him the lowest form of life. Why? Why didn't he tell her the truth? Why couldn't he have told her that he *had* to sell Ivy House, instead of allowing her to hope? She would never have the money in time. It was impossible!

Ahead was a shallow creek about three feet across. Elliot leaned forward as he felt Rico's muscles bunch in readiness. Adrenaline rushed into his veins. Would the horse attempt the jump? Or would he change his mind at the last moment and throw Elliot headfirst?

He welcomed the suspense of the moment, gripping the reins tightly and preparing to fly with the horse.

Rico jumped as if he performed the feat every day. As they landed on the opposite bank with a jarring thud, Elliot suffered a slight pang of guilt at the risk he had taken with someone else's horse.

But then, what would one expect from a blackguard such as he? The wind snatched the derisive laugh from his mouth before it could startle the horse. A man such as he! He avoided creditors, broke engagements, snatched homes from orphans, and had attempted to seduce an innocent woman.

Natalie. God, how he wanted her. She was everything he'd ever dreamed of—and more. Holding her in his arms was like finding his own personal slice of heaven.

Why didn't he tell her the truth? he asked himself

again. But he knew why: pride. He'd wanted to keep that last shred of pride to himself. To tell her he lacked money was one thing; to reveal just how dire his circumstances was quite another.

He slowed Rico to a trot, letting the animal cool down from his mad gallop as he struggled with the logic in letting her believe the worst. She would hate him—probably already did. Was this the logic? That he *knew* they had no future, so he wanted her to hate him? Because he wasn't strong enough to resist temptation, to resist the attraction that sprang between them each time they met? Something about Natalie Polk sizzled his brain and made rational thinking a mere afterthought.

Or was a part of him hoping fate would lend a hand? The dollhouses . . . They *could* possibly make him enough money to stall the creditors until he thought of something else. It would at least give them time to find homes for Jo, Cole, Brett, and Lori.

And Natalie. Where would she go? Elliot turned Rico around and headed in the direction of Noah's place, his mood grim. Marla would take Natalie in, he knew, but he feared Natalie possessed the same flaw that *he* did: pride. If only . . . if only he could regain lost ground without selling Ivy House.

Elliot shook his head, wondering why he continued to beat a dead horse. It was no use; he'd thought and thought until his head ached. He had to sell Ivy House to the highest bidder, and he had to find homes for the orphans. If his grandfather were alive, Elliot knew he would personally ensure their future with the right family. Rico snorted and blew through his nose as if to agree with Elliot's sad assessment.

But knowing he had explored every single possibility didn't stop Elliot from hoping and dreaming that fate *would* intervene before it was too late.

As he rode into the yard to return the horse, Elliot found Noah in the barn cleaning the stalls. He slid from the horse and began the task of unsaddling him.

Noah pitched fresh hay into a clean stall, then settled his hands on his hips as Elliot began to brush Rico. "Gonna be a beautiful day, would be my guess," Noah said, wiping his sweaty brow.

Elliot nodded. "It already is." *No sense in spreading gloom around to cheerful folk,* was his sour thought. "Thanks for the horse. He rides good." Tossing the brush on a table, he slapped Rico on the rump to direct him into his stall, thinking he could use a few hours of tension-easing hard labor. "Can I be of help?"

Noah looked startled by the offer but recovered quickly. He shrugged. "Boy that usually does the work didn't show up. That's twice, so I won't be using him again." He cast a doubtful glance at Elliot's fine linen shirt and creased trousers. "You ain't dressed for mucking out stalls, though."

But Elliot had already removed his jacket and had begun rolling up his sleeves. His smiled tightly. "The clothes will wash."

"You'll have to accept pay," Noah warned as he retrieved a pitchfork from a small enclosure.

"It's not necessary. I owe you one for letting me ride Rico."

Noah paused in handing him the pitchfork, his jaw set. "Rico needed the exercise, and I can't seem to find the time, so you did me a favor. You'll accept pay or you won't work."

"I—" Elliot clamped his mouth shut as an image of Lori's pensive, pale face popped into mind. A child her age should be playing with dolls or a toy of some kind. He'd also noticed the boys needed a haircut, and that Natalie's dress had worn thin.

They needed a milk cow. He could use the extra money for a number of things.

Swallowing his pride, he reached for the pitchfork. "All right. It's a deal." As they began to work in harmony, Elliot suddenly paused to add, "And if your boy doesn't show up, I'll take the job for however long I'll be in town, if it's all right with you."

Noah reached for his hand and gave it a hearty shake, but he was clearly puzzled. "Don't understand why a man of your means would want to muck stalls, but you've got the job."

Elliot hesitated. He knew Noah to be an honest, trust-worthy man from what little time he'd spent with him, but he was also Marla's husband, and Marla and Natalie were friends. He couldn't take any chances. Forcing a dry chuckle, he recited the old cliché his grandfather used to say: "Idle hands make the devil's work." And in his case, it was true. His hands wanted to be all over Natalie. He doubted mucking stalls would change his mind about that.

"She can be as stubborn as a mule sometimes," Noah commented out of the blue.

Elliot stopped mucking to look at Noah in confusion. What was the man talking about? "Pardon me?"

Noah took his pitchfork and spread the pile of hay around in the stall before answering. "Natalie Polk. She can be awful stubborn when she sets her mind to some-thing."

Ah, Elliot thought. The man was astute, and obviously had heard the news. "So can I," he muttered, throwing a forkful of hay with enough force to land it against the far wall of the stall. "So can I."

9

"*I* refuse to take charity from that black-hearted, pretentious—'' Uttering a low, frustrated squeal, Natalie swept her hand over the pile on the table: a jug of honey, a sack of flour, bacon, sugar. No, Elliot Montgomery was *not* going to buy their respect to ease his conscience!

For the last few days, she had steadily stockpiled the items, waiting for the perfect opportunity to throw the gifts back into his face and tell him exactly what she thought of his bribes.

If only she could *catch* him at his dirty deeds! The ornery man seemed to know when she was out in the garden, in the attic, or gone to town.

"But, Natty, we need—"

Natalie sliced her hand through the air, effectively cutting off Jo's entreaty. "No, we do not *need* anything from Mr. Montgomery! How can you say that, knowing he's closing the orphanage?"

"Well, I—"

"He's trying to *buy* us, Jo! Look at these things. They're bribes."

"I think you're wrong about Mr. Montgomery. He wants the best for us—*and* for you."

Natalie's eyes stretched wide. She gazed at Jo in open horror. "The *best* for us? How would *he* know what's *best* for us?" she demanded. She couldn't believe this was happening!

Before Jo could reply, Lori bounced into the kitchen with more energy than Natalie had seen in weeks. She clutched a doll tightly in her arms, her face glowing.

Natalie groaned at her delighted expression and cursed Elliot beneath her breath.

"Look, Natty, Mr. Montgomery brought me a doll! He's nice, ain't he? He's gonna find me a nice ma and pa, too." She sidled up to Natalie and held out the doll for her inspection. "You reckon my new ma and pa will buy me a pony? Hickory has one."

Natalie opened her mouth to blast Elliot Montgomery for raising a little girl's hopes, but she caught Jo's warning look in time. No, she couldn't spoil Lori's dreams, and she couldn't spread her resentment to the children. It was bad enough that she tried to force Jo to change her opinion.

Feeling ashamed, Natalie ruffled Lori's hair. "Yes, it's a nice doll, and I'm sure your new ma and pa"— Natalie choked on the lie—"will buy you a pony." Inwardly, she seethed with mounting anger. How dare Elliot raise their hopes this way? Did he truly believe folks would crowd the porch begging to adopt the orphans of Ivy House?

As if to mock her thoughts, a knock sounded at the door. Frowning, Natalie made as if to answer it. "I wonder who that could be?" she mused. Behind her, Jo cleared her throat loudly and shuffled her boots along the floor. Natalie froze in the middle of the room. "Jo?"

"It's likely to be Mr. Montgomery. When he brought Lori the doll, he said he'd be back."

"You didn't invite him to dinner?" Feeling irrationally betrayed, Natalie turned to look at Jo. "Did you?"

Jo twisted the apron in her hands, her face flaming. "You didn't give me a chance to tell you, Natty. Mr. Montgomery said he was coming back to finish the inspection."

"Jo!" Natalie's mouth opened and closed in disbelief. "You know we can't let him—"

"Let me what?" Elliot asked from the doorway.

Looking tanned and handsome, he gave her a heated once-over with eyes far too knowing before his gaze settled on her glowering face. Brett stood beside him, wearing a suspiciously innocent expression.

He must have let Elliot in, Natalie thought with fresh amazement. Had they all turned against her? It seemed so, but *why*? Didn't they realize what losing Ivy House meant? They would have no home, unless a miracle happened and they found couples willing to adopt half-grown children! It hadn't happened in the years they'd lived at Ivy House, so it wasn't likely it would happen now. What cruel game was Elliot playing? Didn't he know the heartache he was causing?

Aching inside for the children, Natalie gathered her strength for the battle ahead. He would not continue his cruel games, and he *could not* inspect the house. She would find a way to halt both his intentions or die trying.

Clearing her throat, Natalie turned a withering gaze in his direction as if they'd never kissed. "I'm afraid you caught us at a bad time, Mr. Montgomery. You'll have to come back later." She walked stiffly to the table and gestured to the items. "And you'll have to take these with you. I can't accept them."

Elliot spoke for the first time, his voice soft and edged with anger. "I didn't bring them for you. I brought them for the children."

Natalie stiffened. Her cheeks warmed with embarrassment, but she wouldn't give him the satisfaction of seeing her face. "The children don't need them, either.

We've got plenty of food, so this will go to waste." It was a horrible lie, but pride drove Natalie.

Brett didn't know the meaning of the word. "But, Natty, I was looking forward to spreading some of that honey on one of Jo's biscuits," he grumbled.

"I like honey, too," Lori added with a plea in her voice. "I thought *you* liked honey, Natty! You said the other day—"

"Lori, isn't it your turn to feed the chickens?" Natalie gave her a meaningful push in the direction of the back door. Lori shuffled out reluctantly. A small jerk of Natalie's head prompted Jo to disappear. She took a protesting Brett with her.

When they were alone in the kitchen, Natalie folded her hands before her and faced Elliot. Their gazes clashed. She lost her breath at the naked want in his eyes before he quickly masked it.

Her heart suddenly pounding, Natalie inhaled deeply, praying he wouldn't notice how much he affected her. "I know what you're trying to do, and it might work with the children, but it won't work with me." She held her ground as Elliot closed the space between them. Her breath hitched when he lifted a hand to cup her face.

"What am I trying to do, Natalie?" he questioned softly as he gazed into her eyes.

Natalie felt the rough pads of his fingers caress her skin, her mind absently registering the different texture. The last time he'd touched her, she hadn't noticed the calluses. She restrained the urge to grab his hand and explore the change for herself.

What was she thinking? She started to lick her dry lips but stopped the motion abruptly as his gaze dipped to her mouth. "You're—you're trying to ease your conscience by bringing this stuff." His low chuckle made her bones go soft. She stiffened her spine.

"So I'm easing my conscience, am I? Just as I kissed you to soften the blow. Must I always have a motive for everything I do?'' Ever so slowly, his fingers filtered through her hair and over her ear. He began to pull her close.

Natalie jerked back, her voice sharp to stop its trembling. ''Don't touch me! I won't fall for your tricks again, Elliot!'' He let her go so abruptly that she stumbled backward. She caught herself against the edge of the table. Yep, she'd made him mad. The realization sent a surge of victory into her heart. Maybe now he'd stop—stop *tempting* her. ''I want you to leave,'' she declared bravely.

The amusement had faded from his eyes, leaving them as unpredictable as the weather. Natalie suppressed a shiver. She suspected that Elliot Montgomery was a formidable foe when challenged.

''I'll leave,'' he agreed, then added almost casually, ''when I finish my inspection.''

To her horror, he turned on his heel and made for the stairs. Natalie rushed after him, catching up with him as his foot landed on the first stair. ''Where—where do you think you're going?'' she demanded, hurrying to block his way. Her heart sank when she saw the deepening suspicion in his eyes.

''I'm going to look around upstairs.''

''Why?'' she asked breathlessly. *Stall him,* her mind commanded. Unfortunately, nothing came to mind. ''It's just a few bedrooms. . . .'' He continued to wait patiently for her to move. Natalie grew desperate. *He could not see the upstairs!*

Finally, her paralyzed brain began to function. She stumbled backward up the stairs, then allowed herself to fall on her rump. She clutched her ankle and cried out, both relieved and ashamed when she saw how quickly his bland expression turned to one of genuine concern.

''Here, let me see.'' He knelt before her on the stairs.

Gentle, prodding fingers explored her ankle. Natalie closed her eyes and tried to ignore the sensations his touch caused. Heat, fierce and stunning, swept into her bloodstream and coursed through her body, making her ache in strange, forbidden places. Feigning an injured ankle had been a bad idea, she thought in dismay. A very bad idea.

"I don't see any swelling. Try to stand." He grabbed her arms and gently helped her to her feet.

With her guilty gaze lowered, Natalie pretended to put her weight on her ankle before she winced and sank to the stairs. "It hurts. Oh—!" Instinctively, she gripped his shoulders as he swung her into his strong arms and carried her to the parlor.

Natalie tried to breathe softly; their faces were only inches apart. Helplessly, she stared at the strong profile of his jaw, then trailed her gaze to his lips. Firm, yet soft, and oh, so passionate. When he kissed her, she felt as if she were drowning in a soft cloud of cotton, that with little effort she could lean into him and make their hearts beat as one.

She gave her head a little shake to dispel her disloyal and totally ridiculous thoughts, but a telling sigh escaped her as he lowered her to the sofa.

He knelt in front of her, his arms still holding her and his face close to hers. She could see the darker rings of blue around his pupils and the sudden flare of fire in the center of his eyes.

She caught her breath and held it.

"Stop fighting me, Natalie."

The warmth of his breath tingled over her face. Was he talking about the orphanage or just the two of them? she wondered, unable to look away from the deep intensity of his gaze. She sought an answer that would cover both meanings. "I have to." For the children, she must fight him; for herself, she *had* to fight him. Elliot Montgomery was ruthless. Why else would he continuously ignore the fact that he was an engaged man? He shouldn't be here, looking at her as if—as if he could *devour* her! In return, *she* should be thinking about poor Suetta and how that woman would feel if she discovered how faithless her fiancé was!

"Suetta—" she began desperately, only to find her mouth sealed with his. Her heart thundered as he kissed her silent. When he broke the kiss, she was breathing so rapidly she thought her chest would explode. What had she been thinking? Something about—

"Suetta," Elliot announced softly, "is gone."

"Gone?" Natalie struggled to a sitting position, relieved and bereft when his arms dropped away. "Suetta's gone? Where? Why?" Had she found out? Lord, what must Suetta think of *her*?

Elliot drifted to the cold fireplace and propped a foot on the hearth. He kept his back to her. "She left town the day after she arrived. She won't be back."

Natalie felt ashamed as hope leaped in her breast. She quickly squashed it, wishing he'd turn around so that she could see his face. Was he happy? Sad? Clenching her hands in frustration, she asked, "But you'll be meeting her in Nashville?" *Stop hoping, Natalie, of course he will.*

"No. We broke the engagement. It's over."

She didn't believe him. How could she, after what she'd heard outside the hotel room? Suetta had declared her love quite passionately! Yet . . . yet he'd kissed *her* on the porch as if he never wanted to let her go.

"Physical attraction," Natalie murmured firmly. According to Mrs. Boone, a man didn't care about the harbor itself, as long as he could dock his ship.

"We . . . had a disagreement."

About the orphanage, Natalie thought with certainty. Suetta had all but stated she wanted Ivy House for a summer home. Did this mean that Elliot had refused to go along with his fiancée? Natalie slowly unclenched her fingers as hope began to blossom in her heart. Until this

moment, she hadn't realized how badly she wanted to
believe in Elliot's goodness.

"After a long discussion, we decided we weren't
suited for one another. I think I've known for a while."

The heavy sigh that followed his announcement
tugged at her heart. She braced herself against it. It was
possible he lied, and there was still the matter of Ivy
House. She couldn't just sweep it under the rug because
she was falling in love—

"Oh!"

Elliot swung around. "What's wrong?"

Natalie was certain she'd turned pale. She *couldn't* be
falling in love with Elliot Montgomery! Why, it was the
most hopeless situation she could imagine for herself—
much worse than losing Ivy House! Natalie swallowed
hard, praying her expression didn't give her away. "I—I
was just expressing my sympathy," she stumbled out.
"You and Suetta seemed so . . . so suited to one another." And they had, she thought in despair. The realization made her own discovery seem all the more
hopeless.

"I'm surprised Marla didn't tell you. She sold Suetta
the ticket."

"*My* Marla?" Natalie squeaked.

Elliot smiled slightly. "Is there more than one Marla
who works at the Thompson Mercantile?" he teased. He
waved his hand over his stomach to outline a burgeoning
belly. "That Marla?"

Natalie blushed, feeling irrationally lighthearted.
"Yes, that's the same one." The same Marla she intended to have a firm talk with. Not for a second did
she consider that Marla had simply forgotten to tell her
about Suetta's leaving.

Lost in her musings, Natalie jolted to the present as
Elliot's shadow swept past her. She jerked her head up.
"Where are you going?"

He paused and turned, one hand thrust deep in his

pocket. His gaze lingered caressingly on her flushed cheeks. "I'm going to finish my inspection," he stated casually.

"No! You can't. Jo's taking a bath upstairs." Her hasty fabrication backfired when, over Elliot's shoulder, she saw Jo appear in the parlor doorway. But Jo must have overheard her desperate comment, for she skidded to a halt and quickly backpedaled out of sight, no doubt urged on by the look of horror on Natalie's face. Elliot frowned, turning his head to follow her line of vision.

The doorway was blessedly empty.

Natalie let out a slow, shaky breath. That was close! "Maybe you could save the inspection for another time?" she queried with studied innocence. Beneath the folds of her dress, she crossed her fingers. She'd never told so many fibs in all her born days!

After a moment's hesitation, he said, "I don't suppose I have a choice." He glanced at her ankle. "Maybe we can plan a picnic when your ankle heals sufficiently."

"We?" Natalie repeated.

His grin was so wicked it made Natalie's toes curl inside her slippers.

"We—you and the children. I wanted to spend time with them, remember? I thought a picnic would be nice while the weather's still warm."

Disheartened at the reminder, Natalie shrugged to hide her dismay. Not for the first time, she was appalled at the way she kept forgetting Elliot's true reason for being in Chattanooga. "*They* would enjoy it."

He laughed at her disgusted tone.

Natalie grabbed the beautiful pillow Lori had been working on and threw it at him.

Marla tried to read through the paper, but it was too thick. She sidled around the counter and came up behind Elliot, unabashedly trying to peer over his shoulder. He was too tall. Smothering a growl of frustration, she moved a little to the side and craned her neck.

His arm was in the way.

She let out a shriek as Elliot suddenly whooped with joy and thrust the letter into her hands. Before she could read the first word, Elliot told her everything.

"Warren was successful! We need three more dollhouses by the end of the week," he announced with a boyish grin. "Warren says the stores are fighting over who's going to get the bid. A *bid*, Marla! Do you know what that means?" Before Marla could begin to guess, he continued, his excitement contagious. "It means the dollhouses are going to sell for a small fortune! I never dreamed they'd be this successful."

Marla knew someone who *did* dream. Natalie was going to be one very happy woman when she heard the news. She thrust the letter into his hands. "Mind the store for me, will ya? Noah should be back any minute. I'm going to tell them—"

"Them?" Elliot's brows rose in question. "Them?" he repeated.

"I mean *him*—Mr. Smith," Marla quickly corrected, breathing a sigh of relief when Elliot's brow cleared. "He'll be delirious, I'm sure."

"I'd like to meet him."

Marla paused at the door. "It's not possible."

"Will you ask him?" he persisted.

Without turning around, Marla nodded. She suspected she looked mighty guilty, because she *felt* guilty. "I'll ask him, but don't hold your breath. You might suffocate."

With his deep chuckle ringing in her flaming ears, Marla quickly left the store.

Relishing his small success, Elliot leaned against the counter as he waited for Noah to appear. When he heard the back door to the store open and close, he automatically assumed his relief had arrived. He turned with a ready smile to find Hickory watching him curiously.

"Hello, Hickory."

Hickory's face screwed into a fierce frown. "Where's my mama?" he demanded, plopping his hands on his hips.

Elliot chuckled. Hickory reminded him of Natalie, which in turn reminded him of how badly he wanted to share his good news with her. But he couldn't—not yet. Telling her would mean confessing all, including the part about definitely having to sell Ivy House. He hoped that by then, the children would be happily ensconced in homes of their own, thus eliminating Natalie's reason for wanting to keep the house.

"She's gone to visit Mr. Smith," he told Hickory.

"Who's Mr. Smith?"

"The one who makes the dollhouses," Elliot reminded him. To his confusion, the little boy continued to look puzzled. Maybe Hickory had never met Mr. Smith. He supposed it was possible, if the old man was *that* introverted. But Hickory's next words dashed those possibilities from his mind.

"Natty and Cole and Jo and Brett and Lori make dollhouses, Mr. 'Gomry." He poked a proud finger at his chest. "Sometimes they let *me* help." Suddenly, his eyes grew round. He clamped a dirty hand to his mouth. "Oops," he mumbled. "Mama told me not to tell nobody. I forgot."

Too late, Elliot thought, stunned into immobility. *Natalie* was responsible for the dollhouses? But why the secrecy? What possible reason could she have for not wanting him to know? And Marla . . . Elliot glanced at the door she had vacated only moments ago, speculating. Marla had deliberately led him to believe a hermit had crafted the houses, so she was in on the conspiracy.

He lifted the letter in his hand, the words blurring as his mind continued to work the puzzle. The dollhouses were selling, and Natalie was probably counting on us-

ing the profits to buy Ivy House. A logical plan—if there
was enough time. Warren had asked for *three* of the
miniature houses—a far cry from bringing in the amount
of money it would take to buy Ivy House.

Three months was not enough time.

Elliot started to curse, caught sight of Hickory from
the corner of his eye, and quickly muffled his oath. At
least the profits *he* made would keep the creditors at bay
for the time being.

Long enough to find homes for the orphans.

10

The occupants of Ivy House were exhausted but triumphant by the end of the week. Moments after Marla delivered the wonderful news about the order for the dollhouses, they had set to work in a frenzy of excitement and hope, heedless of the grueling hours spent in the warm attic.

Natalie steadfastly ignored the pangs of guilt she suffered each time Brett or Cole ripped away a cypress board from the walls dividing the rooms. It didn't matter, she told herself, for in the end, they would own Ivy House, and unlike the high-and-mighty Elliot Montgomery, *they* wouldn't care if it was cypress or ordinary old pine.

She caught her lower lip between her teeth and carefully swept the brush over a tiny windowsill, then stood back to admire their handiwork. The third and last dollhouse was finished. After the paint was dry, Cole would fetch Noah with the buckboard, and they would take them to the mercantile. From there, the investor would put them on a steamboat, and they would begin the first leg of their journey to New York.

Rubbing absently at a dried patch of paint on her chin, she blew an errant curl from her forehead and prayed that more orders would follow. Elliot had promised to give them—reluctantly, she recalled with an annoyed sniff—three months to get the money, but she wasn't dense; she knew the profits from these dollhouses wouldn't begin to be enough. In fact, in three months, the most she could hope for would be to offer a down payment. Oh, it wouldn't be enough to stagger the heart, but maybe it would be enough to appease a greedy, heartless—

"That dress is ruined."

Natalie swung around at the sound of Marla's chiding voice. "Oh, you startled me." She swiped a self-conscious hand down the faded old cotton dress she'd outgrown years ago. "This ol' thing was ready for the rag pile ages ago."

Marla stretched and groaned. "What about Jo? I've got a feeling she might be changing her mind about never wearing a dress." She arched her brows and nodded toward the window.

Curious, Natalie dropped the brush into a bucket of turpentine and moved to the window. She heard the creak of steps on the attic floor as Marla joined her.

"Remember Sod Warrick's boy? I believe his name is Jeb or Jake or something."

"Hmm." Natalie craned her neck and looked below to the porch, her eyes widening at the sight of Jo lounging against the porch post, talking to a tall, gangly lad of seventeen or so with a shock of reddish brown hair that glinted copper in the sunlight. "Well, I'll be," she whispered, delighted with the scene. "Maybe there's hope for her yet."

"Yep. Let's just hope he doesn't break her heart. Wouldn't take much to break it, I expect."

Marla was right, Natalie thought, feeling the sudden urge to race downstairs and yank Jo inside. But she knew she couldn't compete with Mother Nature. God knows, she had tried to convince her stubborn heart that she had made a mistake about being in love with Elliot Montgomery.

She *couldn't* be. But she was.

Giving the young couple their privacy, Natalie moved away from the window. She folded her arms and speared Marla with a stern look. She had a bone to pick with her best friend, and now was as good a time as any. "Why didn't you tell me Suetta left town?"

With a telltale guilty start, Marla sputtered, "I thought you knew."

"Hogwash. What else haven't you told me, Marla? When I remember how horrible you made me feel for keeping secrets—"

"Okay, okay." Marla sighed, looking obligingly contrite. "I didn't tell you . . . well, because I thought it would do you good to suffer a little jealousy."

Natalie began to tap her foot, beginning to understand and not liking it. "Is that so? Now, why would you think I'd be jealous?"

"I was *hoping* you'd be jealous. I'm entitled to hope, aren't I?"

Marla tried a cajoling smile, but Natalie wasn't falling for it. "What else haven't you told me that you think I shouldn't know for my own good?" Tap, tap, tap went her foot on the floorboards. She began to glower at Marla as Marla hesitated.

"Well," Marla finally said, relenting and looking like a child caught with her finger in the pie. "I guess I should have told you that Elliot's working for Noah."

"Working?" Natalie squeaked in disbelief.

"Yep. He's mucking out stalls."

"Mucking out—! What on earth for?" She shook her head. She tried to imagine Elliot shoveling horse manure and failed. Not that he didn't have the muscle, but why would he? Contrarily, she set her jaw. "It's a trick,

Marla, and you did exactly what he hoped you'd do."

"I did?" Clearly, Natalie's meaning was lost on Marla.

Her certainty growing, Natalie nodded. "Yes, this is probably a lowdown stab at gaining our sympathy. He wants us to think he doesn't have any money, and he was counting on you telling me." She darted an accusing look at Marla before adding, "But I bet he wasn't counting on it taking *this* long. Speaking of which, why *did* you take so long?"

"Because I—" Marla clamped her mouth shut. She shrugged and thrust out her chin. "A man's pride is a delicate thing, Natalie. I didn't think it was right to go 'round telling his business to everyone—"

"Everyone?" Natalie was genuinely hurt. "You consider me *everyone*? And here, all these years, I thought I was your best friend."

"You are, Natalie Polk, and you know it." Marla's voice gathered strength as her guilt subsided and her ire rose. "And to prove it, I came over to show you this before you heard it from someone else." She pulled a folded piece of paper from her dress pocket and held it out.

Filled with foreboding, Natalie took the newsprint torn from *The Chattanooga Express*. Marla reached over and tapped a small area near the bottom of the page.

Natalie read the announcement in silence, growing more horrified with each word. She snapped the paper together and threw it across the room, gasping for breath. She'd never, ever in her life felt such outrage, such stunning fury! For a long moment, she couldn't make her voice work. "He's—he's *selling* the children!"

Marla grabbed her arm. "Now, Natalie, I'm sure Elliot thinks—"

But Natalie couldn't hear over the roaring in her ears. He was offering money to anyone interested in adopting the orphans of Ivy House. Why, it was nothing short of slavery! A—a bribe, plain and simple!

With an enraged hiss, Natalie began stomping across the attic floor, then back again. She clenched her fists and her teeth so hard it brought tears to her eyes. Such impotent rage made her head ache, and she wouldn't have been surprised if steam rolled from her ears. "I can't believe it; I just can't believe it. First he declares the children are *his* responsibility and that he knows what's best for them. Ha!" she snorted. "He doesn't know the first thing about what's best for them. Why didn't he just stay in Nashville where he belongs?"

"Now, Natalie," Marla began in her best soothing voice, "if he had, then you would never have met—"

Natalie stopped to stare at Marla, silencing her with a single, eloquent look. Her voice was low and filled with pain and heartache that mirrored her expression. Tears burned and brimmed in her eyes, but there was nothing she could do about that, either. "Don't you understand, Marla? I wish I *had* never met Elliot Montgomery. I'm ashamed that I could . . . that I have these feelings about such a heartless, selfish—"

"Handsome—"

"Conniving—"

"Sensitive—"

"Ruthless scoundrel!" Natalie's voice ended on a shout.

A shocked silence fell between them. Natalie took one look at Marla's distressed face and did something she rarely allowed herself the luxury of: she cried. Swiftly, Marla crossed the room and gathered her like a child, crooning nonsense and patting her shaking shoulders.

Natalie didn't have the heart to tell Marla that it didn't help. She was afraid nothing would.

Oh, why didn't Elliot leave well enough alone?

• • •

In the shadows of the stairwell, Jo shrank against the wall, blinking tears from her eyes. She had heard everything and was more convinced than ever that Natalie loved Elliot. Natty *never* cried. In fact, she couldn't recall a single time.

And Elliot certainly made no bones about his feelings for Natalie, she thought with a blush. Natalie didn't sound anywhere close to admitting it, though, which meant that it was up to them to make Natalie see reason.

Yes, she, Brett, Cole, and Lori had some planning to do if they were going to prove to Natty that they could get along just fine without her. Marla would help.

With a decisive nod, Jo wiped an impatient hand across her eyes and quietly crept down the stairs. She was convinced that once they were out of the way, Natalie would stop fighting the truth and admit that she and Elliot were meant for one another.

Why, it was as plain as Jane to everyone but Natalie!

As Jo went in search of the others, she found herself thinking about Jeb Warrick and wondering if he'd ever kissed a girl before, the way Elliot had kissed Natalie.

To her great surprise and consternation, she also wondered if Natalie would mind if she borrowed a dress.

Just to try on, mind you.

Elliot watched the steamboat until it was nothing more than a speck of white against the brilliant, orange horizon. The dying sun gave a final wink good-bye before dusk stole over the land.

He turned away and tried to put the dollhouses from his mind, knowing it would take weeks for them to reach their destination and several more weeks after that before he could expect to hear from Warren. These things took time, and Elliot knew success largely depended on the whim of the public. Time wasn't something he had a lot of, unfortunately. He was grateful that Marla had suggested he take the dollhouses and pay for them when they sold.

If they sold, he silently corrected. There was no guarantee.

So far, he'd seen no sign of his grandfather's creditors—*his* creditors now—but he knew the vultures would eventually bully his lawyer into telling them where he'd gone, or they'd hear the news from someone else. Once they arrived in Chattanooga, they'd discover quickly enough that he'd left out one rather large detail that would go a long way in settling his grandfather's debts: Ivy House, a house his grandfather had built for the woman he loved. A house that was now home to a ragtag pack of orphans and one very determined little house mother.

He reached for his pocket watch, then remembered he'd sold it. With a grimace, he quickened his pace. Tomorrow, he planned to hold to his promise and get to know the children before the adoption interviews began. A smile tugged at his lips as he thought about spending the day with Natalie. She challenged and tempted him, and he felt a lifting of his soul at the prospect of chipping away at that stone wall she insisted on throwing up between them. Natalie, he was fast discovering, was a unique blend of woman and warrior.

He wanted to seduce the woman and conquer the warrior, but most of all, he wanted to convince Natalie of her worth, force her to look inside her own heart, and realize what a fine, special person she was. Maybe if he could convince her, she would no longer feel as if she had to take on the world to prove herself.

Yes, tomorrow couldn't get here fast enough.

''I'm gonna use my money to rent a room at Clyde's boarding house, then I'm gonna get a job at the eating place in town. Mrs. Leavens said she could use an extra hand in the kitchen.''

"That sounds like a swell idea, Jo!" Brett crowed. "I wouldn't mind living on a farm and raisin' cattle or something, or being a lumberjack. How about you, Cole? Wouldn't that be all right with you? Wanna learn to rope a cow?"

Lori didn't give the quiet boy time to reply. "I want to live in town and wear fancy dresses," she stated. "Maybe go to a fancy school like Marla did." There was a moment's pause, then, "Course, I want a pony, too. Can I have a pony if I live in town, Jo? Oh, and I want lots of dolls and a dollhouse like the one with the evator."

"Elevator, you dolt."

"El-e-vator," Lori pronounced carefully, oblivious to Brett's scorn. "Maybe you and Cole can make me one, and I can ask my new ma and pa to buy it for me."

Finally, Cole joined the conversation, his voice soft and sad. "You wouldn't have to pay us, Lori. I wanted you to have the last one, but we needed it for the money."

"I know."

Natalie, shamelessly eavesdropping outside the parlor, bit her lip at Lori's solemn acceptance. She was reminded of the little girl in the mercantile who had wailed and stomped until her parents had relented and bought her the dollhouse. Natalie knew that Lori would never think to demand anything. She just accepted the fact that she couldn't have it.

"Well," Jo said, "I just hope we get this over and done with before winter sets in. I'm not lookin' forward to freezing my butt off all winter."

"Yeah, we never have enough wood for heating."

"Or food."

"Or clothes," Jo concluded with such gloom that Natalie winced. "It's downright humiliating having to rely on folks to feel sorry for us and give us their hand-me-downs."

Dazed, Natalie pressed her suddenly hot face against the wall. They sounded so miserable, as if they hated living at Ivy House. How had she missed knowing this? Just because she had matured and realized how fortunate she was to have a home, it didn't mean that everyone else realized the same. They were children, something she had apparently forgotten somewhere along the way.

She knew why she had forgotten; because they seldom got the chance to *be* children. It wasn't right. It wasn't healthy.

Firm hands landed on her shoulders. Natalie jumped in shock and opened her mouth to scream. A gentle hand silenced the sound. The breath from Elliot's soft, amused whisper tickled her earlobe and sent a shiver of a different kind down her spine.

"It's only me. I knocked, and when no one answered, I tried the door. It wasn't locked, so I came on in. Imagine my surprise to find you eavesdropping outside the parlor."

Natalie removed his hand and shrugged the other one from her shoulder, ignoring the traitorous leap of her heart. With the newspaper announcement still fresh in her mind, her whisper came out more of a hiss. "If I had known you were coming, I would have locked it. And what I'm doing is none of your business."

"Haven't you heard eavesdroppers never hear good about themselves?" He stroked her neck with his finger, chuckling when she batted it away.

Well, he spoke the truth, as much as she hated to admit it. While the children hadn't been discussing her in particular, the innocent things they'd said hurt to the bone. She'd thought—selfishly, she supposed—that the children were happy with her here at Ivy House. She was not only selfish, but also foolish for forgetting what it was like to view the world through a child's eyes.

Not so long ago, she had hated this place as well.

And she'd take a bullet before she'd repeat any of it

to Elliot Montgomery. Sighing, Natalie moved away from him. He had a curious way of muddling her thoughts. "What are you doing here? Don't you have stalls to muck or something?" She watched the startled look come into his face, swiftly followed by a flush. Natalie mentally braced herself. She wasn't falling for his tricks again.

"I came to see if you and the children would like to go on that picnic," he drawled, ignoring her reference to work.

Natalie shrugged as if it didn't matter, which she staunchly told herself was the truth. "I'm sure the children would love to. They've fallen for your tricks, but I haven't."

He took a step in her direction. "You still think this is a game, Natalie?"

"Isn't it?" She lifted her chin, recklessly ignoring the sudden blaze in his eyes.

Before he could answer, Lori caught sight of them and came racing from the parlor, her face alight. Jo, Cole, and Brett followed more slowly, but Natalie noticed their faces held the same eager expressions. All for Elliot.

"Mr. Montgomery!" Lori stopped just short of jumping into his arms. She held out her doll for his inspection. "Look, I made Gloria a new dress and a bonnet. Isn't she grand?"

Elliot dutifully looked, a strange expression flickering across his handsome features as he studied the fine stitching in the doll's dress. "Remarkable, Lori. You say you made this?" When Lori flushed with pride and nodded, he shook his head. "You're a fine seamstress, and that's a fact."

Natalie made a strangling sound in her throat. Elliot glanced at her sharply. She glared back at him, telling him without words that *she* wasn't fooled by his smooth tongue.

Without taking his piercing gaze from her face, he said to the children, "How about a picnic?"

Lori bounced up and down with excitement. "At the creek? Can we go swimming?" Then, as if she realized Elliot wasn't the one to ask, she cast Natalie a pleading look. "Can I, Natty? I'm much better."

Natalie didn't hesitate, remembering the little girl in the mercantile with the dollhouse. Swimming cost nothing. "Yes, you can swim." When Lori squealed, Natalie added firmly, "But you'll have to change into dry clothes the moment you finish."

Elliot smiled at the other children. "Well? Any more takers?"

Takers, Natalie repeated silently. Yes, Elliot was a taker. And a rotten scoundrel, to boot. Suddenly, she realized they were all staring expectantly at her. She shook her head, chagrined to feel a stab of regret. "I've got work to do. It's wash day."

"If Natty's not going, neither am I," Jo said, folding her arms across her middle and assuming a stubborn stance Natalie knew well.

Cole and Brett echoed her sentiment. Lori's face crumpled with disappointment, but after a meaningful glance from Jo, she hung her head and mumbled, "Guess I don't want to go, neither."

Smothering her exasperation, Natalie threw up her hands in surrender. "All right. I'll go." She was bombarded with squeals and hugs, and over their shoulders, she met Elliot's smug gaze. She stuck her tongue out at him. When he laughed, Natalie vowed to ignore him the entire afternoon. Elliot would discover that despite the warmth of the sun, the day would be quite chilly.

At first, Elliot was amused by Natalie's stoic determination to ignore him. Deciding he could wait her out, he entertained himself by admiring the lush scenery. It was curiously quiet and still, with not a squirrel or a bird in sight and not even the faintest of breezes blowing to stir the enticing curls at Natalie's neck.

Angling his head, he squinted against the sun's glare as he admired the frosted mountain peaks. Winding down from the mountain, the creek was a sparkling silver ribbon, flanked by thick trees and an occasional cluster of sun-bleached boulders. The place they'd chosen for a picnic was a natural clearing and, according to Brett and Cole, a regular watering hole for the local wildlife. On arriving, Elliot had studied the various animal tracks with interest, wondering if his grandfather had once done the same,.

Perhaps Gill Montgomery had crouched in the bushes with his trusty rifle, waiting for a buck or a doe to venture from the forest to drink. Elliot closed his eyes and easily visualized the image of a young Gill waiting for his chance to bring home a hefty deer. The picture made him smile and wonder why his grandfather had never returned to stay—or at least brought his grandson back to visit. He'd never wondered until now because he hadn't known what his grandfather had left behind.

As one hour turned into two, irritation began to push amusement aside. His interest in the surroundings waned. Natalie sat beside him on the blanket, her back rigid, her face set, staring straight ahead at the children gamboling in the creek. She'd hardly eaten any of the succulent ham and had only nibbled at the cheese he'd purchased from a local dairy farmer with money he'd earned mucking stalls. With a disdainful sniff Suetta would have admired, she had refused the sweet red wine he'd bought with her in mind.

Yes, he was growing very weary of her childish actions and was slightly piqued at the way she turned her nose up at his hard-earned offerings. Elliot grunted to himself, wishing he could explain to her the sense of accomplishment he felt, knowing he'd earned the money by hard work. He suspected she'd never believe him, would quite probably laugh in his face. His grandfather had been adamant about his education and later insisted he see as much of the world as he could before taking over the business. Gill wanted his grandson to experience everything he had missed. As a result, Elliot had never worked a day in his life for actual pay until coming to Chattanooga.

Elliot turned to admire Natalie's smooth, creamy skin shadowed by the broad brim of her bonnet. Although her face was in profile, he could see the tension in her thinly pursed lips and the angry tilt of her chin. He knew that if she looked at him, her eyes would be as dark as storm clouds and just as threatening.

Lounging beside her on the quilt, he chuckled, watching the quick stiffening of her spine. Her fingers curled into the blanket at her side and tightened. A tremor of desire shot through him as he remembered those fingers tangled in his hair, her firm, straining breasts flattened against his chest. He wanted to reach up and pull the pins from her proper bun and watch the silken tresses tumble down her back.

He stirred restlessly to ease the sudden tightness in his trousers, cursing his undisciplined body. He kept forgetting how easily this she-cat aroused him. "How long are you going to punish me?" he asked abruptly. When several taut moments passed in silence, Elliot leaned a fraction of an inch closer. "If you don't answer me, I'm going to tumble you onto your back and kiss you senseless." With satisfaction, he watched her jerk in reaction to his low-voiced threat.

"I don't know what you mean," she whispered tightly, her gaze unwavering on the children splashing in the water.

He gave in to the pressing urge to touch her, running the pad of his thumb over the top of her tightly clenched hand. "Are you still angry because I kissed you on the front porch?"

"I was never angry."

No, he realized with a vicious curse, she hadn't been angry; she'd been ashamed. "So, if you're not angry about that, then what *are* you angry about?"

"I'm not angry."

"Liar," he snarled softly. Jumping to his feet, he reached down and grabbed her around the waist, lifting her up. "Come on."

Sputtering, she tried to twist out of his embrace, her eyes flashing fire. "Let me go!"

"No." Elliot's voice hardened. His patience was at an end. "We're going for a walk. Alone. I want to see if I can find the cave my grandfather told me about."

Natalie apparently decided struggling was useless. She stilled in his arms. "I'm not going with you."

Elliot pressed a hard kiss on her lips, instinctively grabbing her hand as she drew back to slap him. He lifted his head, bringing her clenched fist between them to lie against his chest. He switched tactics. "Go with me?"

"And if I don't?" she demanded breathlessly, proving to Elliot that she wasn't unmoved by the kiss.

A wry grin twisted his lips. He'd have to resort to blackmail after all. "Then I guess I'll have to keep kissing you until you agree."

Her beautiful blue eyes narrowed. "You're despicable."

"Does that mean you'll go?"

"I can't leave the children."

"Jo's perfectly capable of watching Lori." He lowered his head as if to continue his persuasion.

"All right!" She leaned back, her chest rising and falling rapidly in her agitation. "I'll go, although you should know that I hate dark places."

With a triumphant grin, Elliot reached into the basket and withdrew a candle and a tin of matches. "We'll be prepared if we find it."

11

"$\mathcal{L}$ori will get sick again if she stays in the water too long." Natalie kept her distance, still shaken from his kiss and determined not to unbend. But it was difficult to remain angry on such a beautiful day, especially when walking with a man who could charm the birds from the trees. She wasn't immune, but she was aware and on her guard. "And Brett and Cole will get carried away and douse her—"

"I get the point," Elliot said as he took her elbow to lead her around a boulder. "If we don't find it soon, we'll go back."

"Are you sure about this cave? I've never heard anyone mention a cave in this area." Obviously, he sensed her skepticism, for he smiled. She frowned and concentrated on lifting her skirts to keep from tripping. Better to watch her step than to watch that smile of his.

Instead of answering right away, Elliot paused and shaded his eyes. He glanced slowly around the area, then pointed to a pile of boulders at the base of the mountain. "There. I think that's the landmark my grandfather spoke of. He said it was behind a pile of rocks with a tall pine on either side."

Natalie followed his pointing finger, still doubtful. It looked exactly like any other old pile of rocks to her, and there were trees all around them. "I don't see it."

He took her hand and approached the boulders. "Of course you don't see it," he chided. "That's why no one knew about the cave but my grandfather."

Intrigued despite herself, Natalie couldn't resist asking, "So how did your grandfather find it?"

Elliot chuckled. "I'm not sure I believe the tale, but he said he was out hunting one day, and a bear ran him up one of those trees. For hours he sat in the tree, waiting for the bear to give up. He fell asleep, and the next thing he knew, he woke up on the ground." Elliot halted at the boulders and glanced at her. "When he fell, he fell *backward* out of the tree and landed in front of the cave."

"Which is hidden by the boulders and the trees," Natalie concluded. "Why didn't he just shoot the bear?" She loved God's creatures, but when she pictured herself in Gill's place, she thought she might be tempted to shoot the bear.

"She had cubs. Speaking of bears—wait here. We don't want to startle one if it happens to be using the cave for an afternoon nap."

Natalie's protest died on her lips as he brushed a branch aside, squeezed between the biggest boulder and an old pine tree, and disappeared from sight. After a long, tension-fraught moment filled with images of Elliot becoming a snack for a hungry grizzly, he emerged again, his handsome face filled with boyish excitement. Her heart tripped at the sight.

"I found it."

"I gathered," Natalie said, forgetting that she was supposed to be angry and grinning at the expression on his face. "Is it safe?"

"I made some noise and didn't get a response, so I think it's empty."

He reached out as if to take her hand and pull her along, but Natalie stepped out of reach. "I think I'll just wait out here." The discovery of the cave was exciting, but she felt no desire to go inside. It would be dark, and she'd be alone with Elliot—two very logical reasons why she should remain right where she was.

Unfortunately, she didn't think Elliot would accept either reason. A little desperately, Natalie said, "Bats! I don't like bats, Elliot. Oh!" She found herself pulled tight against his chest, her face inches from his.

"Don't you trust me?"

A slow, sweet shiver skirted down her spine at his husky question. Natalie firmly closed her eyes. True, she couldn't close her ears to that persuasive voice of his, but she *could* close her eyes to the tempting promise in his gaze. Why did he keep battering away at her defenses? Didn't he see what it was doing to her?

Of course he did.

"You've got to learn to trust someone sometime, Natalie."

"And you think I should trust you?" came her caustic reply. She kept her eyes tightly closed, forcefully reminding herself of every reason *not* to trust Elliot Montgomery—or to like him.

Or love him. They were worlds apart, extremely unsuited, and destined to remain at odds. They both wanted Ivy House, and they couldn't have it together. She could never give up the children, and she couldn't imagine Elliot cheerfully accepting a ready-made family. Why would he, when he could have his pick of single, unattached, carefree women? And his home was in Nashville, not Chattanooga.

"Yes, you should trust me," he whispered somewhere dangerously close to her mouth. "Sooner or later, you're going to have to admit that there's something powerful between us."

"Can it—can it be later?" Oh, she hated this weakness he caused with so little effort! Easing her lower body away from the disturbing hardness of his, she opened her eyes. "I'll go into the cave with you if you'll forgot this nonsense about us."

"Nonsense?" He smiled slowly and wickedly before letting her go. "That sounds like a challenge, Miss Polk. I've always loved a challenge."

"It wasn't any such thing," she denied. "Now, if I have to go with you into that—that awful cave, then let's go. It's getting late." She trembled at the thought but wasn't willing to admit her fear to Elliot. If he sensed it, he would just use it to his advantage.

Let him think she didn't like the dirt and the damp. Let him think she didn't trust him. Let him think anything he chose. With her head held high and her insides quivering with dread, she gestured for him to proceed. He chuckled and took her hand as if he didn't trust her to follow. Natalie didn't blame him; she thought about bolting the moment his back was turned, but he wasn't giving her the chance.

The opening to the cave was small, maybe four feet high and two feet across. With some trepidation, Natalie watched Elliot bend his tall frame and duck inside. She took a deep, fortifying breath and did the same, grateful now that their hands were linked.

A musty smell greeted her as she straightened carefully once she was inside the cave. She wrinkled her nose. "Light the candle," she whispered, twisting around to face the dim light filtering through the trees and into the mouth of the cave. She wasn't taking another step away from that light until she could see what was ahead.

Elliot let go of her hand. Although she could not see more than his faint outline, she heard him searching through his pockets for the candle and the tin of matches he'd taken from the picnic basket. Finally, a match flared. He stuck it to the candle wick and it sputtered, then caught. She exhaled slowly so that he wouldn't hear. Elliot would enjoy mocking her fears.

"Better?"

"Yes."

"Come on. I want to see if I can find the treasure."

Natalie reluctantly took his hand again and followed, her gaze fixed on that wonderful, wavering light in his other hand. "Treasure? What treasure?" Had the man taken too much sun? she wondered, trying not to think about what could be hanging above them or what was on the cave floor where she stepped. Maybe, she assured herself, the bats didn't know about the cave, either.

The musty smell grew stronger as they went deeper into the cave. It smelled of age and damp and something else she shuddered to imagine. Elliot felt her tremble and squeezed her hand for encouragement, letting her know without words that he knew of her fear. Natalie vowed to do a better job at hiding it.

"My grandfather used to play in this cave—sometimes camped here overnight. He kept his treasures here, things like Indian arrowheads and old coins and such. You know, trinkets that boys collect."

Natalie didn't know, and she didn't think Brett or Cole collected anything but blisters and calluses. It was a shame, she thought, that they had missed out on so much of their childhood. If Elliot could find someone to adopt them, then maybe they would get the opportunity to recover those lost years before it was too late.

She stopped dead in her tracks. Was she beginning to believe in Elliot's promises as well? She, the only one left who appeared to have a lick of sense where Elliot was concerned?

A gentle tug on her hand got her moving again. With an incredulous shake of her head, she thrust those dangerous thoughts from her mind. "Is it much farther?" she whispered, then wondered *why* she whispered. Perhaps because she didn't want to alert any creatures to their presence. She suppressed a shiver and picked up her pace.

"I think it's close. He said there was a ledge at the back of the cave where he slept. He hid his treasures nearby. There, see the ledge?"

Natalie peered around him and saw the shelf of rock jutting from the wall at the back of the cave. It did, indeed, look like a bed, but an uncomfortable one. She bit back a protest as Elliot released her hand and stuck the candle into a crevice in the wall. She watched him as he knelt at the end of the ledge and moved a rock aside. After a moment, he came back to her and shook something out of a tattered cloth sack into his hand. With something akin to reverence, he held it out for her inspection.

"Arrowheads. The Indians used them to make spears and tools. My grandfather said they were as common as rocks when he was a boy."

Dutifully, she touched one of the cool, triangular stones, her mind on getting back into the blessed sunlight. "Interesting. Now can we go? I'm sure the children would love to come back with you another day." She thought her hint came through loud and clear, but Elliot merely chuckled. The sound had her eyes narrowing with temper. Strange, she'd never considered herself easy to anger until she met Elliot. When she was around him, she seemed to be in a constant state of agitation.

"Scared, Natalie?"

"You've got a cruel streak in you, Elliot—" Natalie's tantrum ground to a halt as she caught a movement out of the corner of her eye. Something had darted at the candle then whipped away, something fluttery and dark. Something that made her heart jerk painfully. "What was that?" The whisper was back, shaky and fearful. She moved closer to Elliot until her arm brushed his sleeve. "Elliot?"

"I didn't see anything."

He didn't sound worried about what *she* had seen, either, but that didn't stop Natalie from continuing to sidle closer. Slowly, knowing she shouldn't but unable to resist, she tilted her head and looked at the ceiling of the cave. She quickly closed her eyes.

She was right; she shouldn't have looked. In the circle of light from the candle, hundreds of rustling, evil-looking bats crawled and scrambled over one another for a space. A shudder shook her frame hard enough to rattle her teeth.

She felt something brush against her neck and tried to convince herself it was her imagination. It didn't work. She screamed, and it wasn't a little shriek of fright; it was a full-blown scream of uncontrollable terror.

Suddenly, the air was thick with flying, anxious bats as they dived for the cave opening to escape the strange noise. Natalie kept screaming because she couldn't stop. Elliot grabbed her and shoved her under the ledge. She stuffed her fist in her mouth to muffle her screams.

"Stay down," he ordered. "You startled them when you screamed."

She startled *them*? Natalie fought the urge to laugh hysterically as she cowered under the ledge, trembling so badly she knocked her head against the rock. She didn't dare remove her hand because she could feel her throat aching to let loose.

Suddenly, above the harsh whispering of bat's wings, she heard a different noise. Louder, deeper, and very close, a rumbling that shook the ground beneath her knees and took her terror to new heights. It lasted perhaps thirty seconds before it finally stopped. When she could see that the air was clear of bats, she scrambled out from under the ledge with Elliot's help, her gaze locking with his.

Simultaneously, they turned toward the cave entrance. No light could be seen, not even the slightest trickle of sunlight. If not for the candle, they would have been left in total darkness.

The cave entrance was blocked.

"Rock slide," she strangled out, her throat closing up. She stared at the candle firmly stuck in the wall and muttered a short, heartfelt prayer for its presence.

"The noise from the . . . bats must have caused it."

Natalie stiffened at his hesitation, forcing herself to be honest. "You mean my screaming caused the rock slide. If I hadn't screamed, the bats wouldn't have panicked." It was true, every single word of it, and it made her feel awful. They were trapped inside a cave nobody knew about, and it was all her fault.

"It wasn't your fault, Natalie. Anything or nothing can set off a rock slide. I'm not an expert, but I've traveled extensively, and I've seen it happen. Besides, this was my idea, remember? Stop blaming yourself."

"I'll blame myself if I please," Natalie shot back, driven by guilt and burgeoning fear. She glanced at the candle again. Her mouth went dry as she saw how quickly it was melting. Halfway gone in what—fifteen, twenty minutes? "What are we going to do?"

With his mouth pressed into a grim line so unlike the Elliot she knew, he locked an arm around her shoulder and hugged her close. Natalie leaned into him, too afraid to worry about what was proper. Elliot wouldn't be thinking about seduction at a time like this—and neither was she.

"They'll find us. In the meantime, we search for another way out. Come on."

Keeping his arm around her, he retrieved the candle and began retracing their steps. Every few feet, Elliot stopped and swept the candle from one side of the cave to the other, looking for a crack, an opening, anything that might give them hope. They were about ten feet from the blocked cave entrance when Natalie felt Elliot tense.

She quickly followed the light of the candle. It was a ragged opening in the cave wall, she saw. Rocks lay scattered around the cave floor, and Natalie realized that it must have happened during the same rock slide that had trapped them here; the rocks hadn't been there before or they would have tripped over them on entering the cave.

"It looks like another tunnel," Elliot said. He handed her the candle. "The slide must have dislodged the rocks from the entrance. I'm going to take a look. When I step inside, stick your arm through with the candle so that I can see—and watch those rocks. You don't want another twisted ankle with the last barely healed."

"Elliot—"

"Yes?"

Natalie licked her lips. She'd been about to confess that she'd never twisted her ankle, that she had tricked him. But now was not the time. "Be careful," she said instead. She edged closer, her heart pounding with fear for his safety. They had no way of knowing what lay beyond that opening, yet Elliot seemed unafraid. She almost envied his courage.

Once again, he disappeared from sight. Natalie clutched the wall and carefully stretched out her arm through the jagged opening. "See anything?" She kept her voice prudently low.

Long, tense moments passed without an answer. Natalie's imagination had time to conjure several terrible scenarios. Had he fallen into a deep, yawning hole in the cave floor? Had there been some wild, half-mad beast waiting to pounce as he stepped inside? Or . . . the candle trembled wildly in her hand as she came to the last, most frightening possibility; had Elliot left her behind?

"Natalie?"

She jumped at the sound of his voice, then stifled a shriek when his face suddenly appeared. One look at his flustered, grim expression in the flickering candlelight, and her heart took flight. Clamping her free hand over it to keep it still, she gasped, "What is it? What have you found?"

He shook his head. "You don't need to see this, Natalie."

"See what? What *is* it, Elliot?"

With the image of what he'd found branded on his brain, Elliot attempted to join Natalie and distract her from looking. She wasn't so easily appeased, he soon realized when she remained firmly in place.

"I will not move until you tell me what you found in there! I'm not your average coward, Elliot."

He arched a brow. She flushed, and he knew she was remembering her reaction to the bats.

"That's not the same," she said with rising heat. "Any sane woman would be frightened of bats. If you had any sense, you would be, too. Everyone knows bats spread madness and God knows what—"

"I found a skeleton, Natalie."

"—else." Her eyes rounded. The color drained from her face, leaving it ghostly pale in the sparse light. "A—a skeleton of . . . a *person*?" she whispered in horror.

Elliot nodded. He hadn't wanted to tell her, but she was so damned stubborn.

"Elliot, if this is a joke . . ." The candle wavered in her hand as Elliot continued to stare at her in bleak silence. "I want to see."

"That's not a good idea." Elliot tried once again to push through, but she pushed him back with surprising force.

"I can make up my own mind, thank you. Now, move."

He had no recourse but to stand back, his disgusted sigh loud and eloquent. She ignored him and moved slowly into the small room. He tensed as she held out the candle, ready to clamp a hand to her mouth if she attempted to scream. It would mean certain death if she caused another rock slide while they were in the small room. Their chances weren't exactly promising now. The skeleton could attest to that, Elliot thought sadly.

When she gasped, he knew she had sighted it propped against the far wall. Softly, he told her his theory. "I'm thinking he took shelter from a storm or was traveling and camped here for the night. Maybe there was a rock slide, or perhaps a small earthquake, and he got trapped in here."

"It's horrible."

There were tears in her voice, tears for a man she didn't know. Elliot was curiously touched and understood perfectly. He felt the same wrenching sadness when he saw the skeleton. How terrible it must have been for the man to know he was going to die without a single soul aware of his passing.

"Look, he wrote something."

Lifting the candle higher, Natalie moved closer, and Elliot moved with her, curious to see what she was talking about. The yellow glow of the candle revealed a shaky message scratched onto the rock above the tattered remains of the man's hat.

"My beloved Adell—" Elliot broke off with a startled curse, catching Natalie in his arms as she crumpled in a dead faint. "Damn it, I feared this would happen! Damn stubborn woman."

He continued to berate her as he cradled her tenderly in his arms and retrieved the candle, which thankfully the fall had not extinguished. "If you had only listened to me . . . but no, you couldn't do that one simple thing." He shouldered through the entrance and picked his way carefully over the rocks, marching to the ledge at the back of the cave. "You're not a coward, you say. Wouldn't be bothered, you declared. Well, you're not so tough now, are you my little warrior?"

So mad he could spit—mainly at himself for getting them into this situation in the first place—Elliot gently lowered his unconscious burden to the ledge. His hand trembled annoyingly when he smoothed the hair from her brow. Why hadn't he stopped her? She was a gentle woman with tender sensibilities. Hadn't he discovered this about her when he upset her with tales of his grandmother during that ride on the trail? She'd turned so pale he thought she'd faint right off her horse.

Yes, she was spirited and brave, even hardier in mind than most women he knew, but everyone had a limit, and Natalie had obviously reached hers. They were trapped in a cave no one knew about with a few unlucky bats and a great possibility of dying.

That alone was enough to stagger the stoutest heart, but he had to go and find a skeleton. Then he had to go and let her see it. He should have been more adamant with her. He should have used physical force to stop her.

Elliot thrust a weary hand through his hair as he stared down into her pale face, willing her to open her eyes.

He shouldn't have brought her to the cave in the first place, and he'd spend the rest of his days—possibly hours—wallowing in guilt for acting on what had been an impulse. Yes, he'd wanted to look for the cave, but he'd also wanted to get Natalie alone.

A brute, a clod, a black-hearted fool. Irresponsible, yes, that also applied to him. Was it any wonder that Natalie spurned his advances, that she repeatedly hinted she wanted nothing to do with him? He'd been a block-head for ignoring the harsh truth.

He didn't deserve her, plain and simple, and if they got out of this mess, he would exercise his self-restraint and treat Natalie with the respect she deserved. She was by far the noblest person he knew, other than his grand-father. Who else did he know who would fight so gallantly to save a home for children who weren't even her own?

Nobody he knew, and nobody he would ever know.

Elliot's heart gave a curious leap as he watched her lashes flutter. She was so beautiful, he thought, stifling the urge to press his lips to hers before she came to full consciousness.

Natalie opened her eyes, and the opportunity to taste her one last time slipped by him. She blinked, then focused her gaze on him. He watched the blue of her eyes darken in remembrance. Heaving a regretful sigh, he took her hand in his. "I can't apologize enough for getting us into this mess and for letting you see that horror. How do you feel?"

To his great astonishment, she reached up and circled his neck with her arms, pulling him to her. Her enticing mouth lingered less than an inch from his own as she whispered, "I feel wonderful, and you have nothing to apologize for. In fact, I should be thanking you—at least for finding him."

Elliot hung back, not because he didn't flat-out ache to taste her sweet mouth, but because her response completely baffled him. "Him?" he echoed. She moistened her lips, and despite his recent vow and his present confusion, he groaned.

"Him," she whispered, tugging on his neck, "My father. You found my father."

She smothered his startled exclamation by crushing her mouth to his. After an all-too-brief hesitation, Elliot's willpower disintegrated as if it had never been.

When he'd made those promises to himself, he hadn't counted on having to deny Natalie. Somewhere in his subconscious mind, he had known that would be impossible. He just hadn't allowed himself to believe it could ever happen.

As the warmth of her mouth seeped into his and their tongues collided in a heated rush, Elliot surrendered without a fight.

12

"We've had worse than that ol' shaker," Brett scoffed. "That wasn't enough to jiggle a baby's butt."

"Brett!" Jo admonished, slanting a meaningful glance at Lori. She was in charge with Natalie gone, and she took her job seriously. When she had noticed the water trembling, she'd herded them out of the creek, deaf to their groans and protests. It had stopped by the time they reached the bank, but Jo knew it didn't necessarily mean it was over.

Brett gave her a wide-eyed look. "What? Lori's never heard the word *butt*?" He grinned when Jo continued to glare. "All right, I'll watch my mouth—not that you're big enough to soap it." Before she could retaliate, he hurriedly asked, "What do you reckon's takin' them so long, anyway?"

Jo combed her fingers through her short, damp hair and rolled her eyes at Brett's innocent question. She knew, but they were memories she would rather forget. "You know. Stuff." She glanced at Lori again, who was listening with interest. "Lori, go change out of those wet clothes and get your dry ones on like Natty told you.

Go behind that tree over there. If you feel the ground shaking again, you get away from it." When Lori reluctantly did as she asked, Jo continued in a low voice. "They're probably kissing again."

Brett made a face. "Why would they keep doing that? It doesn't sound like nothing I wanna do when I get older. How about you, Cole?"

Cole grunted and opened one eye. He lay sprawled on the bank of the creek, letting the sun dry his britches. "Don't know until I try it," he muttered.

Jo remembered having the same opinion as Brett about kissing—before she met Jeb. Now, she wasn't so certain she'd mind. If she could just forget about the past . . .

Changing the subject because it made her uncomfortable, Jo said, "You boys did a good job in the parlor with Natty listening. She *has* to think we want to be adopted now."

"Yeah." Brett signed and rubbed at a patch of dried mud on his foot. "But I wish they'd come on back. I'm hungry."

Jo snorted. "You're always hungry." She craned her neck to look down the trail where Natalie and Elliot had disappeared over an hour ago. "I wonder if they found that cave Mr. Montgomery was talking about. I'd like to see it some time." Maybe she could show Jeb. Maybe he'd be impressed enough to kiss her. And just maybe she'd let him.

She sat up with a jerk as a thought suddenly occurred to her. Reaching over, she grabbed Cole's shoulder and shook him. "Cole! What if Natty and Elliot were in that cave when the quake hit? What would happen?"

Cole reacted instantly to the alarm in her voice, proving that he hadn't been as uninterested in their conversation as he'd like for them to believe. He leaped from the blanket and began tugging his boots on. "Don't know much about caves, but I'm thinkin' *I* wouldn't want to be in there when a quake hit. We'd better go lookin' for them.''

"Lori!" Jo bellowed. "Hurry up!" She yanked Brett to his feet, fear streaking through her. "They might have gotten trapped or they might be hurt. Come *on,* let's go!" She grabbed a bewildered Lori's hand and forced her to run in the direction the couple had taken, praying they'd meet up with Natalie and Elliot along the way.

What if they didn't? What if they couldn't find the cave?

What if it was already too late?

The kiss went on and on, and in Natalie's opinion, even that wasn't long enough. She wanted it to continue and to develop into something more satisfying, more quenching. She had a sudden, powerful thirst to learn all there was to know about making love with Elliot Montgomery.

When he broke away, she whimpered a protest. "Don't stop." She kept her arms around his neck and held him when he would have pulled away. He gently grasped her hands, holding them tightly in his own. She might have been embarrassed if she hadn't witnessed for herself the intense struggle on his face.

He wanted her. *He wanted her.*

When he spoke, his voice was husky and heavy and echoed her thoughts. "I want this as much as you do." He shook his head. "No. More than you do. But I've got to know what changed your mind. If it's the situation, then we need to talk. I don't want you hating me when we get out of here or feeling ashamed of what we've done."

"But we won't get out, will we, Elliot?" Surprisingly, Natalie felt no immediate panic at the possibility. If she was going to die, she wanted to die in Elliot's arms.

Finding her father had freed her from the shame and guilt she had carried in her mother's place.

"Yes!" He grabbed her hands until she winced. "Yes, we *will* get out of here. Don't even think that we won't. Just because *he* didn't get out doesn't mean we can't hope."

"You mean my father," Natalie murmured, watching Elliot's eyes widen. So, she was right; he hadn't been paying attention when she told him earlier. She smiled as she remembered the reason he *hadn't* been paying attention. He was forgiven. "Yes, my father."

When Elliot quickly felt her forehead as if checking her for a fever, she laughed softly, reaching up to smooth his frowning brow. "I'm not delirious, Elliot. He is— was—my father. My mother's name was Adell." She rose to a sitting position, and he sank onto the ledge beside her, his expression stunned, as she continued. "I always thought he didn't want my mother and didn't want me, that he just left her after he'd had his pleasure. I'm sure my mother thought the same when he didn't come back for her." Pity for her mother momentarily darkened her mood. She shook it off. It was a long time ago, and it wasn't easy to forgive her mother for leaving her and taking her own life. Someday, maybe she could, but not yet.

"So, you see, Elliot, he was coming back to her. He didn't make it."

"How can you be sure he's the one? Adell isn't an uncommon name—"

Natalie shook his hand for emphasis. "I *know* that's him, Elliot." She caught a flash of pity in his eyes and stood, tugging him with her. "Take me back to him."

"Natalie, I—"

"I won't faint again," she promised. "When I saw my mother's name scratched on the wall and realized who he was, I was shocked." She straightened her back and smiled. "I'm fine now."

Elliot stared at her for a moment longer as if to assure himself that she told the truth. He must have realized that she did, for he rose and retrieved the dwindling candle from the wall. Turning, he held out his hand again, his eyes alight with a tenderness that made Natalie go soft inside.

Her heart suddenly aching for what might have been, she clasped his hand and followed him through the cave. Once inside the small room, Natalie took the candle and knelt beside the skeleton of what had once been her father. With a trembling hand, she grazed the brim of his hat and murmured a soft prayer.

"I didn't even know his name," she said quietly, comforted by the knowledge that Elliot stood behind her. Just as she started to rise, she caught the glint of gold on the cave floor near the man's hand. With a cry, she picked up the gold wedding band and held it out to Elliot. "See? He *was* going to marry my mother!"

Elliot took the ring and examined it. "There's an inscription on the inside of the band, but I can't make it out in this light." He glanced at her excited face, his smile crooked. "Seems you were right, Natalie. The man obviously intended to marry your mother."

Natalie took the ring and slipped it into her pocket. She turned and approached the wall with the candle, reading the message aloud. " 'My beloved Adell. I'm sorry. I will love you through eternity.' " It was signed "Nate." Natalie let hot, cleansing tears fall unheeded. When she felt Elliot's hands on her shoulders, she leaned back with a shuddering sigh.

"She named me after him, Elliot. My mother left a note telling Nelda my first name, but she didn't leave a last name. Nelda said she didn't want me having *her* name on account of how she took her life. That's when she started naming us after the presidents."

"Hmm," Elliot murmured with interest. "So she named *you* after President Polk. I wonder how she knew? He was a brave man who didn't hesitate to voice his own opinions and stand up for what he believed, no matter who he angered.'' He slowly turned her around in his arms and kissed her tears away. ''Remind you of someone?'' he asked with a soft chuckle, brushing his lips against hers.

''I guess she did the best she knew how.''

He frowned. ''I'm not convinced of that. Come on, let's go back to the ledge. You're cold.''

Natalie shivered, confirming his guess. It *did* seem to be colder in the smaller cave. She gave the remains of her father one last sad glance and followed Elliot through the opening.

When they reached the ledge, he pulled her onto his lap and began to rub her arms. She didn't give a thought to protesting, her mind returning to their predicament. Death was so final, and there were many things she had yet to experience.

Such as making love with Elliot.

Even before the thought slipped quietly into her mind, Natalie began to heat up with a different kind of warmth. His slightly rough hands stroking her bare skin, his breath warm and scented with sweet red wine as it drifted over her neck, and his incredibly strong thighs beneath her own all combined to awaken her senses, make her feel alive and aware.

Need flooded her body and soul. Need for this man, for what he could make her feel and for what he could make her forget.

With a gasp of longing, she turned in his arms.

Their mouths met, clung, devoured, tasted, and nibbled, growing more frenzied by the second. It was as if he shared her desperation, Natalie thought. There wasn't any need to worry about tomorrow, because tomorrow might not come.

There was only now, and she was here with Elliot.

''Natalie?'' he muttered against her mouth.

''Yes.'' She knew the meaning of his unspoken question. ''Yes, Elliot. Make love to me fully. I don't want to die without sharing this with you.'' And she meant it.

''We're not going to die,'' he argued, but he began to work the buttons on her dress with feverish intensity, his breath quick and ragged. Natalie continued to stroke her fingers through his hair and plant moist kisses on his neck, his ears, his jaw, his eyes. She wanted to touch every inch of him. When he pushed her dress from her shoulders, she arched into his hands, gasping as his rough fingers rasped across her nipples.

His mouth soon followed, torturing her. She locked a scream in her throat and moaned instead. When he suddenly set her on her feet, her eyes flashed open in protest.

''Let's get out of these clothes. I want to see all of you, Natalie. But first . . .'' He yanked the pins from her hair and watched as the wild curls sprang free and tumbled about her shoulders. The soft candlelight caught just a hint of fire in her golden tresses. ''So beautiful.'' He speared his hands in her hair and slowly raked his fingers through.

She thrilled to the sound of his husky, aching voice. He wanted her as she wanted him, and there would be no stopping, no doubts, and no regrets. This was right. She belonged to Elliot, and he belonged to her. She knew this as certainly as she knew the sun would rise tomorrow, even if it meant it would rise on their graves.

Natalie wasn't sure how they managed to get undressed without parting lips, but within moments, Elliot broke away long enough to spread their clothes on the ledge in a makeshift blanket. He picked her up and gently laid her down, then stood back to look at her, his chest heaving with pent-up emotion.

She boldly studied him in return. Finely muscled with dark blond hair furring his chest and flat belly, he was a breathtaking sight. His skin seemed to glow a deep gold as if he'd spent time in the sun. Her gaze dropped for an electrifying instant on the evidence of his desire, then swiftly she looked away.

He chuckled, reaching out to cup her face with his hands. Desire and tenderness deepened his voice. "Don't be afraid, Natalie. I won't hurt you."

She forced herself to meet his gaze, her body trembling in anticipation, despite the trickle of fear she felt. "I trust you," she said simply. How could she not? She loved this magnificent man with all her heart.

Too late, a sinister voice whispered. Despair tried to dig its ugly claws into her heart, but Natalie willed it away. She wanted nothing to dim this joyous union. Since death was inevitable, it could wait.

Her body seemed to leap of its own free will as Elliot stretched out beside her and took her into his arms again. His mouth crushed hers, demanded, sought, and received what he wanted. While his mouth began their journey into love, his fingers continued it, sweeping across her belly and tangling in the silken curls between her legs. Skillfully and ever so gently, he parted her moist petals and stroked the very core of her desire.

Natalie arched against him with a startled cry of pleasure, her hands clenching over his arms, then sweeping, seeking, touching. She gloried in the satin feel of his skin and the rough hair on his chest, reveled in the rough bristles of his chin against her lips. When she brushed a curious hand against his thrusting manhood, she caught her breath. She held it as she hesitantly closed her fingers around him. The skin was smooth and velvety and oh, so soft.

Her lips parted in awe.

He groaned and rose over her, his face suddenly taut, his eyes blazing in the glow of the candlelight. Lowering his head, he covered a straining peak with lips warm and exciting as he gently nudged her knees apart.

Natalie unfolded without hesitation or fear. If what

was to come was anything like she'd felt thus far, then she was more than ready to participate.

Elliot sank slowly and carefully into her, capturing her whimper of pain with his mouth and soothing the hurt with a deep, satisfying kiss. When he fully possessed her, he held his trembling, eager body still, but Natalie had passed the point of hesitation and surged against him.

She demanded.

He gave.

Both savage and tender, Elliot moved with her, clenching his teeth in an effort to hold onto his control. Each time she met his thrust with sweet abandon, he groaned and fought the release his body ached for. His lips roamed hers, then traveled along her arched throat to the madly beating pulse at her neck.

That symbol, that one tiny proof of her pleasure, pushed him over the edge. With a final groan, he lowered his mouth onto hers and convulsed against her. She tumbled after him, clutching his hair and stifling a bewildered, joyful cry against his mouth.

Tears trickled from her eyes and ran into her hair, but they were glad tears. Her breathing ragged, she framed his face with her hands and planted a soft kiss on his lips. "Thank you."

He let out a shaky chuckle. "I'm not sure you should be thanking me. This ledge is solid rock; you're probably black and blue."

She shook her head at his apologetic tone, her eyes luminous. "If I am, then it was worth every bruise." He dipped his head to nuzzle her neck in silent appreciation. Natalie took a quick, shallow breath, loving the feel of his weight on her, loving *him*.

"Elliot, if we don't get out of here—"

"We will. You've got to believe that. I'd like to try this again on a soft bed."

Her heart hitched at his fierce look, so in contrast with

his halfhearted attempt at humor. She wondered if he knew it. "There's a chance we won't, and it's time we faced it." She murmured a protest as he rolled to the side but changed it to a contented sigh when he gathered her against him.

"I'm too heavy; I've already crushed you," he explained, kissing the top of her head.

"Was I complain—oh!" Natalie tensed as the candle fizzled and spluttered out, plunging them into a darkness so black it felt thick. "Elliot?" She hated the wobbly, cowardly sound of her voice, but she was helpless against the gripping fear that began to creep over her.

"I'm here, darling." His arms tightened in reassurance; his lips nuzzled her jaw. "Don't be afraid."

She might have listened had she not heard the despair in his voice that he tried and failed to hide. With her heart tripping against her chest, she pressed against him and buried her face in his neck, holding on for dear life.

They were going to die.

Everyone gathered silently around Cole as he dropped to his knees and studied the tracks. Behind them, the sun sank perilously lower in the sky. They wouldn't be able to track them after dark, and the urgency inside Jo grew stronger with the knowledge.

Finally, Cole turned his head. His eyes narrowed. "Looks like they stopped here, then went that way."

Jo followed his gaze, frowning at the pile of rocks at the base of the mountain. A tall pine flanked either side; the one on the left leaned drunkenly to one side. "They couldn't have, Cole. There ain't nothing but rocks and trees in that direction—and the mountain."

"Could be a cave under those rocks," Cole mused. "See that tree? Looks like something hit it and knocked it sideways. Maybe those rocks fell when the quake hit."

"Dear God." Jo took a step in the direction of the rocks. What Cole said made sense. "Dear God," she whispered again. She ran to the base of the rocks and began screaming. "Natalie! Elliot! Can you hear me? It's Jo!"

"We ain't sure there *is* a cave, bird brain. And if there *is* a cave behind that pile, then they'll be dead before we get them out."

Jo whirled to face Brett, panic skittering just below the surface. It would do Natalie and Elliot no good if she became hysterical, she reasoned, fighting the urge to shake Brett's teeth loose. Instead, she reminded herself that Brett hated to be afraid, and this was his way of hiding it. As she looked at his pale face, she realized that she was right; he was terrified. "We'll get them out, Brett. Even if we have to dig all night!"

"We don't even know if—"

"Be quiet." Cole didn't have raise his voice to get their attention; the urgency in his softly spoken words froze them in place. "Brett's right, Jo. If they're behind those rocks, we need to start digging. We might not have much time. Brett, you go back to town and get help. Find Noah and tell him we'll need everyone who can come."

Lori, who had been listening in round-eyed silence, began to cry. "Is Natty gonna die, Jo? Is she?"

Jo sprinted to Lori and cuddled the frightened girl close. She swallowed a ball of tears and said in her firmest voice, "No, Lori. Natty and Mr. Montgomery ain't gonna die. We won't let them. Now, you sit over here so we can start getting those rocks out of the way."

"No! I'm gonna help, too." Lori knuckled her eyes and pushed at Jo, her expression both fierce and frightened. "I can pick up the little rocks."

Cole began lifting rocks and pitching them aside. He paused long enough to glance at the two girls. "She can help."

Realizing they were wasting precious time arguing, Jo said, "Okay, but be careful. Some of those rocks might fall on us when we move the others." She led Lori to the side of the pile and pointed. "You start there, and if you see any rocks moving, you jump out of the way. We ain't got time to be tendin' you if you get hurt."

Battling tears, Jo set her mouth in a determined line and went to work alongside Cole. Many of the rocks were too big for them to budge, but with any luck, help was on the way.

She prayed they weren't too late.

Raising her voice as loud as she could, Jo began to call out again. If they were alive, maybe they'd hear her.

"Natty! Elliot! We're here! We found you!"

Inside the cave, Elliot awoke to the faint sound of someone calling his name. Cold sweat beaded on his skin as he thought of the implications of that voice.

Was this the end, then? he wondered, tightening his arms around Natalie, who dozed beside him. Alone with his thoughts, he let despair sweep over him. Just when he found the woman he could spend the rest of his life with, they would die. It hardly seemed fair.

He tensed and lifted his head. There came that voice again, but this time, he thought he recognized it.

"Elliot! Natty! It's Jo!"

Abruptly, he rose to a sitting position, bringing Natalie with him. He shook her gently. "Natalie, I think they've found us. I hear us. I hear Jo." When he was certain she was awake and steady, he let her go and scrambled in the pitch black for his trousers.

"Hmm?" The sleepy sound of her voice suddenly sharpened with fear. "Elliot? Elliot!"

He cursed and captured her flaying arms, pulling her close. "I'm sorry. I'm sorry. Here I am." Holding one arm around her trembling shoulders, he continued his search. Finally, his fingers closed around the outline of the matches. He dug inside the pocket and drew them out. "I'm going to let you go for one second, sweetheart.

Just long enough to light a match.'' When she didn't protest, he slowly let her go and struck the match. She winced at the sudden burst of harsh light but didn't close her eyes.

''Get dressed quickly before the match is gone,'' he urged.

Natalie's gaze never wavered from the light as she gathered her clothes and began to slip them on. ''Are you sure, Elliot? You really heard Jo? You didn't dream it?''

''Damn!'' Elliot dropped the match and sucked the end of his scorched finger, then quickly pulled another match from the tin. He couldn't see Natalie's face, but he could feel her panic building. ''I'm right here, and I'm lighting another match.''

''I know,'' came her brave and unsteady whisper. ''I'm not afraid.''

Elliot found himself grinning at her bravado. Even while she trembled, she denied being afraid of the dark. His warrior woman, so brave and determined, so fearless in the face of death. A faint thumping noise distracted him. He cocked his head and listened. *They're digging us out*, he realized with an inward shout of joy.

He and Natalie weren't going to die.

He lit a match and found her shaking hand in the dark, closing her fingers around the base of the match. The meager light flickered wildly. ''Hold this. I'll be back before it goes out. I promise.''

''Where are you going?''

Over the yellow flame, Elliot met her panicked gaze. Her eyes were large and luminous. Beautiful, he thought with a fresh ache of need. ''To tell them we're here,'' he managed around the thickness in his throat. ''Don't move.''

''Don't you—don't you need a light?''

He smiled at her envious tone. ''I can manage. We've only got a few matches left.''

Relying on instinct, he made it to the entrance using the wall for his guide. He shouted at the top of his lungs until he heard an answering, indistinguishable shout that confirmed his success, then returned quickly to Natalie. When he drew close, he followed the small flame Natalie held in her hand.

Just as he reached her, she dropped the match with a soft cry of pain. Elliot reached out and brought her finger to his lips, soothing the hurt. He closed his eyes at the slightly salty taste of her skin, fighting a wave of desire. Just her taste, her touch, and he was ready to love her again. His lips moved from her finger to her wrist, then along her arm until he felt her quick, uneven breath on his face. Beneath the old, musty smell of the cave, he could smell the fresh, flowery scent of her hair. He inhaled deeply and with great enjoyment.

He was alive, and he was with Natalie.

"Elliot?"

This time, she was asking.

He captured her lips, his passion exploding as if they had never made love. She responded with equal passion, her mouth soft and pliant but greedy. With a deft twist, he pulled her up and turned with her in his arms as he sat on the ledge, pulling her between his hard, powerful thighs. With his hands circling her waist, he tightened his thighs against her hips to hold her there.

"It'll take them a while to move that pile of rocks," he whispered between breathless kisses. They had narrowly escaped death; surely they had earned the right to celebrate life.

Natalie melted against him willingly, breaking the kiss to lay her head against his chest. He felt her smile, and while his heart pounded fiercely, she twirled lazy circles around his nipples with her finger, sending sharp daggers of desire into his groin. Would her touch always have this effect on him? he wondered in a daze.

"You have something in mind to while away the

time?'' she finally asked, tiptoeing those torturous fingers down his belly.

He sucked in his breath, anticipating where those fingers would end. She was more woman than he could ever have hoped to find: sensuous, inventive, eager to learn and enjoy. He felt a moment's panic, wondering if he would ever be worthy of this beautiful, unselfish woman.

In the next instant, his doubts vanished as her soft, moist lips nuzzled him with such sweet hesitation and curiosity that he shuddered. When he felt the tip of her tongue flicking against the hardened peaks, he buried his fingers in the wild, sensuous tangle of her hair and brought her mouth back to his, growling, ''I most certainly do.''

13

$\mathcal{B}$lacksmiths Bobby Brewster and Joel Kincaid were fierce competitors and mortal enemies, yet they worked side by side, grunting and heaving as they lifted the heavier rocks away from the cave entrance, their rough curses muffled in deference to the ladies present.

Marla held Lori against her side and watched the two hefty blacksmiths, along with about a dozen other men from town, as they worked to free Natalie and Elliot. Cole and Brett worked at the base of the rock pile and out of harm's way; Jo stood to the side, her fists clenched and her youthful face reflecting hopeless anger because she wasn't allowed to help.

Silent tears rolled down Marla's cheeks. Hysteria hovered just below the surface, but she fought it for the children's sake. What if the cave collapsed before they could dig them free? What if they ran out of air?

When she had answered the door to find Brett out of breath and stammering something about Natalie and Elliot buried alive, the edges of her vision had grayed alarmingly.

Leaning against the doorjamb, she had silently fought

the weakness until she was certain she wouldn't faint. If she had fainted, she wouldn't be here; Noah would have insisted she stay in town, and that would have driven her mad.

"Are we sure they're in there?"

"Of—" Marla swallowed the sharp retort and glanced at Mrs. Newberry, who stood beside her, cooling her face frantically with a fan trimmed with ivory-colored lace. Marla remembered the day at the mercantile that she had haggled with the woman over the fan and lost. A few other women, mostly gossips like Mrs. Newberry, huddled in a small circle a few yards away. *Probably busy shredding Natalie's reputation,* Marla thought scathingly. To Mrs. Newberry she said with careful patience, "Where else could they be? They've been missing for a few hours now. Besides, Jo said she heard someone shouting."

"Maybe they eloped," Mrs. Newberry suggested with a hint of hope, completely ignoring Marla's latter comment.

"Natalie would never leave the children." Marla's patience began to wear thin. She suspected that Mrs. Newberry would rejoin her group of pecking hens the moment she squeezed enough information out of her. "And Natalie wouldn't leave without telling me," she added stiffly. Lori sniffled and stirred against her; Marla tightened her arms around her.

"I've heard Mr. Montgomery's been spending a lot of time at Ivy House."

"He owns the house, Mrs. Newberry." Marla gave her head an impatient shake. "Perhaps that's the reason." It wasn't; or at least Marla didn't think it was the *only* reason, but she wasn't about to feed the chickens. They would love nothing more than to nod their hypocritical heads and whisper that blood followed blood.

The fan became a blur in Mrs. Newberry's wrinkled

hands. "Well, they've been in there an awfully long time . . . alone."

"Should I have Noah fetch the shotgun on the off chance they're still alive and able to stand before a preacher?" This time, when Marla glanced at the woman, she held her gaze until Mrs. Newberry looked away. The tears came faster now and trembled in her voice. She caught a sob and swallowed it. If Noah turned and saw her crying, he'd force her to go home. She couldn't bear it. "I think our time would be better spent praying for their safety, rather than dwelling on crude speculations."

Mrs. Newberry sucked in an indignant gasp, but Marla didn't wait for a reply. She clutched Lori and moved away from the snippy woman and the other gossips. Natalie *had* to be all right. She couldn't imagine life without her best friend.

In fact, she *refused* to imagine it.

Looking first at the pile of discarded rocks growing larger by the moment, then at the small mountain of rubble still to be moved, she clasped her hands and bent her head. Her lips moved fervently in prayer.

It was only a very thin sliver, and at first Natalie thought her mind played tricks on her, but as she strained her eyes in the dark, the sliver of golden light grew and winked against the cave wall. Her excitement grew along with it. She clutched Elliot's arm to get his attention. "Elliot, look! I see light!"

He went still beneath her fingers. Natalie knew he had been struggling with the buttons on his shirt from the steady stream of muffled curses. It had taken him forever to refasten her dress in the dark.

"I think you're right. They've managed to dig us out."

"Do you think they heard you?" she asked, thinking of how frightened and worried the children would be. If they had gone for help, then Marla and Noah would be waiting, too. Natalie bit her lip, thinking about Marla's condition. The distress wouldn't be good for her.

"I think they did, but maybe we should try again."

He found her hand and clasped it, pulling her slowly toward that wonderful splinter of light. They neared the entrance, and Elliot moved to the right to avoid the scattered boulders from the hidden tunnel. As they passed the room where the remains of Natalie's father lay, a wave of sadness washed over her. He'd died alone, his bones the only reminder that he ever existed. She should give him a decent burial, she thought, now that she'd found him.

Elliot paused several feet from the light. Natalie pressed against the warm, solid wall of his back, knowing their time together was at an end and determined to make every second count.

"Can anyone hear me?" Elliot shouted. Then to her, he warned softly, "Get ready to run. My voice might set these rocks rolling."

Natalie tensed and waited. She heard a muffled shout but couldn't make out the words. She squeezed Elliot's hand. "They heard us. I wonder how much longer it's going to be?"

"Not long." Elliot lifted their entwined hands and pointed to the entrance. "Look."

The light became a hole, and now they could hear the cheers and shouts more clearly. Natalie recognized Noah's gruff voice, raised in excitement. Within moments, the opening grew larger as the men cleared away more rocks.

"I think we can crawl through!" Elliot shouted.

He turned to her. Natalie could make out the faint outline of his face, but not his expression. Her heart leaped at the memory of his lovemaking, her skin growing hot. She wasn't certain she wanted to leave now that they could.

"I'm going to lift you up."

She nodded over the lump in her throat, then realized he probably couldn't see her. "All right. Elliot?"

"Hmm?"

"I . . ." She stumbled to a halt, needing to say the words but fearing his response. Would he say he loved her in return? She had wanted to say it when he was deep inside of her, then later when he loved her again. Why hadn't she?

As if he sensed her deep, emotional turmoil, he took her face in his hands. His eyes gleamed with an unidentifiable emotion. Passion? Pity? Love? There was only one that would send her heart soaring.

"We'll talk later." He pressed a hard, possessive kiss on her mouth and released her. "Now, I'll help you climb up. Watch your step."

Natalie shoved her chin forward and willed the tears away. At least she still had her pride; she hadn't told him she loved him. Yes, they had made love—passionate, tender, unforgettable love—but Natalie knew it didn't mean the same for a man. They didn't have to love to *make* love. Hadn't Nelda explained this to her?

A deep, tearing ache blossomed in her heart. She feared it was just the beginning, because for Natalie, loving and making love went hand in hand.

Strong hands clasped her waist—hands that had caressed her body with infinite tenderness and arousing expertise—and lifted her to the opening. She grasped the rocks and scrambled for a toehold. Poking her head through the opening, she snapped her eyes closed against the blinding, hurtful light. Someone grabbed her arms and lifted her effortlessly out.

When Natalie felt the ground beneath her feet, she cautiously opened her eyes. Noah grinned down at her, keeping his hands on her shoulders until she was steady.

"Glad to see ya, girl," he said gruffly.

After that, Natalie was squeezed and battered by the

children, then nearly choked to death by Marla. When she finally disentangled herself, her gaze found Elliot. He was surrounded by the men, shaking hands and stumbling beneath hearty back slaps from a few of the more enthusiastic congratulators.

As if he sensed her watching him, his head shot up. Their gazes locked. His slow, lazy smile hinted at secrets and promises yet to be fulfilled. Voices receded; people blurred and disappeared. They were alone, remembering, wondering, and anticipating.

When the ground began to tremble, it was a few seconds before Natalie snapped out of her daze and realized what was happening. Frozen, she watched as the boulders blocking the cave entrance shimmied and rumbled. All around her, people began to scream and shout, running to escape the tumbling rocks.

Natalie couldn't move. The cave entrance was collapsing, and the remains of her father—her only proof that her mother was not what everyone believed her to be—would be lost to her forever. She had to stop it! She took a stumbling step in the direction of the collapsing cave.

The air left her lungs in a squeaky rush as Elliot slammed into her, knocking her to the ground. He rolled them to safety as rocks thundered perilously close.

"You idiot! What were you thinking?"

Natalie, quelled in the face of his raw anger, struggled out of his arms and got to her feet. She automatically brushed at her dress, tears blinding her. "My father . . . my father's in there, Elliot."

He stood and grasped her shoulders, anger hardening his features. But as she watched, compassion gradually overshadowed the anger. He gentled his grip.

"He's dead, Natalie. Dead. Let him rest in peace."

She looked away from his burning gaze to the crowd of women who stood huddled together, pointing at the collapsed entrance and clutching their trembling bosoms, apparently marveling over their narrow escape. Without proof, they would never believe her, she thought. They would continue to whisper and speculate.

Did it really matter?

She knew, and Elliot knew. Marla and Noah would believe her, not that they cared one way or another. The children loved her unconditionally and didn't give a fig about her past.

Natalie slowly unfurled her clenched fists and wiped the tears away. Her chin came up. Her spine grew rigid. She looked at Elliot. "You're right. He's dead. I should let him rest in peace."

Three days.

Natalie watched him approach from her bedroom window, her hungry gaze sweeping over his broad, strong shoulders and muscled thighs as he strode up the lane. Three days since she'd last seen him. Three days that had seemed like a lifetime. She had floated on a cloud, her mind constantly reviewing their time spent together in the cave.

Every touch, every murmur, each and every kiss remembered, relished, and cherished. She was a woman in love. She had experienced the marvelous passion between a man and a woman and wouldn't soon forget it.

No, she'd *never* forget it.

Checking her hair and smoothing her dress, she raced downstairs and opened the door just as he was poised to knock. Her bright, happy smile faltered at his solemn look. "Elliot?"

"Natalie." He nodded and stepped past her. When she shut the door, he gestured to the parlor. "I need to talk to you."

Natalie swallowed a ball of fear. Something was obviously wrong. He was supposed to be happy to see her, as she was him. He was supposed to be looking at her with hot need, having missed her as she had missed him. He was supposed to *remember*.

She stared at his tightly compressed lips, searching for a glimmer of affection or that familiar, lazy desire. Her heart spasmed painfully when she found nothing but a guarded expectancy.

Yes, something was terribly wrong, and as he turned to go into the parlor, Natalie had to force herself to follow. Whatever it was, it was obvious that Elliot knew she wouldn't like it.

Once in the parlor, he prowled the room restlessly. Her eyes followed him. She caught herself twisting her fingers together and firmly put them behind her. Clearing her throat, she said, "You have something to tell me?"

He picked up the stool Brett had been working on and examined it. "He's good at this, isn't he? He really ought to be a carpenter's apprentice, don't you think?"

Natalie nodded. "Yes, he should." Where was this leading? Why didn't he just say whatever he had come to say? And where was the man she loved? Had he forgotten her so soon? Maybe he regretted what had happened between them. Behind her back, she quietly kneaded her fingers until they burned.

"And Cole. He's bright. He should be doing something as well, learning a trade."

"He—" Natalie clenched her jaw. No, now was not the time to tell him about the dollhouses, not until after she heard what he had to say, and maybe then she wouldn't want to. "They're both very talented," she managed instead and waited.

Elliot set the stool down and picked up the cushion Lori had finished, the very same cushion she had thrown at him a lifetime ago. So much had happened between them; so much had changed inside of her.

She couldn't say the same for Elliot. Natalie blinked her burning eyes and continued to wait. Obviously, he wasn't in any hurry to tell her, and she certainly wasn't in any hurry to hear it.

He trailed his fingers over the fine stitching, then abruptly met her gaze.

Natalie drew in a harsh breath at the stark regret in his eyes.

"We have an interview, a couple interested in meeting Brett and Cole."

"No." Her chest hitched. She brought her clenched fists out of hiding. "No. Surely you can't—not after we—" Natalie trailed off with a shudder before she made a complete fool of herself. She wouldn't open herself to more humiliation.

Welcoming the numb cold that crept in to block out the pain, Natalie forced herself to remember the conversation she'd overheard. The children had sounded eager to leave Ivy House, and despite the hurt she felt, she had to face the truth. Whatever her faults, she wanted the best for the children.

"You're right, of course." Triumph flared briefly at his surprised look. At least she'd managed to stir *something* in him, she thought with bitter anguish. Trying not to choke on the bald-faced lie, she continued, "I'm looking forward to meeting them. When will they be here?" *And how much did you offer them?* she screamed silently.

He quickly recovered, his bland expression slipping back into place and proving to Natalie that he was indeed a master of deceit. Why didn't she listen to her instincts? Inwardly, her broken heart wept. Outwardly, she remained as cool and composed as he. Pride and pride alone kept her from slinking away to her room so that she could wail like a baby.

"They should arrive any moment. Where are Brett and Cole? Are they upstairs?"

When she nodded, he moved to the parlor doorway as if to fetch them, but Natalie quickly stepped to block his path. She was proud of the polite smile she summoned. Now, if she could keep it from cracking . . .

God, it hurt! She felt as if her chest would split open and reveal her broken, bloody heart! "I'll get them. You'll want to answer the door when they arrive." Because *she* wouldn't. "I'll be back in a moment."

Or an hour. Amazingly, she didn't cry as she started for the stairs. If she did, she was convinced her tears would freeze on her cheeks, so cold did she feel.

He was going to sell the children. He was going to sell the children, then sell Ivy House. Then . . . leave.

Natalie squeezed her eyes so tightly it hurt. How stupid could she be? He felt no love for her . . . only lust.

Lust in the guise of love, the bastard.

Unlike her mother, she had been taken in by a scoundrel.

"You'd better be right, Marla," Elliot mumbled, staring after Natalie as she stomped up the stairs. He swore softly, then turned away from the sad sight, propping his foot on the cold hearth. "Yes, you'd better be right, damn it."

He braced himself against the mantel and closed his eyes, letting out a shaky breath. It had been sheer torture standing so close to her and not pulling her into his arms. He wanted—no, he *craved*—her mouth like a drunk craves wine. The last three nights had been spent tossing restlessly, aching for Natalie and cursing fate for keeping them apart.

But he couldn't offer for her because *he* had nothing to offer, not yet. With a lot of luck and a little skill, he hoped to change that situation very soon. He had very little time, and he had to perform a miracle.

A knock at the door brought a wry smile to his face. *The beginning of the miracle,* he thought, going to answer the door.

Determined to be optimistic—since he was certain

Natalie wouldn't be—he greeted the aging couple with a warm smile and waved them into the parlor. Before he had the opportunity to question the farmer and his wife, Natalie returned with Brett and Cole.

The show began.

An hour later, Natalie and Elliot faced each other in the empty parlor. Elliot had sent the couple on their way with completely false promises that he would get in touch with them soon. Brett and Cole had been banished from the room by a furious Natalie.

"How dare you be so rude!" she began.

Grim-faced and more than a little aggravated himself, Elliot assumed a defensive stance with arms folded and feet spread. His eyes narrowed on her flushed face and glittering eyes. She'd never looked so beautiful. "Rude? And you think Mr. Hatchet wasn't being rude when he hinted he needed a couple of strong backs to replace the mule that died?"

"It's Mr. *Hacket*," Natalie corrected. She paced up to him, then whirled furiously away as if she couldn't stand the sight of him. "They're getting old. There's nothing wrong with them needing strong sons to help on the farm. Didn't you notice that Brett and Cole liked the idea of living on a farm? As for working, they're used to it. Mr. and Mrs. Hacket are nice folks. They would take good care of the boys."

Elliot snorted, hiding his bewilderment over the turn of events. He had expected Natalie to find fault, but instead *he* had taken an instant dislike to the stone-faced couple. There was something about them that set his teeth on edge. "And just what, exactly, happened to their three dead children?" he demanded, his suspicions resurfacing.

Natalie's eyes widened in disbelief. She stopped pacing long enough to shrink him with an incredulous glare. "You have an overactive imagination, Elliot Montgomery, and thanks to you, you've ruined Brett and Cole's chance at happiness.''

Elliot dropped his arms and leaned against the mantel. He wasn't about to admit she was succeeding in making him feel foolish. Maybe he *had* overreacted, but what if he hadn't? He clung to that slight possibility and tried to distract her by turning the tables. "I thought they were happy here with you. Why are you suddenly so eager for the adoptions? If I remember correctly, you were very opposed to my plan from the beginning." He cocked a brow for emphasis. "*Strongly* opposed, I might add."

"Did I have a choice? Do I have one now?" Natalie asked, going still.

Looking into her hopeful eyes, Elliot wished he could give her the answer he knew she wanted to hear, but he couldn't. His frustration bled through. As a result, he was harsher with her than he intended. "Damn it, Natalie, *I* don't have a choice. Neither of us do. What would have happened to the children if we had died in that cave? Did you think about that? Where would they have gone? Who would have taken care of them?"

"Marla—"

"Marla has a family!" Elliot all but shouted. "Would that be fair to Marla or Noah? Taking on four children is a major responsibility."

"Not everyone is afraid of responsibility," she flung at him, leaving him in no doubt of her meaning. "As I recall, you weren't thinking about the children in the cave."

"As I recall," Elliot retorted with uncharacteristic malice, "you weren't, either." He spat out a vicious curse when she went pale, reaching her in three angry strides. Instead of shaking her as he wanted to do, he ran his hands up and down her stiff shoulders, soothing, apologizing without words. "Natalie, I want what's best for the children, and I want what's best for us." He lowered his voice, his gaze straying to her mouth. "Finding homes for them is the only way."

She kept her gaze lowered. "You said—you said you'd give us a chance."

She had whispered the accusation, yet it was ten times more potent than a shout. Elliot did shake her then, but gently. She was the most stubborn, bull-headed, determined female he'd ever met, he decided, torn between frustration and admiration. "And you believe you'll sell enough dollhouses to buy Ivy House?" he queried softly. When she lifted her stunned gaze to his, he nodded. "Yes, I know about the dollhouses." He considered telling her that he was the investor now that he knew the whole story from a chastened Marla, but he decided against it. One step at a time.

"I admire your determination, Natalie, but I don't think—"

"Don't patronize me," she spat, jerking free, "and stop telling your lies. You care nothing about the children or Ivy House—or me. Why don't you try being honest for a change? At least Nelda was honest. Well, the children are counting on me, and I won't let them down the way she did, as this town has, and as you're doing."

Elliot gritted his teeth. How much patience did he have left? He searched and found none, and that left him with but one choice: to tell her the truth. It would be the ultimate test, he knew. Perhaps—no, probably—it was one of the reasons he had avoided telling her. When she found out, would *he* find out that she really cared nothing for him? That her one and only interest in him had been Ivy House all along?

He inhaled slowly, holding her gaze with his own. He wanted to see her eyes when he told her. Only then could he be sure. "I *have* to sell Ivy House, Natalie. My grandfather owed a staggering amount of money to the railroad—people who had invested in his venture—and they want their money.'' Elliot watched the shock come into her eyes and braced himself. ''They don't know about Ivy House yet, but it's just a matter of time. If they find out before I sell it, they have every legal right to take it. It's worth more than I owe them.''

Her eyes continued to widen until Elliot thought surely they would swallow her face. Her lovely lips parted, then closed as if she wanted to speak and couldn't.

To hide the pain her reaction caused, Elliot growled harshly, ''So not only am I a pauper, I'm also up to my suspenders in debt.''

She found her voice. ''We never had a chance, did we? You let me believe we had a chance, but we never did, not even from the beginning.''

Hating to but knowing he had no choice, Elliot slowly shook his head. ''No, you never had a chance to buy Ivy House.''

14

"You should talk to him, Natalie," Marla said, gripping the edges of her sweater tightly against the chill breeze. The weather had turned; winter was on its way. "You can't solve a problem by ignoring it."

Natalie knew evasiveness wouldn't work with Marla, but she tried, anyway. "I've got to get these potatoes up before the first frost." As if to emphasize her point, she jabbed the shovel into the ground, grunting as she pushed through the earth in search of potatoes. She could have given the chore to Brett or Cole or even Jo, but she had needed the distraction. Maybe if she worked hard enough, she'd sleep tonight.

From the corner of her eye, she caught sight of Marla's swollen ankles. They reminded her to stay calm. She turned the earth from the shovel and bent over to pitch the dirt-crusted potatoes into a basket. "We have nothing to say to one another, anyway. He's going to sell Ivy House."

"He has no choice," Marla reminded her.

Slowly, Natalie straightened. Her back ached as well as her heart. She'd been avoiding Elliot for three weeks,

and Marla constantly nagged at her for it. She leveled
her gaze on Marla. "Maybe he doesn't have a choice,"
she conceded, "but has it occurred to you that *I* don't
have a choice, Marla? When Nelda Boone left, I made
a promise to myself and to the children. What kind of
person would I be if I went back on my promise, even
for love?"

Marla smiled smugly. "So you do love Elliot."

"I never said I didn't." Natalie resumed her digging,
refusing to acknowledge why her eyes burned. Of course
she loved Elliot, and it hurt like the devil. "Have you
forgotten the vow we made just before you were adopted
by the Masons? Even if Elliot *did* want to marry me,
he's made it clear that he doesn't want the children. We
said we wouldn't marry anyone who thought like that."

"But if he finds homes for the children—"

"Will he? Do you really think he will?" Natalie
stared at Marla until she shifted her gaze away. They'd
had this talk before. "All of them? Yes, someone might
adopt Brett and Cole because they can work, but what
about Lori? She's sick more often than not. And Jo?
What will happen to her? Don't you care, Marla?"

Marla gasped. "That's not fair!"

Immediately contrite, Natalie apologized. "I'm sorry,
I didn't mean that. I know you care." She shrugged her
weary shoulders. "I'm just so confused lately. Let's go
in for a cup of tea." Marla stopped her before she could
turn in the direction of the house. Her shrewd eyes
searched Natalie's face. Natalie felt a blush begin to
build. There was seldom anything she could hide from
her best friend, and although she had told Marla about
finding her father, she had left out the most important
part of the adventure. She planned to tell her when she
could talk about it without falling apart.

"What else happened in that cave, Natalie?" Marla
asked gently. "You're hurting, and I want to know
why."

Natalie closed her eyes. "Something that shouldn't have happened. Something that changed everything for me, but I can't talk about it yet, Marla. Please understand."

Marla stared at her for a long moment. Seemingly satisfied by what she found, she relented and changed the subject. "I didn't tell Elliot about the dollhouses, you know. Hickory did."

"It doesn't matter." Natalie sighed, leaning the shovel against the fence that surrounded the garden to protect it from critters. She tried to summon her optimism, but that seemed to fail her. "We'll never get the money we need, so it really doesn't matter." Her smile felt weak. "The most we can hope for is enough to rent a room at the boardinghouse for myself, Lori, and Jo until we figure out what to do. I expect Brett and Cole'll have new parents by then."

"You're always welcome to stay with us," Marla began, only to be interrupted by Natalie's fierce reply.

"No, no, we won't stay with you, but thanks for the offer," Elliot's blunt comment still lingered in her mind like a splinter buried just below the skin. He was right; it wouldn't be fair to Marla. "We'll be fine at Clyde's. He runs a decent boardinghouse, and maybe I can strike a deal with him. Room and board in exchange for cleaning and washing." If her words lacked enthusiasm, Marla didn't seem to notice.

Each lost in her own thoughts, they strode into the house.

"And you say you've always wanted a little girl?" Elliot eyed the fidgeting couple perched on the edge of the sofa in his hotel sitting room. Just a few questions, he thought, before he took them to Ivy House and introduced them to Lori.

Mrs. Thorton, a short, plump woman who wore her rouge like war paint, twisted the handkerchief in her lap.

She exchanged a nervous look with her husband before saying, "Yes. When Ace and I saw your ad in the paper, we discussed it. We'd love to meet her."

"Why?" When they looked at him blankly, Elliot explained, "Why do you want a little girl? Why not a boy?"

Bewildered, they exchanged another glance. "Well, I don't rightly know," Mrs. Thorton stammered. "I guess because girls are quieter than boys." Warming to her theme, she added, "Boys get dirty and fight. They're noisy, aren't they, Ace? Isn't that the reason we decided on a girl?"

Elliot smiled thinly at the well-dressed couple, thinking of how rambunctious Lori could be when she wasn't sick, and how much she enjoyed playing in the mud. Which reminded him . . . "Mrs. Thorton, have you had any experience at nursing the sick?"

"What? Oh, no. Not really." She swallowed visibly, the twin slashes of red standing out like flags against her pale cheeks. Her voice quavered. "Why do you ask?"

"Lori seems susceptible to colds." He didn't see the need to mention the strange fevers because he wasn't entirely convinced they existed. Marla would know, however. He made a mental note to ask her the very next time they spoke. "Nothing serious, but she does require a little extra care. Her room has to be kept warm and draft-free, and in the winter, it's best not to take her out—"

"Ruth," Mr. Thorton suddenly burst out, snatching the handkerchief from his wife's hands and mopping his sweating brow. "I think we should give this a little more thought." He grabbed his wife and hauled her to her feet. "I'm sorry, Mr. Montgomery. We'll get in touch and let you know what we decide. These—these things shouldn't be rushed. Don't you agree?"

His mouth curving in a cynical smile, Elliot nodded as the couple dashed to the door and disappeared. He knew they wouldn't be back, which was just as well. Lori needed quality care, like the care Natalie gave her. Mrs. Thorton didn't appear to have the backbone it would take to raise a special child like Lori.

Yes, he'd done the right thing by questioning the couple before raising Lori's hopes. He had enough on his conscience without giving the children over to just any strangers who happened along.

His growling stomach reminded him that he hadn't eaten lunch. Pleased with himself, he snatched his hat from a chair and made his way downstairs to the hotel dining room.

He'd ordered from the menu and was sitting back to enjoy a cup of coffee before his meal arrived when the banker approached his table. Elliot calculated swiftly, then relaxed as he realized that he wasn't late on the small loan he'd made with the bank. He smiled at Camper McCormick and stood, shaking the portly gentleman's hand.

"Mr. McCormick."

"Mr. Montgomery." The banker took the proffered seat across the table from Elliot. "I'm not interrupting your lunch?"

Elliot shook his head, taking a cautious sip of his coffee. Instinct told him this wasn't a chance meeting, but he couldn't for the life of him figure out what the banker wanted.

Mr. McCormick signaled the waitress and ordered coffee. When she'd brought it, he stirred an enormous amount of sugar into the black brew, then took a scalding gulp. His mustache gleamed with moisture. "I've heard you might be selling Ivy House," he said, lifting a bushy brow in question.

Elliot hid his surprise. He guessed it was common knowledge, but after living anonymously in a big city, small-town antics still amazed him. "I might," he ventured with a touch of reserve. It was too soon.

"I'm interested. My wife and I have thought about building something bigger, but I'd like to take a look at your house before we decide." Mr. McCormick leaned closer, his voice lowering to a conspiratorial whisper. "Got seventeen grandchildren, and I can't begin to tell you how deafening that can be when we all get together. I'd like a house big enough to get lost in, if you get my meaning."

Elliot got his meaning, all right. In return, he gave the banker his silent understanding. Seventeen grandchildren! He shifted in his chair. "Well, like I said, I haven't decided. But when I do, you'll be the first to know."

That appeared to be good enough for the banker. He drained his cup and stood, grabbing Elliot's hand again. "Don't take too long, sonny. Can't hold the missus off forever." With a friendly wink, he strode away, leaving Elliot alone with his brooding thoughts.

He shouldn't have hesitated. He should have taken the banker out to Ivy House the moment he mentioned his interest in buying it. How could he let an opportunity like that pass him by? Had he lost his mind? It was suicide to wait, and he knew damn well two or three months wouldn't make any difference. Didn't he? In the end, the men he owed would get Ivy House, one way or another. But this way he could choose how it was done rather than leave Ivy House in the ruthless hands of his debtors.

Elliot sipped and thought, vaguely aware that his meal had arrived. He picked up his fork and began to eat, no longer hungry but knowing his belly would not stop quarreling until he fed it. Why did he hesitate when a golden opportunity practically fell into his lap? Well, first, he needed time to find homes for the orphans. Then Natalie would need time to look for lodging and adjust to the change. With the money he earned helping Noah, he could just manage to make the small payments on the loan and pay for his own lodging until everything was settled.

Muttering a disgusted curse beneath his breath, he speared a potato and popped it into his mouth, chewing with more force than the tender vegetable warranted. Excuses, he admitted. They were all excuses. Just the thought of selling Ivy House made his gut clench in rebellion, and *that* was the truth.

Then, there was Natalie. . . .

She had become the most important thing in his life, beyond Ivy House, beyond his future security, beyond his own well-being.

Natalie Polk, orphan, woman, and warrior. The keeper of his heart. Elliot's laugh was humorless as he left his meal unfinished and threw some coins on the table.

Natalie was all those things and more, and certainly worth the enormous hell she was putting him through by pretending to hate him. Elliot frowned. At least, he hoped she only pretended. According to her best friend, Natalie suffered from guilt, believing she had failed the children. If she acknowledged her feelings for Elliot, then it would be the same as deserting them, at least to Natalie.

Elliot shook his head as he made his leisurely way to Noah's house, perplexed over Marla's twisted logic. He supposed it made sense . . . if you were a woman.

"You'd better be right, Marla," Elliot grumbled.

"They're gone," Natalie announced, surprised to find her voice steady. She didn't feel steady. She felt betrayed, unloved, a failure, and perilously close to tears after reading the note the boys had left in their room. "They're gone because of me."

Jo and Lori had come running from the kitchen at Natalie's call and now stood at the bottom of the stairs. Lori had been helping Jo make biscuits, and from the looks of her flour-dusted arms and face, she had dived in with gusto. Jo, too, had flour everywhere, including a smudge on her forehead and a slash of white on her cheek.

"They're gone? After I made extra biscuits for that sniveling, whining—"

"You really didn't know they were going, Jo?" Jo's answer was important. If Natalie knew she had just one ally in a world gone mad, then she'd make it, she thought.

When Jo flushed beneath the fine layer of powder sprinkling her cheeks, Natalie flinched inwardly and switched her gaze to Lori. Lori buried her face in Jo's apron and sniffled.

She had her answers.

Jo wiped her hands on her apron, her expression earnest. "I didn't know they were going today—right now, Natty. Honest, I didn't. Neither did Lori."

Jo looked down at Lori as she spoke, patting her head. The protective gesture made Natalie swallow a sob. Jo was protecting Lori from *her*. Damn Elliot Montgomery. This was all his fault!

"We heard Cole and Brett talkin' about that nice couple that wanted to adopt them, and how they wanted to live with them, but Mr. Montgomery messed things up, and they just decided to strike out on their own. Ain't that right, Lori?" Lori nodded her head but didn't look up. Jo's face darkened. "Believe me, if I had known, I wouldn't have went to all the trouble of makin' extra biscuits for that pig."

Natalie knew Jo referred to Brett, who could eat twice the amount of food as Cole, despite his diminutive size. The memory brought a sharp ache to her chest. Brett . . . Cole, alone out there in the big, cruel world. What if the farmer and his wife changed their minds and rejected them? Natalie would never forget how *that* felt and wanted to protect them from ever having to feel the same, hopeless anguish.

She had failed them, failed them all. If Brett and Cole hadn't been so concerned about their future, they wouldn't have gone to the farmer and his wife. They hadn't believed she could save Ivy House.

And they were right.

"Guess maybe this ain't the right time, or maybe it is," Jo began, pushing Lori in the direction of the kitchen. "Go check on them biscuits, Lori. I'll be right in."

Natalie gripped the hand railing and wondered what could possibly happen next. Everyone was deserting her, it seemed. Would Jo desert her, too?

"I'm gonna get that job at the restaurant, and soon as I get my first pay, I'm rentin' a room at Clyde's." Jo's voice trailed off breathlessly, as if she had to push it all out in a hurry.

"Why?" Natalie was so stunned, she couldn't think of anything else to say. Stunned and hurt. Yes, the possibility had entered her mind, but she couldn't believe it now that she heard it with her own two ears. "Why?" she repeated, descending the last three steps.

With an effort, Jo looked her in the eye. "Well, because Mr. Montgomery's sellin' Ivy House, and it's the only think for me to do." She shuffled her feet and dropped her gaze to the floor.

"I'm going to take care of us, Jo." With a hand that trembled, Natalie reached out and brushed flour from her pert little nose. Her throat was tight with tears. "Did you think I wouldn't?" *Did you think I couldn't?* That thought hurt above all.

"Well, it's not that I didn't think you would, Natty, it just ain't your place to. I'm nearly a grown woman now, and I can make my own way." There was a gleam of pride in Jo's eyes behind the lurking fear.

Where did the children get such ideas? Natalie wondered. Jo was obviously frightened of her plans, no matter how bravely spoken, so why did she insist on doing this? Why had the boys taken it upon themselves to run away?

Suddenly, Natalie had had enough. Something very strange was going on, and she meant to find the cause. "Go fetch Mr. Montgomery for me, will you? Ask him to borrow Marla's buggy."

Jo's eyes widened in alarm. "What are you gonna do?"

"I'm going to fetch Cole and Brett back home where they belong," she announced. She crumpled the note and flung it across the hallway entrance. "Then I'm going to get to the bottom of this. While Ivy House is ours, we're going to stick together, through thick and thin."

Within a short time, she and Elliot were on their way to the Hacket farm several miles outside of Chattanooga. Despite the jostling of the carriage, Natalie kept her back ramrod straight and her shoulders firmly away from Elliot.

He glanced at her from time to time but kept silent until they'd traveled some distance in the gathering twilight. "How long have they been missing?" he finally drawled.

Natalie closed her eyes tightly, then opened them again. She blamed everything on the scoundrel sitting beside her, handling the reins with casual expertise. "The last I saw of them was right after lunch. About four hours, maybe."

Elliot nodded thoughtfully. "They've had time to get here, then, even on foot."

"I imagine so. Brett and Cole are good runners."

"Hmm."

She slanted him a bitter glance, unable to contain her gathering anger. "You put them up to this, didn't you? Brett and Cole would never have thought of doing this on their own."

Elliot gave a start. The look he swung her way was incredulous. "Have you forgotten that I didn't *like* the

Hatchets? I had nothing to do with this, Natalie.''

"Hackets, not Hatchets! And you could have been pretending, hoping I'd be contrary and like them just because you appeared not to.'' It was a fresh possibility, and Natalie thought it sounded just like something Elliot would do. Oh, he thought he was so smart—

"So you think I'm the mastermind behind this plot, hm? My, my.''

His sarcastic tone made her stiffen. At that precise moment, a wagon wheel hit a pothole in the road. Natalie grappled for a handhold as she was pitched in Elliot's direction, expelling her breath in relief when she found one in the nick of time. While she might hate him at the moment, she didn't want to challenge her endurance. To her disgust, every night her dreams were filled with Elliot, and every morning she awakened aching and miserable.

Just as she suspected, it was impossible to forget what they'd shared together in the cave. And sometimes . . . sometimes she didn't *want* to forget. Those were the times she hated herself the most. He'd waltzed into town with his honeyed words and empty gifts with nothing more on his mind than closing Ivy House—and having fun in the meantime.

Having fun with *her*. Why else would he insist on selling Ivy House after what they had shared? Unlike poor, disillusioned Marla, Natalie didn't believe his sad story about debts and debtors. Or maybe she didn't want to. Maybe it was easier to convince herself she didn't love him if she believed the worst.

A flash of heat swept up her neck. Natalie resolutely turned her head away from his probing gaze, wishing she could forget how willingly she had turned in his arms, how eagerly she had accepted his kisses, and how joyfully she had taken him into her body. A foolish romantic, thinking he made love to her because he loved her. A foolish, foolish woman.

She shivered and drew her shawl together against the cool evening breeze, pushing those punishing thoughts from her mind. It was useless to dwell on what she should have done and too late to change the past. Right now, she would think of nothing more than getting her family back together, even if they didn't have long before Elliot shut Ivy House down.

At least they would have until Christmas, if Elliot's word could be believed at all. Natalie thrust her chin up and narrowed her eyes on the road ahead. She was going to make it the best Christmas the orphans of Ivy House had ever seen, a memory they would cherish for the rest of their lives.

"We're here."

Lost in her dismal thoughts, Natalie jolted back to earth at the sound of Elliot's low-voiced announcement. The shiver that ran through her wasn't from the cold this time. "Oh." Bracing herself, she allowed him to help her from the carriage. Knowing she shouldn't let her guard down but unable to hide her uncertainty, she fixed her diamond-bright gaze on him and blurted out, "What if they don't want to come home, Elliot?"

His eyes softened at her terrified look. "If that's how they feel, we'll deal with it."

With those encouraging words, Natalie suddenly felt stronger, more confident. She squared her shoulders and took his hand, declaring a truce for the time being. For the first time in weeks, she sensed an ally. How ironic that it turned out to be Elliot Montgomery.

"I'm ready when you are," she said.

15

When Mrs. Hacket opened the door, Natalie quickly peered around her while Elliot explained their presence. She spotted Brett seated at a rough-hewn table that dominated the spacious room, eating from a plate piled high with sliced ham, yams, and greens. The fragrance of baking bread permeated the air, along with the more subtle smells of lye soap and lemon.

Of Cole there was no sign. Recalling Elliot's suspicions about the couple, Natalie panicked, forgetting how she'd laughed. She clutched at his sleeve as she whispered, "Elliot! I don't see Cole."

He glanced down at her, then back to Mrs. Hacket. "If we could just talk to the boys, make sure they're all right?"

Mrs. Hacket hesitated. "They came of their own free will," she stated. "The boys want to stay with us."

"We're aware of that, Mrs. Hatch—Hacket, but Miss Polk and I would sleep better tonight if we spoke with them."

"All right. Mr. Hacket will be back shortly. He's calling the cows in." She stepped aside and waved her hand.

"Come in. I've got supper on the table if you're hungry. That Cole don't eat much, but Brett, he's got a hollow leg, I believe."

Her smile was full of pride, Natalie noted with a pang of shameful jealousy. Why, the woman couldn't have known the boys an hour, yet she showed them off as if they were her own. A glance at Elliot told her he'd noticed. He not only looked surprised but a bit chagrined as well.

Brett caught sight of them as they stepped over the threshold. He dropped his fork and leaped to his feet, grinning. "Natty! Mr. Montgomery, what are y'all doing here?" Then, as if he suddenly remembered the circumstances, his expression fell. "Me and Cole, we—that is, we thought we'd come on out and visit with the Hackets and see if—" He shot a quick glance at Mrs. Hacket. "Well, we thought—"

"It all right, Brett," Natalie said, realizing she meant it. "But where's Cole?"

"I'm right here, Natty," came a muffled reply.

Natalie gave a start of surprise and looked in the direction of the voice just as Cole backed out of the fireplace against the left wall. He was covered in black soot from head to toe.

Trying to brush at his clothes only made things worse. Finally, he gave up, his sheepish grin a shocking white in the black of his face. "I noticed their chimney wasn't drawing well, so I put out the fire and took a look. Sure enough, it needed cleaning. So I cleaned it."

Mrs. Hacket clucked over his ruined clothes, giving his ear a friendly pinch. She shooed him outside to undress and turned back to Natalie and Elliot, her tone unmistakably hopeful. "They've been so helpful since they've been here. Brett fixed that wobbly table leg, and Cole, well, you see what Cole's been doing. My Andrew's already planning on building an extra room onto the cabin for them. We hope you'll let them stay," she added, bustling to the cookstove. "Would you like some coffee or tea?"

Natalie looked at Elliot and saw the same battle in his expression that she suspected was in her own. The boys appeared to be happy here, and the Hackets seemed to not only need them but to want them. It was hard letting go. She slipped her hand in Elliot's and gave it a small squeeze. At his slight nod, she took a deep breath for courage.

"All right, they can stay—"

"Yippee! Did you hear that, Cole?" Brett shouted through the door. "She said we could stay!"

"—on one condition," Natalie concluded.

All eyes turned to her. She cleared her throat and looked into Mrs. Hacket's anxious eyes. "If they change their minds, you'll let me know? You won't force them to stay?"

The good woman was already shaking her head. "No, we won't force them to stay, but we hope they will."

For the first time since entering the cabin, Elliot spoke. "I'll bring the money tomorrow."

Again Mrs. Hacket shook her head, this time emphatically. "No, sir. I don't mean to be rude, but we don't want the money. We do pretty well for ourselves, and Andrew doesn't think it's right to take money for children."

Natalie heard the hint of disapproval in the woman's voice. She totally agreed with her. Tugging at Elliot's hand, she said, "We'd better be getting back. Jo will worry."

"We'll come to visit," Brett promised around a mouthful of food.

"Don't talk with your mouth full," Natalie and Mrs. Hacket said simultaneously.

Brett grinned. "See, Natty? She's just like you."

"Yes, she is, isn't she?" Natalie managed a smile when all she really wanted to do was cry. She didn't understand it. Why should she be sad when it was obvious the boys were happy? Why did she feel like sobbing, while they were smiling? Was she being selfish? She'd never thought of herself as selfish before, but she couldn't justify her feelings.

Once outside, they said their good-byes to Cole, who stood shivering in his long johns while Mrs. Hacket found him something else to wear. Natalie promised to send the rest of their meager things over the next day. Cole looked happier than she had seen him in a long time, she noted. Happy and hopeful.

She managed to hold back the tears until they could no longer see the cabin. Silently, Elliot guided the horses to the side of the road and pulled the brake.

Natalie turned away. She'd hoped to hide her misery, but apparently he was more observant than she thought.

"Come here, you," he said softly, pulling her into his arms.

Natalie went. She told herself it was only because she needed comforting, but her heart didn't believe the lie. Snuggling into his broad, strong shoulder, she wept.

Elliot patted her back and soothed her with words. "They *will* be all right, Natalie. Didn't they look happy to be there?"

Natalie sobbed harder.

"You're going to miss them," he guessed accurately.

She nodded her head, reluctant to look at him. She felt foolish for crying when she should be overjoyed. Foolish and selfish.

"They'll miss you, too, but they deserve a future, a new family, don't they, Natalie?" he reasoned. "Both Brett and Cole are fine young boys, soon to be fine young men. Chances are the Hackets will adopt them, and they will inherit the farm."

Yes, Natalie thought, taking a deep, shuddering breath. They had a future now. And she *was* happy for them, but she was going to miss them. When her sobs subsided, she drew back and looked at Elliot, intending to thank him for his kindness and firmly remove herself from the danger of his arms. The words died in her throat at the look of utter tenderness on his face. Then his expression became blurred as he lowered his head and kissed her. His lips roamed hers, gently seeking a response.

Natalie answered his request without thought, pressing herself against him, her body joyously remembering every hard angle, every firm muscle, and exactly what those hands could do to her. Her lips parted, allowing him to deepen the kiss. His tongue collided with hers, fused and retreated in a teasing game of love. Passion flared; heat burst inside of her, rocketed through her system, and sent her senses spinning out of control.

In a matter of moments, he made her forget her grievances against him and think only of what was happening now in his arms. As a woman, she loved him fiercely and without judgment, but Natalie Polk couldn't love him without sacrificing what she believed in.

That last thought gave her the strength to pull away. She didn't want to, and the small whimper that escaped her throat proved it, but she was determined to win the battle between her heart and her ethics. It was the only way she could live with herself. It was the only way she could *like* herself.

"I—we shouldn't have done that."

Elliot's eyes were soft with passion. "I don't agree," he said, tracing her swollen lips with his finger. "You haven't forgotten what we shared inside the cave any more than I have."

Natalie pursed her lips and scooted away, putting distance between them on the hard seat. "It shouldn't have happened then," she repeated firmly, "and it will not happen again."

He slapped the reins and got the horses moving, his expression smooth and unreadable. "Would it make a difference if I told you that I wasn't going to sell Ivy House?''

"No." It wouldn't, Natalie thought, because she'd still be responsible for the children, and Elliot didn't appear to want to share that responsibility. "We were— we were carried away by the possibility of dying, and—"

His mocking laugh startled her into silence.

"You really think that's the only reason we made love, Natalie?"

Her face warmed, but she doggedly stuck to her excuse. "Yes, I really think it was. What else could it be? We have nothing in common. In fact, we have more reasons *not* to like each other—"

"I can't think of a single reason not to like you," he said softly, throwing her a glance hot enough to set her dress on fire. "And if you weren't being so bull-headed, you'd realize that you really don't have any reason not to like me."

"I do so."

"Name one reason."

Natalie huffed and scrambled around for a reply. It was disconcerting to have to think. Didn't she have dozens of reasons, and didn't she repeat them to herself several times a day? "Well, you're arrogant," she finally sputtered.

He laughed. "I might be. Or maybe you're having trouble remembering because there aren't any reasons."

"Not a chance!" she said, then forced herself to calm down. Elliot would gain enjoyment by riling her. "You're a scoundrel—a perfect reason for any intelligent woman not to like you." There, let him swallow that one.

"Am I? What is your definition of a scoundrel?" When she didn't answer, he continued, with a soft, dangerous edge to his voice, "Does a scoundrel seduce innocent young women?"

"Yes."

"And did I? Seduce you? Think carefully before you answer," he warned.

Natalie did think carefully and hated him immensely. "No, you didn't seduce me," she admitted.

"And?" he prompted.

If she were a man, she thought furiously, she'd bash him in the nose. Through gritted teeth, she said, "And our . . . coupling was by mutual agreement."

"Coupling?" He chuckled. "I like to think that we made love, Natalie."

She gripped her fingers together and imagined his throat between her hands. She ignored the delicious shiver his tone and words evoked. "Think what you like. I try not to think about it at all."

"Hmm."

To Natalie's relief, they arrived at the edge of town. "Just drop me off at Marla's so that I can let her know the boys are okay."

"I'm going there, myself," Elliot countered.

"Then I'll walk to Ivy House from here. *You* can tell Marla what happened." As she scrambled down from the carriage with unladylike haste, her ears burned from the sound of his amused chuckle. *Awful man,* she seethed, marching down the street in the direction of home.

It was a downright shame she loved him.

Jo stood before the mirror in Natalie's room. With hands that trembled, she smoothed her dress and tugged at the neckline, then tucked her short hair behind her ears. She was going into town to apply for that job and maybe talk to Clyde about renting a room at the boardinghouse. If she happened to run into Jeb . . . well, she'd consider it fate, just like Elliot and Natalie, according to Marla.

Brett and Cole had been gone a week. It was past time she did her own part to bring Natalie and Elliot together by going her own way and showing Natalie that

she wasn't needed. Oh, she *was* needed—the thought of
supporting herself terrified Jo, as did the thought of
wearing the dress—but she wasn't going to let that stop
her. Natalie deserved to be happy, and as long as she
felt responsible for the orphans of Ivy House, then Natalie's stubborn nature wouldn't let her care for Elliot.

Jo twirled around, watching the folds of the faded
dress she'd borrowed from Natalie settle around her bare
feet. It was the very first time she'd attempted to wear
a dress, and now that she found the courage to put one
on, she couldn't bring herself to leave the room.

Old, ugly memories surfaced. Jo backed up until she
felt the edge of the bed hit her weak knees. She sat down
abruptly, wishing she could block the memories but
knowing she couldn't.

They were always there, hovering like a threat.

Her mother's hesitant, frightened voice filled her head
like thunder. *"Don't let them know you're a girl, Jo. If
they think you're a boy, they'll leave you alone. Me, I
gotta do whatever it takes to put food in our bellies."*

More memories followed, uglier and more frightening. Jo clamped her hands over her ears and squeezed
her eyes tightly shut. Despite the protective action, she
could hear her mother's screams and that savage, ugly
voice cursing her.

Jo wasn't likely to ever forget the face that went with
that voice. She also wasn't likely to ever forget the sight
of her broken, bleeding mother. After that, she had lost
days where she couldn't remember what she'd done or
where she had gone. Then one morning she found herself outside of Ivy House without having a clue how she
came to be there.

Abruptly, Jo stood and mimicked Natalie's stubborn
stance. Back straight, shoulders square, chin firm. When
she darted a shy glance in the mirror, she noted that her
eyes glistened with the light of battle. She'd march into
town and get that job, and nobody would bother her. Of

course they wouldn't. This was Chattanooga, and while people appeared indifferent to the lost orphans of Ivy House, Jo didn't think they would stand by and let someone attack her.

What was she thinking? She was silly for dwelling on something that would never, ever happen! Laughing at herself and spurred by an unaccustomed excitement, Jo went to fetch her shoes from her room.

A half hour later, she emerged from the restaurant simply named Mama's Kitchen, grinning foolishly. People passed her on the boardwalk, some curious and some too busy to notice that the orphan girl who dressed like a boy wore a dress for the first time. Or maybe, Jo thought, those who knew her didn't recognize her. The possibility made her giggle. Would Jeb know her? Would he like her this way? Or did he only like her as a friend and felt comfortable around her because she dressed like him?

Standing in front of the door enjoying her newfound independence, Jo nodded at those she knew and smiled at those she didn't as she pondered her future. She was to start her new job on Monday at five o'clock sharp. Tapping her foot, Jo cast her thoughtful gaze on the boardinghouse just down the street. Why wait? Why not go ahead and ask Clyde for a room with a promise to pay him at the end of the week? Clyde was a round, jolly man, well-liked by everyone; his wife was a perfect match. They ran a respectable business, and their friendly manner and comfortable lodgings couldn't compare with the cold hauteur of the fancy new hotel that had sprung up last year.

No, the hotel hadn't hurt the Nolens in the least.

Deciding she'd take the challenge while her confidence soared, Jo made her way to the boardinghouse, a two-story affair squeezed between the jewelry shop and a funeral parlor. Clyde answered her knock with a welcoming smile and a wave of his thick, hairy arm. His eyes twinkled kindly.

"Aren't you little Miss Jo from Ivy House?"

Jo nodded, nervous now that the moment had come. "I—I'd like to let a room. I've gotten a job at the eatin' place, but I won't get paid until the end of the week. If you could just let me stay until then, I'd pay you the moment I—"

"Whoa, girl!" Clyde's laugh boomed through the house. "That's a lot to follow, and at such a speed!" He turned and bellowed, "Mama! Come here! Come see this pretty little lady on our doorstep."

A woman came through a doorway Jo suspected led from the kitchen, wiping her hands on a food-splattered apron. She was frowning. "What is it, Clyde? You know I've got to get those pies baked before—Why, isn't that Jo from Ivy House?" she asked as her gaze lit on the young woman standing in the doorway.

Jo studied her in return. She had warm brown eyes like her husband's, set in a kind, wrinkled face. Thinking of her own brown eyes, Jo thought, *I could have been their daughter.* Startled more by the wistfulness of her thought than by the fact that she had thought it at all, Jo gave her head a slight shake. She'd gotten over those ridiculous dreams a long time ago, hadn't she?

"What on earth are you doing here, Jo?" Mrs. Nolen asked, pulling her inside. She smelled of apples and cinnamon, familiar, comforting scents to Jo. "Shut that door, Clyde, it's gettin' cold."

She kept her arm around Jo, and Jo decided she didn't mind at all. In fact, it gave her a warm feeling in the pit of her stomach. Looking into those welcoming, friendly eyes, Jo found herself pouring out the entire story.

By the time she had finished, Clyde and his wife were clutching each other, nearly helpless with laughter. Watching them, Jo began to chuckle. Before long, she was laughing as heartily as they were. Yes, it *was* funny to hear it told. A passel of matchmaking orphans and a well-meaning pregnant woman acting as general.

When the laughter finally died down, Mrs. Nolen wiped her streaming eyes and said, "Well, I thought I'd heard it all, girl! 'Pears I hadn't! Of course you can stay. We want to do our part in bringing those two together. You can take the room opposite ours, top floor, last room on the left. That way we can keep an eye on you."

Jo started to protest that she didn't need looking after, but then she remembered the fear that came upon her at night sometimes. She clamped her lips shut. "Can I see the room?" she asked instead.

"Sure can. Go on up. I've got to check on the pies, but I'll be along in a minute." Mrs. Nolen shoved her gently toward the stairs. "Clyde, you need to set the table for dinner."

Left alone at the bottom of the stairs, Jo glanced up at the shadowed stairway and began to climb the steps, nearly tripping over her skirts before she remembered to hold them up. She'd rather have waited for Mrs. Nolen, but if she was going to become independent, she had to learn to put her fear behind her. Just like Natalie said, there wasn't any shame in being a woman. And besides, she continued to assure herself, Chattanooga was a safe town.

On the second-floor landing, Jo hesitated, then started down the hall to the last door on the left as Mrs. Nolen had instructed. Halfway there, she heard the sound of muffled, male voices. She paused, her heart pounding. The voices came from the other side of the door directly to her left.

Keep going.

Her body ignored the order. A cold, terrified sweat popped out along her spine. The tiny hairs at the nape of her neck rose in warning.

She recognized that voice!

"He's here, mark my words, and we'll find him.

We're not leaving until we get the boss's money.''

"Does this hole in the ground sport a brothel? I didn't notice on that bone-jarring drive from the river—''

The man who opened the door snapped his lips closed the moment he noticed Jo frozen in the middle of the hallway. He held a cigar clamped between his teeth. Shoving it to one side of his mouth, he drawled, "Well, who have we here?'' His watery, bloodshot gaze trailed up and down her slim form in bold appraisal. He wiggled his eyebrows suggestively and glanced over his shoulder at his partner. "We didn't order room service, did we, Evans?''

Jo didn't hear him; she was watching the other man. He'd aged, but he hadn't changed so much that she didn't recognize him. She'd never forget as long as she lived. The same cruel, black eyes, and the same twisted mouth caused by a scar that lifted his lips upward in a permanent snarl.

Paralyzed with horror, Jo dropped her gaze to his hands. Yes, he still wore the rings. He'd cut her mother's face beyond recognition with those rings.

"Hey, don't I know you?''

She jerked her gaze back to his face, her eyes widening in shock. "I—I—'' It was no use. She couldn't make her throat work, just as she couldn't make her legs move. It was the same nightmare come true for Jo, one she'd lived in fear of repeating for a very long time.

The man she knew as Randal Evans brushed past his partner and stepped into the hall. He reached out and grasped her chin, jerking it roughly from side to side. "Yes, I know you. Aren't you the brat of that whore who thought to rob—''

It was the feel of his cold, slimy fingers on her skin that released her muscles.

Jo whirled and practically fell down the stairs. She snatched open the front door and raced down the steps, hiking her dress high and not giving a fig who saw her.

Her heart pounded in rhythm with her shoes on the warped and scarred boardwalk. She let out a gasping sob and rubbed at her chin, trying to erase the horror of his touch as she raced toward Ivy House and safety.

Those same hands had killed her mother.

Painful sobs began to build in her throat. People stopped to stare, but Jo continued running, her one single thought to get home and lock the door, hide under the bed . . .

Ivy House came into view, but just as a sob of relief bubbled in her throat, she heard footsteps behind her. Not daring to look back, Jo picked up her pace, her harsh breath whistling in and out of her lungs.

He was behind her!

She tripped on the blasted dress she'd never wear again and pitched forward, flinging out her hands to catch herself. Strong arms circled her waist and snatched her up just inches before she hit the ground. With the last, tortuous breath left in her lungs, she screamed.

16

Elliot pounced on Natalie the moment she entered the parlor. "How is she? Is she all right? What in the hell frightened the child?"

He was a wreck, she thought, letting her gaze travel over him. His hair stood on end where he'd raked his fingers through it; the top few buttons of his shirt were in the wrong buttonholes as if restless fingers had worked them loose, then carelessly rebuttoned them. His face looked haggard, and his eyes held a wild gleam she recognized as panic.

He'd never looked so handsome, and she realized something in that moment, something she'd been too blind to see or too proud to admit; Elliot did care about the children. He really cared. She sighed and passed a weary hand over her own frazzled hair. Yes, Elliot cared, but if not for him and his determination to sell Ivy House, Jo wouldn't have felt the need to apply for a job in town, and she wouldn't be in the state she was in, for whatever reason. "She won't talk, but I do know that she applied for the job at the restaurant. She also mentioned something about checking with Clyde—"

"Clyde?" Elliot strode to her, his expression growing wilder. "Who's Clyde?" he demanded.

"Clyde runs a boardinghouse," Natalie said in a soothing voice meant to calm him. It didn't work. Elliot swung around and paced to the fireplace, rubbing the back of his neck. Natalie held still, fascinated with this new side of him. He always appeared so controlled, while she seemed to leap from one emotion to the next.

"You should have seen her face, Natalie, when I caught her as she was falling. She looked at me as if I were the devil himself! And that scream—" His mouth twisted in a grimace that was more anguished than puzzled. "Something or someone frightened her, and I'll know who it is before the day is out!"

Natalie believed him, and she pitied whoever was responsible. "I'll talk to her again, see if I can find anything out."

"Yes, yes, do that. If someone hurt her—laid a hand on her, I'll—" He let out a string of oaths that made Natalie's eyebrows rise. "I'm going into town to get some answers," he growled, stomping past her.

Natalie watched him go, her heart aching with a fierce love she knew would never die. It didn't seem to matter to her heart that he had turned their world upside down.

When the door slammed shut, Natalie slowly climbed the stairs. Maybe when Jo's fear subsided, Jo would talk to her, tell her what happened.

She could always hope for a miracle.

Mrs. Kelley closed her fingers around the rolling pin, keeping a wary eye on the madman who had stomped uninvited into her kitchen. "I told you I don't know which way she went. I was back here in the kitchen when she left."

"And she didn't mention where she was going from here?" Elliot asked for the fourth time. He knew he repeated himself, but damned if he could help it.

Blowing out a frustrated breath, he looked at Mrs. Kelley. She was a thin woman of about fifty, with dark hair peppered with gray and twisted tight in a conservative bun. From the looks of her skinny arms, she didn't eat much of her own cooking. Still, she appeared harmless, if a little tired.

"I saw which way she went, Miz Kelley."

Elliot jerked his gaze to the huge black woman peeling potatoes over a slop bucket. He'd been distracted when he arrived and hadn't noticed her. Why in heaven's name didn't she speak up when he first asked the question? he wondered with an inward snarl of frustration. "Well?"

She rolled her round, coffee-colored eyes in the direction of the swinging doors leading into the dining area. Amazingly, the knife continued to move around the potato with lightning speed. "I was sweeping the walk out front when dat girl left. Her was headin' south."

"Thank you," Elliot snapped ungraciously, slapping his hat on and stalking out through the swinging doors. South probably meant toward Clyde's boardinghouse, he mused, stepping outside.

A brittle wind whistled around the corner of the building and cut clean through his thin coat, making him long for one of the heavier coats he'd left in Nashville. With a face full of thunder, Elliot ignored the cold and walked the short distance to Clyde's boardinghouse. He'd get some answers, by God, one way or another.

But Clyde and his wife, it seemed, were just as baffled as Elliot. According to the couple, Jo had asked for a room but had left without making arrangements.

"She went upstairs to take a look," Mrs. Nolen explained, "and came racing down—oh, couldn't have been more than five minutes—like the hounds of hell were chasing her."

"Nearly tore the door apart leaving," Mr. Nolen

added on a worried note. "Can't imagine what spooked her."

Elliot glanced upward and narrowed his eyes. "You've got boarders?" he questioned softly. He rested his foot on the bottom stair and contemplated the upstairs landing. Dark, shadowy, but enough to scare Jo? He didn't think so.

"Couple of fellows from Nashville." Mr. Nolen tugged at his beard and added, "Seemed like nice gentlemen."

Elliot was beginning to have his doubts about that. "I'll just have a word with them, if you don't mind. Which room?"

"Well—"

An elbow to his side effectively silenced any protest Clyde thought about making. Mrs. Nolen glared at her husband before turning to Elliot. "Go right ahead. If those men frightened Jo, then I don't want them in my house, that's for sure. They're staying in the second and third rooms on the left."

Elliot left the couple arguing in fierce whispers and took the stairs two at a time. He paused before the second door and listened. Nothing. Stepping a few feet to his right, he listened at the third door. *Ah, voices,* he thought, knocking sharply. Jo's terrorized scream still echoed in his head. He clenched his fists and waited.

The door was yanked open almost immediately by a mustached man dressed in a somber gray pinstriped suit. He'd discarded the coat, revealing black suspenders with a startling slash of red through the center. One look in those watery, weak eyes, and Elliot knew this was not his man.

He shoved the man aside and strode into the room. Bare-chested, Randal Evans stood by the washbasin, his face nearly hidden by thick lather. Apparently, he'd caught Evans in the middle of a shave, Elliot thought without sympathy. His lip curled in distaste. Even without his shirt and his face covered with lather, he recognized the man.

"You found me," Elliot drawled, guessing Evans was the man he was looking for. Anyone who worked for a ruthless tycoon like Bo Carnagie had to sport a mean streak, Elliot concluded silently.

Without haste, Evans grabbed a towel and wiped his face clean, revealing a permanent snarl that turned out to be an asset when collecting unpaid debts.

It didn't scare Elliot. In fact, the thought of this hideous man touching Jo pushed his blood pressure through the ceiling.

"Looks as if *you* found *me*," Evans retorted. With a jerk of his head, he ordered the other man from the room.

Elliot swung around. "You stay. I might have a few questions for you."

Evans shrugged. "This is none of his business, but suit yourself." He pitched the towel onto the washbasin and picked up his shirt. "Carnagie wants his money, Montgomery. We're not leaving this town until we get it for him."

It was Elliot's turn to shrug. "Maybe you will, and maybe you won't. That's not what I want to talk about right now."

Something flickered in Evans's eyes. It might have been fear or it might have been confusion. Elliot really didn't care. He stepped closer, wanting to watch the man's expression as he asked his questions. "Did you accost a girl in the hall an hour or so ago?" Evans gave a guilty start, and even before Elliot looked at the other man to confirm his suspicion, he knew he'd been right in thinking Evans was the cause of Jo's hysteria.

With almost casual ease, he took that last step that brought him to Evans. He grabbed the man's unbuttoned shirt and hauled him against the wall. Eyes blazing, he spat, "What exactly did you do to her?" He shook him for good measure. Evans's snarl became more pronounced. "And don't try to lie," he added, "because I'll know it."

The man standing behind Elliot let out an alarmed squeak. His voice was shrill as he cried, "He didn't do nothing but talk to her, ain't that right, Randal? Didn't you know—"

"Shut up, you fool!" Evans snarled. "I didn't know the wench. I was just making friendly conversation."

Elliot pressed his knuckles into the man's windpipe until his face began to redden. "If the conversation was so friendly, then why did she run from the house as if the devil chased her?"

"She didn't—"

"I have witnesses." Although Evans's partner had answered his question, Elliot never took his eyes from the man before him. He couldn't get the image of Jo's terror-stricken face from his mind. No, the man had not engaged Jo in friendly conversation. There was more, and he intended to find out exactly what it was.

Hauling Evans into a chair, he released his stranglehold on his shirt and stood back. He dusted his hands on his pants as if to wipe away the filth before he fixed Evans with a deadly stare. "Tell me what happened, and I might let you live."

Evans breathed in great gulps of air, massaging his neck and glaring at Elliot. "We found the girl listening outside the door," he rasped. "I simply asked if we could help her with something, and she ran screaming." He darted a glance at his partner as if for confirmation. "Tell him, Jules."

Jules nodded vigorously. "Yes, that's exactly what happened. Just like Randal said."

"Shut up," Elliot said, and the man did. "You'd lie to your mother, I'll warrant. And if this man pays you to hound people, you'd most definitely lie for him."

"No, sir, I—"

"Shut up."

"Yes, sir." The man swallowed audibly.

Elliot regarded Evans as if he were a particularly slimy worm that had crawled out from under a damp rock. "Since I'm certain you'll be staying in Chattanooga, I'm willing to let you live for the moment." He leaned forward until Evans's eyes widened in alarm. "But when Jo decides to tell me what you did to her, there won't be a rock big enough to hide you."

Turning away, he strode to the door and jerked it open.

"This ain't over, Montgomery. You owe Carnagie a lot of money. I'm not leavin' until I get it."

Elliot paused. "So you've said. Seems we've both made promises we intend to keep." He turned his head slightly. "Ever heard of the expression, 'You can't squeeze blood out of a turnip'? I can't give you money that I don't have."

"Your old man was a fool," Evans snarled, growing braver now that Elliot was at the door.

"You'll leave my grandfather out of this." It was a simple statement delivered with a ton of steel. "Or I'll make good my promise right now." He wanted to—oh, how he wanted to! But he didn't relish a night in jail, and words were, after all, just words. If it turned out the slime had touched Jo, then that was an entirely different matter.

"That lawyer of yours said you were here on business," Evans added just as Elliot started to leave again.

Reminding himself that Evans was probably only fishing, Elliot forced a casual shrug. "I pay the man to say what I want him to say." He grasped the knob and opened the door.

"Rumor has it you own property around here."

Elliot stifled a sigh of relief. If Evans knew about Ivy House, he'd make it clear. It was obvious he knew something, though, and it would only be a matter of time, a much shorter amount of time than he'd hoped. He'd have to move things along, tell Natalie, contact the banker, and show him the house.

Without answering, he left Evans to wallow in frustration. He had a terrible suspicion that if Jo started talking, he'd find Evans before Evans had a chance to find him.

The Nolens were waiting anxiously in the hall.

"Well? Did those fiends touch our Jo?" Mrs. Nolen demanded, plump fists planted on her hips.

Elliot shook his head. He had his suspicions, but he had no proof. Natalie had told him that Jo was a troubled young girl with dark secrets in her past. It could have been nothing more than a look, a word, a gesture. Instinct told him it was more, but he couldn't accuse a man on instinct. "I can't say just yet, Mrs. Nolen, but they'll bear watching."

"That I'll do. Why, if it were up to me, I'd pitch them out on their ears right now—"

"Now, Mama—"

"Don't you Mama me, Clyde!" she snapped. "Mr. Montgomery, you let us know if you find out anything. I'll not have those tramps in my house if they're not gentlemen. We run a respectable business here."

"I'm sure you do," Elliot murmured sincerely. He eyed the door and considered his odds. Apparently the couple had not resolved their argument, and he had no desire to referee.

"And tell Jo to come back anytime. We'll hold that room for her, won't we, Clyde?" Without giving him a chance to respond, she sailed onward. "Jo's such a precious girl and right lucky she is to have you looking out for her. Why, you're the best thing that's happened to Ivy House in a long time, ain't that right, Clyde?"

"Of course, dear."

Mrs. Nolen ignored her husband's sarcastic muttering. "Poor Natalie, the way she's had to look after them

young'uns since that no-account sot ran off and left them
in a lurch! Why, Natalie's hardly more than a babe herself.'' She arched a knowing brow at Elliot before adding quickly, ''Not that she's too young for marriage,
mind you. If it weren't for taking care of the young'uns,
she'd probably be married by now, don't you think,
Clyde?''

''Not if she's smart,'' Clyde muttered, winking at Elliot.

His wife poked him with a sharp elbow. ''Clyde Nolen! You rascal, you'll have Mr. Montgomery here
plumb scared to death of matrimony! And with you
knowin' how much you love me. Tell him.'' She poked
him again. ''Go on, tell him.''

Elliot kept his expression bland as Clyde turned red
with embarrassment. The man had his complete and total
sympathy—and a great amount of envy, he was surprised to realize.

''You know I love you, Mama.''

Mrs. Nolen beamed at Elliot. ''See? Ain't love
grand?''

Indeed. Elliot cleared his throat. ''I've got to get going, Mrs. Nolen. It's been a pleasure talking to you.''
During the course of the conversation, Elliot realized
that Jo must have had quite a chat with Mrs. Nolen. He
couldn't decide whether he was embarrassed or amused.
He did suspect the entire town would know before the
day was out. ''Good day.''

''Don't forget to let us know,'' Mrs. Nolen said, following him to the door. Her expression, cheerful only
moments ago, darkened as she added, ''I'll keep an eye
on those two.''

Elliot stepped onto the porch and tipped his hat to the
good woman. He didn't doubt for a moment that Mrs.
Nolen would keep *both* eyes on the varmints staying
beneath her roof.

* * *

Evening shadows darkened Jo's small room as the girl lay huddled on the bed with her back to Natalie. She had changed into her familiar trousers and shirt—presumably while Natalie was downstairs calming Elliot—and the borrowed dress lay scattered in pieces over the bedroom floor. Natalie frowned worriedly at the ruined dress. She suspected it was a silent testimony to the turmoil that boiled inside Jo.

Soundlessly, Natalie lit a lamp before again taking her seat next to the bed, picking up her crochet hook to resume the soothing task of weaving the yarn. She'd been watching Jo and crocheting for well over two hours now, with no change.

Jo hadn't spoken a word since Elliot had brought her home.

Natalie had never seen Jo like this, and it scared her. What if she didn't snap out of it? What horrible thing could have happened to make her this way? Surely, if she'd been attacked . . . by a man . . . someone would have seen or heard? Reaching out, she let her hand hover over the girl's shoulder, then took it away without touching her. She didn't want to startle Jo.

"It's okay, Natty. Nobody hurt me."

Natalie gasped at Jo's soft, reassuring whisper, sensing the pain and fear behind the words. She wasn't fooled; she knew Jo too well. Jo would try to protect her. She knew because she would have done the same.

Forming her words with care, Natalie placed her crocheting on the floor at her feet. "Can you tell me what *did* happen, Jo? Elliot's frantic with worry. We all are. We want to help you." Jo was silent so long, Natalie thought she'd either decided not to answer or she'd gone to sleep. Just as she was about to give up and resume her crocheting, Jo spoke again, her voice soft and curiously devoid of emotion. Natalie suspected she wouldn't have been able to speak any other way.

"It was my mother's idea for me to wear boys'

clothes and to keep my hair cut short. She wanted everyone to think I was boy so they'd leave me alone. It worked, mostly.''

Tears made Natalie's eyes ache. She swallowed hard, watching Jo's shoulder hitch in a sigh or a sob. She desperately wanted to hold her but instinctively knew Jo wasn't ready for comfort. Right now she probably just needed to talk, to lance the poison.

"I never told her about that time Mr. Eubanks caught me takin' a bath. He didn't really hurt me, just tried to—tried to—touch my breasts. I slapped him and ran, and after that he didn't bother me no more.'' As if she sensed Natalie's unspoken question, she explained, ''Mr. Eubanks worked for Miss Lily. He protected her girls if the men got too rough. He collected the money, too.''

Natalie bit her lip, suddenly understanding what Jo meant. She had lived in a brothel, and her mother had been a—

"But the night my mama died, he wasn't there. He'd gone out to get Miss Lily some cigars.''

Jo turned abruptly, fixing her diamond-bright gaze on Natalie. A slight, disbelieving smile tilted Jo's lips, reminding Natalie of how young Jo was. Sometimes, looking into her worldly eyes, it was easy to forget.

"Can you believe that? A woman smokin' cigars? My mama said it wasn't ladylike.''

With her heart in her throat, Natalie kept silent. She didn't think she could have spoken if her life depended on it, nor could she have explained to anyone why it didn't sound absurd for Jo's mother to sell her body yet consider smoking cigars unladylike. Maybe it was the reverence in Jo's voice when she spoke of her mother.

Settling on her back, Jo propped her knees up and focused her gaze on the ceiling. ''Anyways, Mr. Eubanks was gone, and this man''—She raised her hand and twisted one corner of her mouth into a grotesque shape—''who looked like that, came in and asked for

Mama. It wasn't the first time, either. I'd seen him go into Mama's room before, but this time, he was mad and yellin', sayin' Mama took his money. Miss Lily tried to stop him from going upstairs, but he got past her.''

Shimmering brown eyes darted to Natalie's face, then back to the ceiling. Her throat convulsed. ''Mama was brushing her hair, and I was sittin' on the bed countin' her earnings like she taught me. When she heard him comin' up the stairs, yellin' and stompin', she told me to get under the bed and to take the money with me.''

Finally, the tears came. Natalie saw them, a trickle at first, running from the corners of Jo's eyes, then a steady stream. She couldn't stand it. ''Jo, you don't have to—''

''No, Natty. You've always told me I'd have to get it all out someday, and you're right. I gotta. Now.'' Swiping ineffectively at the tears, she continued. ''This man, the one with the funny mouth, came bustin' in the room. At first he only yelled, but when Mama kept saying she didn't have his money, he started hittin' her. He kept on hittin' her and hittin' her and hittin' her.'' She paused for breath. ''I stayed under the bed.''

She looked at Natalie, her eyes huge and filled with guilt and shame and remembered terror. ''I stayed there, Natty, while that horrible man beat my mama to death. I didn't do nothing about it. When he dragged me out and started yellin' at *me*, all I could do was cry.''

''You were a child, Jo! He might have killed you, too.''

She shook her head violently. ''Maybe not. Maybe I could have hit him with something—anything—''

''Don't.'' Natalie felt her own tears falling. She knew what it was like to feel ashamed, to feel guilty for something she couldn't help. ''Don't blame yourself, Jo. Please don't blame yourself. Your mama wouldn't have wanted you to.''

Jo seemed to consider this. Finally, she sighed. ''I know you're right, but I just can't forget about it, thinking about what I should have done, what I could have done.

"He let me go, I guess when he realized I was too scared to talk." She fingered a tiny, crescent-shaped scar at the corner of her eye. "He only hit me once, but he wore rings on nearly every finger."

Natalie slowly curled her nails into her palms until she felt the pain. She knew it could never compare to what Jo had felt.

"Mama was still alive when he left. The other girls— well, they were too afraid to come when he was there, but when he left, they came. Wasn't anything they could do by that time." Her breath hitched on a sob, but she gamely held it back. "Mama told me, right before she died, she said, 'Jo, don't ever let them know you're a woman, or the same will happen to you.' "

"No wonder you've been terrified." Natalie didn't succeed in hiding her anger. "She shouldn't have told you that, Jo. The situation—the place she was in—that's not the same as here, in Chattanooga. At Ivy House."

Jo shrugged as if she didn't care. Natalie knew it was a lie. "I guess she did the best she could. It was her way of protecting me."

Natalie couldn't dispute Jo's logic, even if she didn't agree with her mother's methods. "And today? Did something happen to remind you of those memories?"

After a telling hesitation, Jo said, "I thought I saw the man . . . the same man that killed my mama . . . but it wasn't him. It just scared me, that's all."

"Are you *certain* it wasn't him?" Natalie persisted, sensing that Jo was lying. Her heart began to pound just thinking that such an evil man existed. And he was here in Chattanooga? She shuddered. "If he's here, we need to let the sheriff know. He's wanted for murder, isn't he?"

Jo was silent for a long moment. With a bitter grimace, she finally said, "No. Miss Lily told the sheriff my mama fell down the stairs. She didn't want no trouble with the law; it was bad for business. I left that night. I didn't even wait for her to be buried.''

The sobs came then, as harsh and deep as the river that cut through the mountains. Natalie scooted to the bed and held her close as Jo poured out years of heartache, grief, anger, guilt, and shame onto Natalie's shoulder.

Natalie's tears fell silently as she, too, grieved. She grieved for Jo's horrid childhood and the bitter memories that were Jo's only legacy from her mother.

She understood. Oh, how she understood.

$\mathscr{W}$arm summer days were behind them, Elliot decided, watching his breath turn to plumes of smoke as it hit the cool air. Although it was late in the morning, the early frost still lingered, sparkling like diamonds on the sparse patches of grass and the thick trees that sheltered Ivy House from strong, bitter winds.

Not only had his grandfather used the finest lumber, but also he had chosen the location with care and foresight; Ivy House lay tucked into a hollow at the base of the mountain, surrounded by natural barriers, isolated yet comfortably close to town.

Tethering Rico to the porch post, Elliot dismounted and strode to the door. As he started to knock, Natalie opened it, muffling a startled shriek at the unexpected sight of him. After a brief, unguarded glance, she tightened her mouth and glared.

Elliot made a quick assessment. She clutched a bundle of clothing in one ungloved hand and a jar of honey in the other. Along with the frost in her eyes, he had no trouble identifying the militant angle of her chin. Normally, such a spirited greeting would amuse him; not today. He felt Natalie had every right to be angry with him. She couldn't be more angry with him than he was with himself.

"It seems I've caught you at a bad time," he said, letting his gaze roam over her strained features in brutal self-punishment. There were shadows under her eyes, making him wonder if she had slept at all last night. "How's Jo this morning?"

The frost turned to ice. Her chin angled another notch. "She's better."

She might as well have shouted the words, *No thanks to you!* "Natalie, I—"

"Excuse me. I've got to get these things out to Brett and Cole before they have to go naked." She pulled the folds of the heavy gray cloak over her shoulders and tried to step past him.

Elliot noticed how threadbare the garment was on close inspection. With a silent oath, he covered the hand holding the bundle with his own, ignoring the way she stiffened at his touch. "How did you plan on getting to the Hacket farm? It's too long a distance to walk, and it's too cold."

She tilted her face at him, the brim of her bonnet sweeping his chin. Anguish flickered briefly in her eyes, and the sight of it had Elliot muttering another oath beneath his breath. He was the cause of her anguish, and the worst part was, he didn't know what to do about it or if there was anything he *could* do. He couldn't give her Ivy House.

The fingers beneath his hand tightened on the bundle. "Not that it's any of your business, but Noah's taking me out in the wagon."

"I'll take you," Elliot found himself saying in a tone far more possessive than he intended. "We can ride double on Rico." When she opened her mouth to decline his offer, Elliot hurriedly added, "I'd like to see the boys."

"I don't want to ride with you."

"I don't blame you." Elliot smiled without humor at the surprise on her face. "Would it help if I said please? I was about to ride out and see them myself, anyway." He watched as she battled with her emotions, wanting badly to kiss the hurt and anguish away but knowing he couldn't. Not this time. It would take much, much more. A lifetime, if she would give him the chance. He'd made such a rotten mess of things.

Finally, she sighed. "All right, since you're going that way." The long, cool look she gave Elliot reminded him that as far as she was concerned, their relationship was nonexistent. She thrust the bundle at him and slipped the jar of honey in the pocket of her cloak. "Let's go, then. I don't want to be away from Jo for long."

Masking his triumph, Elliot tied the bundle to the saddle horn, then lifted Natalie into the saddle. He grasped the reins and swung himself behind her onto the back end of the horse. Rico twitched his ears in surprise, but after dancing sideways a few steps, he seemed to accept the unusual distribution of weight.

They set off along the lane at a steady pace, the wind cool at their backs, the clouds a gloomy blanket above them. Elliot eyed the taut line of her spine and resisted the urge to pull her against his chest and force her to remember how she had once—not so very long ago— enjoyed the closeness. He wanted to snatch the prim bonnet from her head and let loose her hair; turn her face around and sear her lips with a long, satisfying kiss; and demand that she remember and stop fighting what was meant to be.

But what right did he have? None.

Instead, he attempted a civil conversation. "Have you learned anything new about what happened to Jo yesterday?" He'd already decided not to tell her about Randal Evans and the confrontation he'd had with the varmint, not until he found out what happened. Knowing

Natalie, she'd probably stomp to the boardinghouse and confront Evans herself, and Elliot didn't want her near Evans.

After a curious hesitation, Natalie said, "She mentioned that someone frightened her, but it was . . . because he reminded her of someone from her past."

Elliot frowned, sensing she wasn't telling everything. "She told you about her past?" Another hesitation deepened his conviction that she was hiding something. He watched her shrug those stiff shoulders, wishing he could see her face.

"Not really. Just a hint here and there."

Fine. If she didn't want to confide in him, then he couldn't force her. Elliot shifted into a more comfortable position and swallowed the angry, demanding words he wanted to say.

"There's a shortcut through those trees yonder," she said coolly, pointing to a grove of pines a few yards from the road.

Obligingly, Elliot guided Rico into the grove of sparse pines. The temperature seemed to drop another ten degrees as they rode into the shadows. He saw Natalie shiver. With an exasperated oath, he pulled her against him and wrapped his arms around her. "You're cold, so stop being stubborn," he growled in her ear when she struggled to pull away.

"I'm not cold," she lied but stopped struggling.

Elliot pondered the inevitable as Rico weaved his way through the trees. Natalie's earlier affection toward him had cooled, it seemed. What would she feel when she learned that they had even less time than he'd first thought? After leaving the boardinghouse, he'd gone straight to the bank and talked to Mr. McCormick. The banker had been surprised by Elliot's quick decision but overjoyed at the opportunity to look at Ivy House.

The appointment was for next Tuesday at one o'clock. A shaft of pine needles spiraled lazily down from the tree above them and landed square in the middle of Natalie's bonnet. Elliot plucked it away before tightening his arms, ignoring her halfhearted protest. Finally, he was rewarded as she sighed and relaxed against him.

Of course she blamed him for Brett and Cole running away and for Jo's misfortune in town. She had every right. If he'd stayed away, neither incident would have happened. They would have managed without him, because he had no doubt about Natalie's ability as housemother.

How could he have prevented trouble? Maybe if he'd stayed closer to his grandfather, he would have been able to talk Gill out of that last, catastrophic investment.

Maybe if he had, he'd be here courting Natalie in the style she deserved instead of tearing her family apart and kicking her out of her home. Elliot closed his eyes against the futility of it all. No use thinking about what might have been. There was only now, and he had come to terms—or thought he had—with the way it would have to be.

He'd sell Ivy House and pay his grandfather's outstanding debts, along with the loan at the bank. With the little money left, he'd buy a small house in town for Natalie, Jo, and Lori. It was the only alternative left.

Then and only then would he think about his own future. Once he set a course in that direction, he would find employment and begin the long, uphill climb to reestablish himself. When the time came, he would return to Natalie and talk about their future.

He'd pray to God she'd wait for him. He had no reason to believe that she would, but he could pray and hope. He also had no valid reason to believe she'd forgive him, but in that, too, he could hope. Perhaps, in time, she would realize that he'd had no choice.

As for the dollhouses, yes, they could become a profitable sideline, but now that he knew the truth about who made them, he couldn't take a penny of that money. It

belonged to Natalie and the children. All of it. No matter
how close the hounds nipped at his heels, he could not
and would not lean on Natalie or the children to get
himself out of this mess.

"We're here."

"Hm?" Elliot blinked and looked around him in
amazement. He'd been so engrossed in his thoughts and
plans that he hadn't realized they'd arrived at the Hackets' farm.

Smoke rose from the chimney of the little house with
its sagging roof and rough-hewn stones; chickens fussed,
pecked, and cackled as they strutted around the yard. An
enormous barn situated several hundred yards from the
house appeared in better shape than the house itself.
Somewhere in the distance, a cow mooed as if in agony.
Probably waiting to be milked, Elliot thought as he dismounted, then reached for Natalie. All in all, it was a
simple, peaceful scene.

He envied this family.

His hands closed around Natalie's tiny waist beneath
the cloak. Their eyes met and held. He slowed his movements and brought her closer, sliding her along his body
as he lowered her to the ground. She dropped her eyelids
to hide her expression, but when she pulled her bottom
lip between her teeth, Elliot knew she wasn't as unmoved by the contact as she wanted him to think. The
realization made his heart ache and his body pound with
need. He wanted her to look at him once more with
wonder and love, as she had in the cave.

He needed her as desperately as a starving man needs
food. Natalie had become his sustenance in life, clouding
his every thought and sometimes his reasoning.

Holding his breath, he watched her gaze travel along
his chest, onto his neck, and finally lift to his face.

"Natty! Mr. Montgomery!"

Together, they turned to watch the boys approach
from the barn. Elliot continued to lower Natalie, then

reluctantly stepped away. What would he have seen in her expression? Pity? Love? Yearning? Hate? If not hate yet, then that would appear after he brought the banker to Ivy House. Of that Elliot was certain. With a heavy heart and a smile that felt stiff on his face, he waited for Brett and Cole to reach them.

Marla set a slice of warm apple pie in front of Elliot, pushing the small pitcher of heavy cream within reach before taking a seat at the table. She and Noah exchanged worried glances before she looked at their guest. "Are you certain Brett and Cole are happy, Elliot?"

Elliot nodded, toying absently with his fork but not touching the pie. "They seem to be. Brett's building Mr. Hacket new stalls in the barn to replace the ones an old bull took down, and Cole's milking the cows. According to the Hackets, both boys are heaven-sent. The feeling appears to be mutual."

"As long as they don't work the poor babes to death," Marla muttered. The mental picture her comment produced brought a frown to her face. She knew how Cole and Brett loved to please. It would be so easy for the Hackets or anyone else to take advantage of their gratitude.

"They aren't babes anymore, Marly," Noah scolded. "They're nearly men."

"Babes," Marla argued, digging into her apple pie with gusto. "And speaking of babes"—with a glance, she dared Noah to dispute the fact again—"how's Jo doing? Did you ever find out what happened in town yesterday?" Busy chasing an apple slice around her plate, it was a moment before she realized that Elliot didn't answer right away. Her gaze shot to his; her eyes widened at his guilty expression. "Elliot, what's the matter?"

As if coming to a decision, he placed his fork by his

uneaten pie and steepled his hands. "I think I need to tell you and Noah what's going on," he began, sweeping his intent gaze between the two, "in the remote possibility that something happens to me."

Marla's heart jumped in reaction to his serious tone, but she managed to hide her quick panic before Noah noticed. He'd order her from the room, and then she'd never find out what was going on. She cleared her throat. "Nothing's going to happen to you, Elliot, but you know anything you say won't leave this room." Beneath the table, she crossed her fingers.

As Elliot began to fill them in on the most recent development, it took more and more effort for Marla to remain outwardly calm. When he told them of his suspicions about Randal Evans and explained who he was, she forgot herself and let out a horrified gasp. "Poor Jo! From the way you describe him, I'm sure just the sight of him would scare the wits out of her! And if he said— if he touched—" Marla fell silent, refusing to voice the ugly possibility. "Poor, poor Jo!"

Elliot's eyes were hard. "If he touched her, I'll make him regret it. You can count on that."

"Amen," Noah echoed. He pointed his fork at Elliot. "So, they've found you."

"You knew about this?" Marla squeaked, glaring at her husband and feeling irrationally betrayed.

Unrepentant, Noah nodded. "I did, and I wasn't at liberty to share it with you." He reached out and patted her cheek, his soft expression belying his stern tone. "Besides, we know you can't keep a secret. Elliot didn't want to make it easy for those men to find him, and you're not exactly the best at keepin' secrets, Marly."

If only he knew, Marla thought, batting his hand away. "So why am I suddenly so lucky?"

"Do you want the man to continue with his story, or should we take the rest of this conversation outside with our pipes?"

Marla swallowed her irritation at the threat and looked at Elliot. "Please go on, if you're sure you can trust me," she added without blinking. Elliot rewarded her with a faint smile. It faded all too quickly for Marla's peace of mind.

"I'm taking Mr. McCormick to look at Ivy House on Tuesday."

Marla closed her eyes and muttered a quick prayer. She prayed that she hadn't heard him say what she thought he'd said, and that if he had, that it didn't mean what she was afraid it would mean. Heaven help them when Natalie found out! "You're not going to sell Ivy House so soon, are you?" she asked hopefully.

"I don't have a choice."

"But didn't you promise Natalie—"

"Don't badger the man," Noah interrupted. "Elliot doesn't have a choice in the matter, Marly. You heard him say his creditors found him. If he doesn't sell before they find out about Ivy House, they'll take it. The house is worth more than he owes, but it won't matter if they get their hands on it. By law they can take it as part of his grandfather's estate."

The ominous meaning behind Noah's reminder quieted Marla. She felt a fresh burst of sympathy for Natalie. "But what about the dollhouses? Any day now, your friend could need more. Couldn't you take your earnings and make a deal with this Evans person? Explain to him—"

"No." Elliot spoke the word gently but with finality. "Don't you think I haven't thought of every conceivable plan, Marla? A man like Evans doesn't make deals, and he won't wait."

Marla couldn't give up, although she suspected Elliot had already set his mind. "But what about Mr. McCormick at the bank? Won't he loan you the money to pay them back?"

Elliot lifted his brows. "And how would I pay the bank?"

"With the money you earn selling the dollhouses—"

"Marla," Elliot interrupted patiently, "even if the dollhouses started selling like phonographs, I won't take a nickel of the money *now*."

His glance was significant. Marla cringed, thinking he meant to tell Noah about her little fabrication. Noah would lecture her for hours if he found out how she'd convinced Elliot a hermit had created the dollhouses. But Elliot didn't rat on her, bless him.

"I'm asking your advice. You know Natalie better than anyone else. Should I warn her about the appointment?"

"No!" The two men looked at her, surprised by her vehemence. Marla flushed. "I mean, I don't think you should. She wouldn't sleep a wink if she knew, and she's not been sleeping well as it is." When Elliot looked pained at the reminder, she hastened to say, "In this case, I think it would be kinder just to surprise her." Hanging onto her composure by a thread, Marla scooted the chair back with a noisy scrape and jumped to her feet. "I'm just gonna go check on Hickory. He should be getting up from his nap soon."

Once clear of their view, Marla stopped and leaned against the wall. She pressed her hand over her pounding heart before dropping it to her burgeoning belly, wondering if pregnancy caused a woman to go temporarily insane. Because of her impulsive advice to Elliot, Natalie would have no warning.

On Tuesday, Elliot would discover that Ivy House had depreciated considerably in value since the very first dollhouse was made.

He would be furious at Natalie, Marla thought, warming to the idea. Her friend would no longer have the market on anger. Best of all, this would perhaps make

Natalie realize that everyone makes mistakes, and that sometimes people have no choice but to make them, just like Natalie didn't have much of a choice when it came to using the lumber to build the dollhouses. The children might have starved had she not thought of the idea.

Marla stepped away from the wall, her heartbeat slowing to normal. An enlightening smile spread across her face. After Elliot discovered what they'd done to the upstairs, Natalie could hardly point an accusing finger at Elliot, now, could she? She had destroyed someone else's property. Oh, not maliciously, but then, Elliot wasn't taking their home out of meanness, either.

Natalie had done what she had to do.

Elliot was doing what he had to do.

Her smile growing wider, Marla sauntered in to check on Hickory, feeling decidedly proud of herself. Sooner or later—she hoped sooner—those two stubborn fools would realize that they were perfect for each other.

Seeing that Hickory was as sound asleep as she suspected he would be, Marla crept from the room and headed back to the kitchen. She had one more harmless suggestion to make to ensure that Elliot and Natalie didn't spend too much time apart.

Very harmless, she assured her skeptical conscience.

The sound was faint, but Natalie's eyes shot open as if she'd heard a gunshot. She'd been lying in the dark, trying to will her exhausted body to sleep, knowing it was a useless mission. She hadn't slept more than three hours in one night since making love with Elliot.

Elliot. Oh, God, how she loved him, and oh, God, how she hated herself for loving him. Why did she have to go and fall in love with someone she couldn't be happy with? Why not a nice, stable, compassionate man like the one Marla had found?

The sound came again. She strained her ears in the dark, trying to identify the noise. It sounded as if someone were attempting to walk across the floor without stepping on the boards that creaked, she decided, and that someone wasn't very good at guessing.

Hickory. With the thought came relief. It had to be Hickory. Throwing back the covers, she swung her legs to the side and stood. Her nose connected with someone's chin. Hands shot out of the dark and grabbed her arms to keep her from falling backward onto the bed.

"Natty! It's me, Jo. I hear someone downstairs."

Natalie clutched her throbbing nose and just managed to stop her sharp remark in time. Jo sounded terrified, and the realization reminded Natalie of what Jo had been through. Her heart softened. "It's probably Hickory, Jo. I was just going down to check."

"No!" Jo grabbed her arm and whispered fiercely, "It's not Hickory."

A violent shudder shook Jo's slim frame. Her nails dug into Natalie's arm. Alarmed at this uncharacteristic reaction from a normally tough Jo, Natalie tried to calm her. "What makes you think it's not Hickory, Jo?"

"Be-because I saw the man come onto the porch."

"How?" Natalie was lost. "Are you saying you were watching from the window?" In her concern, she forgot about the intruder downstairs. "Jo, it's the middle of the night! What were you doing up at this hour?"

"Watching."

If Jo hadn't sounded so serious, Natalie would have laughed. But she was deadly serious, and that tore at Natalie's heart. Before she could form a soothing reply, they heard another loud creak. The sound froze Natalie. "I think I'd better go investigate," she said as calmly as she could. Now *she* was beginning to be afraid, which was silly, wasn't it? Jo was imagining things. She'd find Hickory trying to sneak upstairs into her bed—

"Take this. I'm coming with you."

Natalie automatically closed her fingers around the board as Jo thrust it into her hands. She started to chide the girl but decided against it. If it wasn't Hickory . . . "All right. Let's go. You stay behind me."

As one, they moved silently to the stairs. With any luck, they'd reach the bottom before whoever it was started up. Unconsciously avoiding the creaking boards Natalie knew by heart, she hugged the wall and descended the stairs. Jo followed so close, Natalie fancied she heard the girl's heart banging against her ribcage.

Her own wasn't exactly quiet. Perhaps that's why she didn't hear the familiar creaks from the first and third stair, she thought, freezing against the wall as the shadow loomed before her.

It was a big, dark shadow. Not Hickory, certainly not Hickory. Natalie registered the fact with a sharp jolt of fear, thrusting the impressive length of lumber in front of her. She opened her mouth to demand the intruder identify himself, but Jo, it seemed, had already decided on another form of communication. She screamed, an earth-shattering, ear-piercing scream directly into Natalie's ear.

Natalie let go of the board and clapped her hand over Jo's mouth. The board tumbled down the few remaining stairs end over end, creating a clatter that was sure to awaken Lori. There was a loud, pained oath as the board came to rest, hopefully, Natalie thought, against the intruder's head. Jo struggled against her, clawing at her arms and then finally the hand holding her terror at bay.

She dug her nails into Natalie's fingers and jerked her hand away. "Natty—"

"Shush," Natalie whispered softly to the frantic girl. "I think the board got him. Maybe on the head—"

"Unfortunately, it *wasn't* my head," a deep, drawling voice interrupted.

Natalie shrieked.

18

"Elliot!" Natalie gasped out.

"Mr. Montgomery!" Jo echoed.

"One and the same." Elliot tried for mockery, but suspected he sounded more like a wounded dog. He definitely wanted to howl like one. The board had caught him squarely in the shin with enough force to buckle his leg. There would be a bruise tomorrow, if he wasn't actually crippled from the blow.

"What are you doing here?" Natalie demanded.

Elliot could see nothing but a faint shape, but he responded to the breathless sound of her voice like the besotted fool that he was. She was the siren, and he was the ship, just like in the legends. "I'll tell you, if you'll be kind enough to lend me a hand. I don't think I can walk on my own." He could, but he'd much rather have her near. Eliciting her concern would be the fastest way, possibly the only way.

And his leg *did* hurt.

She reacted as he expected, and since she couldn't see his expression in the dark, he smiled.

"Jo, go fetch a candle, and hurry!"

He heard the sound of Jo scurrying up the stairs, but he didn't hear Natalie come down. One moment he was staring at the spot where he *thought* she was standing, fantasizing about how sheer her gown might be if he could only *see* her, and the next moment he felt a jolt of surprise and pleasure as she pressed her warm body against his side. With efficient movements, she lifted his arm around her and grabbed his waist, grunting as she pushed upward with her shoulder to take the brunt of his weight. He didn't have the heart to tell her it was the opposite leg.

"Here we go, just lean on me until Jo gets back. No sense in taking risks in the dark."

"No," Elliot murmured, turning his head to get a whiff of her hair. He was a beast for fooling her, but he was a happy one. So many nights had he lain awake, thinking about burying his nose in her hair, having her body pressed tightly to his again.

"I'm back," Jo said, out of breath from her swift descent. She struck a match and lit the candle, cupping her shaking hand around the flame until it caught, then handed it to Elliot. She stood shivering, hugging her arms over her chest with eyes round with lingering terror.

Elliot raised the light and studied Jo's face. "What's going on?" he demanded.

Jo stuttered, "I—I saw you and I thought—I thought—"

"Jo, go on back to bed. I'll handle this." Natalie's voice was firm. "You need to get some sleep."

Without another word, Jo scampered back upstairs. Elliot watched her until she disappeared into the shadows. "What happened, Natalie?" he asked softly. "What is it you're not telling me?" He felt her hesitation again, determined to drag it out of her. "I'm not leaving until you tell me. She's still terrified about something, and I don't think Jo scares that easily."

"Let's go into the kitchen, and I'll fix us a cup of tea."

"Coffee, if you have it." Elliot frowned, but turned with her snuggled under his arm. His foot clanked against something on the floor. Ah, yes, the weapon responsible for his bruised shin. "What the hell did you hit me with, anyway?" He lowered the candle as he spoke, running the light along the length of the board. "Where did this come from?" It looked like cypress wood.

"Um, it came from the attic," Natalie said with suspicious haste. "Must have been left over from when your grandfather built the house. Come along, it'll be warmer in the kitchen."

"Don't you have any heating fuel?" He had noticed how cold the house was while sneaking across the foyer.

"Of course, but we don't waste it when we're asleep," she retorted defensively, pulling out a chair and slipping out from under him.

Elliot eased into the chair and stretched his leg out. He set the candle on the table as she knelt before him, her soft, gentle hands probing the area of his shin—on the wrong leg. Ignoring the rush of desire that stole his breath, he said, "It's the other leg."

Her hands stilled. She looked at him, one eyebrow arched. "Why didn't you tell me? You walked in here on your injured leg." Clamping her lips shut, she bent to the task again, probing his shin until he winced. "It's not broken, but then, you knew that, didn't you?"

Elliot couldn't resist stroking her hair, which shimmered like molten gold in the candlelight. It felt like satin beneath his palm. "I've missed you," he whispered huskily.

Her head shot up in alarm. "Why are you here, Elliot? Did you think to sneak in and climb into my bed?"

"No—"

"Did you think I'd just welcome you with open

arms?'' She leaped to her feet, the pupils of her eyes dilated and filled with wrath . . . and something else Elliot was certain she wasn't aware of; a mixture of hurt and suppressed need that struck an answering chord in his own heart.

He knew that feeling well. ''Of—''

''Well, you've wasted your time and mine, Elliot. I don't intend to—to make that mistake again. There's nothing between us. Nothing. There *can't* be!''

''It wasn't a mistake,'' Elliot snapped. ''And that's not what I'm here for, despite what your wicked little mind is thinking.'' He smiled when she gasped at the insult. ''You're good at insulting me, but you're not so good when the tables are turned, are you?'' She continued to study him, her lips clamped tightly together.

Elliot's patience dissolved with her continued silence. He reached out and yanked her to him. He kissed her hard, possessively, leaving her in no doubt about his feelings on the matter. Just as her cool lips began to heat up and soften beneath the onslaught, he thrust her from him. She'd never know—he hoped—how much the effort cost him.

She stumbled and caught herself, running a deliberate hand over her mouth as if to remove the kiss. Her eyes flashed with temper. ''You—you're a bully!''

Elliot stared at her heaving chest beneath the concealing cotton nightgown, his gaze traveling hungrily over the curves outlined at the height of each breath. Curbing his raging need, he forced his gaze back to her face. ''I'm here because I'm worried about you,'' he stated. ''I was hoping to catch you alone so that I could talk to you without little ears listening.''

''Worried?'' She uttered the word in disbelief as she stood trembling before him.

He wondered if she trembled from the cold or from the same need that now tightened every muscle in his body. He'd like to think it was the latter, but he knew he probably fooled himself. Rubbing a hand over the lump on his shin, Elliot said, "Marla hinted you haven't been feeling well." For a telling moment, his gaze dipped to her waist.

She obviously didn't take the hint. "Marla had no right telling you anything. It's none of your concern *how* I feel."

"Maybe it is, if I'm responsible," he said slowly, gazing pointedly at her stomach again. He saw the moment she understood his meaning; her face flushed red, and her eyes narrowed to slits. Those dainty hands curled into fists.

She was furious.

"Marla *told* you that? I don't believe it! Why would she tell you such a lie—"

"So it isn't true? You're not with child?"

"No, I am not *with child*." She spoke between clenched teeth. "Now that you've satisfied your curiosity and appeased your conscience—once again—you can leave."

Elliot settled back in his chair, surprised to feel disappointed. He should be relieved, for he definitely wasn't in any position to become a father. Yes, he was insane, thinking for one moment, hoping for one second that fate would intervene and give them both a reason to overcome the obstacles in their paths.

Giving his head a slight, mystified shake, he said, "Now that we've got that cleared away, you can tell me what happened with Jo." When he saw her stiffen, he lifted his hand. "And don't tell me it was nothing. I saw her face."

Natalie would have told him anything just to get him to leave. How close she had come to breaking her vow, how very close he had brought her to humiliation again. Knowing it didn't make the want go away, either, she discovered. She wanted to fling herself at him and lose herself in his kiss. Her breasts tingled and ached, and her thighs quivered wickedly at the thought of those strong, warm hands stroking her.

And her heart . . . dear lord, her heart physically hurt just knowing he didn't love her. Wanted—yes, that was obvious. And it wasn't enough.

Taking a deep, fortifying breath, she said, "Okay, I'll tell you. Then you'll leave?" His eyes flickered over her like a hot flame before he nodded. Natalie quickly swung around and began to make coffee, trying desperately to forget he watched her. She cursed her traitorous body and slammed the kettle on the still-warm plate. With agitated movements, she stoked the fire and added a small chunk of wood. She was like that fire, banked to embers when Elliot wasn't around; stoked to a fierce flame when he came near.

Why did it have to be Elliot? Someone she couldn't *allow* herself to love? Natalie stifled a bitter laugh. It was as if she had no choice. But she did have a choice, she reminded herself. She did not have to admit, accept, or act on her love.

With this staunch reminder firmly ensconced in her head, Natalie returned to the table and began to tell Elliot what Jo had told her. Throughout the story, she carefully avoided looking at him, although she sensed his intent gaze on her face.

She felt guilty for betraying Jo's confidence, but the girl hadn't really said she shouldn't tell Elliot, had she? And Elliot wasn't leaving her a choice. Surely Jo would understand.

Once during the conversation she paused and got up to pour coffee for Elliot. She pumped a tin cup full of ice-cold well water for herself before returning to the table. "So, you see, for a moment Jo thought the man at the boardinghouse was the very same man who . . . killed her mother. She's been jumpy ever since, and tonight when she saw you coming onto the porch, she thought—''

"I was that man," Elliot concluded coldly.

Natalie looked at him in surprise and confusion. He sounded angry, but why would he be? She had explained that, according to Jo, the man had done nothing but remind Jo of someone she feared.

"Do you believe her?"

At his question, Natalie frowned into her empty cup. She remembered how she'd sensed that Jo wasn't being entirely honest. "I don't know. I can't think of any reason she'd lie, can you?"

Elliot sat forward and wrapped his hands around his cup. "Maybe she's too afraid to tell the truth," he suggested.

She glanced up. A shiver stole over her at the hard gleam in his eye. Elliot knew something, she realized. He knew something—or *thought* he knew something— and he wasn't going to share it with her.

With a weary sigh, she stood. "I'd like to go to bed now, please." He mumbled something and tossed the last of his coffee down his throat. Natalie swallowed, watching him. He was beautiful and totally out of her reach. Her heart clenched painfully. To cover the sudden, crushing sense of loss she felt, she snatched her cup from the table and took it to the counter.

She shouldn't have turned her back on him, she realized with a stifled moan as his arms slid around her. Helplessly, she leaned into him, telling herself it was only for a moment, no more.

His breath scorched her ear while his fingers burned a path from her hips to her breasts. "Normally, I'd take you up on such a tempting invitation, but there are children in the house."

"Oh." It was all she could squeeze from her suddenly empty lungs. He was such a brute, and she was such a gullible fool.

"Lock the door after I leave."

"Hickory—" she began, then stopped in surprise. Was that husky, seductive voice her own? Lord. Best she not speak at all than to give him the satisfaction of hearing how he affected her.

His knowing chuckle told her it was too late.

"Deny me all you will, sweetling. You want me, just as I want you." With a regretful sigh, he dropped his hands away and stepped back. "I doubt Hickory will be out tonight. He was exhausted from riding his pony." He toyed with her loose braid, his fingertip brushing her spine.

Natalie shuddered.

"Tomorrow, I'll talk to him, warn him away from my woman," he added on a teasing note.

"I'm not your woman." *And you're not my man.* She clutched the edge of the counter and bit down hard on her bottom lip. She wouldn't turn around, and she most certainly wouldn't beg him for a kiss. Furthermore, she refused to acknowledge the rush of pleasure his words evoked.

His woman. Ha! She had learned her lesson the *first* time she'd danced too close to the flame. She was strong, intelligent, and didn't need a second lesson.

The first one had hurt quite enough, thank you.

Natalie shot the bolt home with vicious force, then leaned against the cold door. She had to stay away from him—miles away from him. Well, she'd get her wish soon enough. When he sold Ivy House, he'd be on the first steamboat out of Chattanooga. In the city, he'd have his pick of single women who had nothing to do but please him.

Maybe he'd go back to Suetta.

She flinched at the thought, then trudged upstairs to lie awake until dawn. While she was lying there, she would rehearse what she would say to her dear, meddling friend Marla. With child, indeed! She paused on the dark stairs and pressed a hand on her flat stomach, then firmly moved it to the bannister again. Thank God, she could safely say she wasn't. History was *not* going to repeat itself.

Natalie steadfastly ignored the pang of disappointment she felt. It was perfectly normal, wasn't it, to dream of having a child by the man she loved? A dream was, after all, just a dream.

Harmless.

Oh, yes. Marla was in for a long, enlightening lecture on how to give up on a hopeless cause.

Because Natalie already had.

By Tuesday, Jo had begun to relax, Natalie noted with relief. She no longer paused and stared searchingly out of every window she passed, and she had begun to sleep through the night. Natalie knew, because *she* didn't sleep well, and took advantage of her restlessness to check on Jo and Lori frequently. Lori had developed another nasty cold, bless her.

But when the knock came at the door after lunch on Tuesday, Jo, who was in the kitchen making apple butter to take to the boys, shrieked, proving that she hadn't completely recovered from her ordeal. Natalie nearly dropped the jar she'd been drying.

"It's just someone at the door, Jo," she reasoned, frowning at the girl's pale face and wide eyes. "I'll get it."

When Natalie opened the door to find Elliot and Mr. McCormick standing on the doorstep—one looking very cheerful and excited, and the other looking far too solemn for her peace of mind—Natalie turned as pale as Jo had been.

"Good—good afternoon, Mr. McCormick," she stammered before turning to the one who worried her the most. "Elliot?"

His clear blue eyes darkened with regret as he stepped

forward and ushered the banker inside and out of the cold. Stunned, Natalie automatically took their hats and coats and hung them on the coat rack by the parlor door.

What was going on? Why would Elliot bring the *banker* to Ivy House? Unless . . . unless he was hoping for a loan from the bank to keep Ivy House? But if that were true, then why the regret? She glanced at him again, hoping beyond hope that she'd misread his expression.

Elliot stared back at her with something akin to grief. Definitely remorse, too, lurking in his bold blue eyes.

Natalie closed her eyes in denial, then opened them again. "Elliot . . . ? What's this about?" She saw him physically brace himself and knew she was doomed.

"Natalie, I—Mr. McCormick here would like to look at Ivy House. He's interested in making an offer"—he paused significantly, as if he had to force the words out—"to buy it," he finished.

The blunt words hit her like a wave of heat from a hot oven. Natalie covered her mouth with her hand to stem the tide of protests and pleadings that begged to be said. She wouldn't grovel, not in front of the perplexed banker. Elliot had warned her this was going to happen, but she hadn't been expecting it *today*! He'd promised—

"I'll explain everything later. I promise."

Oh, she knew how sincere his promises were. They meant nothing to her, nothing at all. He was a liar and a silver-tongued devil in disguise. The children might fall for his platitudes and promises, but not Natalie. Oh, no, not her. He could make excuses until the sun refused to shine, but it would not make one iota of difference to her.

But he had known she wouldn't fall apart in front of the banker, the bastard! Trembling so hard she was afraid her teeth would knock together, she said, "There's no need to explain. I understand." She did. Perfectly.

She didn't know where she found the strength, but she did. With a sweet smile for the banker, she gestured to the upstairs. "Would you like to start upstairs and work your way down?" Flashing a mysterious glance at Elliot, she added, "That should save us all some time." With a surge of triumph, Natalie saw Elliot's eyes narrow with suspicion at her compliant tone.

Natalie whirled and led the way upstairs, conscious of Elliot following close behind. She could feel those orbs of steel he called eyes boring into her back.

Oh, he'd be sorry he did this to her. Very, very sorry. And extremely furious.

She thrust off a shiver of fear and topped the landing, opening the first door on the left, Cole and Brett's old room. "There are four bedrooms upstairs, and a small bedroom with an adjacent sitting room that Mrs. Boone used for an office. We all sleep up here, as you can see." Natalie stood aside and let the banker step into the room.

She had given Cole and Brett the largest room, since they shared. It was decorated simply with a full-sized bed, armoire, two chests of drawers, and a small desk where the boys studied their lessons. The cold floors were bare of rugs, the boards worn smooth with age and wear. A huge quilt covered the entire wall separating the bedroom from the room next door.

Mr. McCormick gave it a cursory glance, then turned as if to go out of the room.

Natalie took a deep breath for courage and moved into his path. "No need to go out into the hall. We can go through here." She whipped the quilt aside and stepped through the bare framework. It had once been a solid wall of cypress lumber, and it had been the first to go when they began making the dollhouses.

Somewhere behind her—hopefully out of hitting distance—she heard Elliot gasp and mutter a nasty oath. She ignored him.

"As you can see, most of the rooms look the same."

She looked around, anywhere but at Elliot. She fancied she could *feel* the heat of his mounting anger.

When she thought the banker had had sufficient time to study Jo's room, she moved to the far wall and raised another quilt nearly identical to the one separating the boys' room from Jo's, pausing to call out a warning. "Lori, Elliot and Mr. McCormick—the banker—are here to look at Ivy House. We're coming through."

Lori sneezed, then asked in a scratchy, weary voice, "Why's he looking at our house, Natty? Hi, Mr. Montgomery. Did you bring me something?"

They stepped through the skeletal framework one by one, Natalie careful to move to the far side of the room and away from Elliot. She smiled at Lori, who was propped up in her bed, reading from an old and tattered storybook. She looked so small and defenseless amid the mountain of covers that Natalie wanted to weep.

Several safe feet away, she felt Elliot's glare, jumping as he growled a greeting he just managed to temper in time.

"Lori, Natalie didn't tell me you were ill again."

"Just another silly cold," Lori assured him. "I get them all the time, you know."

"Yes, I do."

A small fire burned brightly in the grate, keeping the room warm and adding cheer to the gloomy afternoon. On a small table by the bed sat an untouched bowl of broth Jo had brought her earlier. Natalie frowned severely at her, forgetting the men for a moment as her mothering instincts took over. "Jo's gonna be mad if you don't eat, Lori. You've got to keep up your strength to fight this nasty cold."

Lori managed an elfin grin, then promptly went into a sneezing fit. When she finished, she rubbed her red nose and croaked, "It was too hot. I'll eat it later, I promise." Her watery eyes fixed on the banker with unabashed curiosity. "Are you going to buy Ivy House for us, Mr. McCormick?"

Embarrassed, Natalie intervened before the flustered banker could answer. "No, Lori. Mr. McCormick's thinking about buying Ivy House from Mr. Montgomery." For Lori's sake, she managed to sound matter-of-fact about it. Inside, the pain continued to build. How would the Nolens feel about boarding Lori, who was sick more often than not? They might be afraid she would spread the sickness to the other tenants.

That was something she hadn't considered. Natalie bit her lip, then risked a glance Elliot's way. He was staring at Lori with such an obvious expression of anguish that Natalie felt a moment's shame. True, she hadn't known he was bringing the banker today, but Lori's relapse definitely added to the revenge.

"Oh," Lori said. She lowered her eyes and plucked at the covers. Then, suddenly her face brightened. She looked eagerly at Elliot. "But that's okay, isn't it, Mr. Montgomery? You're going to find me a ma and pa, aren't you?"

Natalie wondered if Elliot was thinking how difficult it would be to find someone willing to take Lori. The shame returned tenfold. Elliot had proved how much he cared about the children, yet she stood by with her mouth firmly closed, letting him suffer. Did that make her any less heartless than he? If she was wrong and he truly didn't have a choice—as Marla seemed to believe—then she was mean and spiteful for making him feel even worse.

So Natalie found herself saying, "Don't worry, Lori, you'll be staying with me until Elliot can find you a ma and pa."

"But where will *you* live?"

Hm. She hadn't anticipated that question. How would Lori feel when she learned she would be living in a boardinghouse after the space and security of Ivy House?

"Excuse me," Mr. McCormick said, speaking for the first time. He sounded as if he'd gotten a frog stuck in his throat.

Lori giggled. "You sound like me, Mr. Banker."

"Hm. Yes." Mr. McCormick cleared his throat. He looked behind him at the makeshift wall they'd stepped through, then back to the small, defenseless girl in the bed. "I don't think I need to hear—see anymore." He turned a stony face to Elliot, who looked as if he'd blow any second.

Natalie searched for the sweetness that is said to come with revenge and found nothing but shame and remorse.

"Elliot, could I speak with you downstairs, please?" The banker gritted the words, his face glowing with righteous anger.

With a stiff nod, Elliot strode through the door. He never glanced her way, Natalie noted, her heart sinking and her guilt increasing.

"They looked mad, didn't they, Natalie? Do you think Mr. Montgomery's mad 'cos we tore down his walls? You said he'd be mad."

Mad? Oh, she'd have to say *furious* would better suit the way Elliot looked. "Um, no, Lori. I don't think they're mad. I think that's the way men look when they're going to talk business."

Lori accepted her well-meaning lie and buried her reddened nose in the book again.

Her feet dragging, Natalie slowly left the room. Now she knew how lambs felt on the way to slaughter. But if there was ever a lamb who deserved to be slaughtered, then she was it.

Guilty as charged.

19

"*I* wouldn't have taken you for a thief, Elliot, but I don't know what to think. The shape this house is in—why, it isn't worth half the amount you quoted! And furthermore," the banker ranted, gathering steam, "you can't begin to know how much it disturbs me that you're turning these helpless people out into the street." His face turned a frightening shade of purple as he fought to keep his voice down. "I've got seven granddaughters, and that little girl reminds me of—"

"Then buy Ivy House and give it to Natalie and the orphans," Elliot interrupted to say harshly. He'd never been more embarrassed, more *furious* in his life.

"What?" Mr. McCormick looked at Elliot as if he'd lost his senses.

Elliot hadn't lost his senses, but he'd lost the last of his patience with one Miss Natalie Polk. "I said, 'Buy the house and give it to them.' "

"Why, I can't do that!"

"Neither can I," Elliot said vehemently in frustration. "This house isn't mine to give or to keep. The moment my grandfather's creditors find out about Ivy House, they'll take it—and believe me, they'll care a whole lot less about what happens to the inhabitants than I do!''

Speechless, Mr. McCormick stared at Elliot.

Elliot, far beyond thinking before he spoke, went on. ''They're waiting at Clyde's boardinghouse as we speak. Waiting to pounce the moment they find out exactly what property I do still own. I've been trying to get the children adopted out so they wouldn't be on the street. Evans won't give a damn—and he won't wait.''

The banker opened his mouth like a fish gasping for air. His entire manner underwent a sudden, startling change. Pity flickered in his eyes. ''I apologize, Elliot. I didn't know you were in dire straits.''

''It isn't something a man likes to brag about,'' Elliot snapped, disgusted with himself and with Natalie for embarrassing him this way. She'd snatched his heart; now she would snatch his pride. Had he been blind to her true nature all along? As pretty as you please, she had led them upstairs, *knowing* what his reaction would be and knowing what the banker would think.

Good God.

''When you—when you applied for the loan, I just assumed you needed some quick cash for investment purposes. Your grandfather was known for his expertise in making money.''

''His *expertise* is the reason I'm in this position,'' Elliot snarled, past the point of worrying about what was left of his pride. He shoved his weary hands through his hair and followed the banker to the door, forcing himself to calm down. It wasn't the banker's fault in any way. ''I apologize, Mr. McCormick. I had no idea the house was in such disrepair. For one reason or another, I never got around to inspecting the upstairs.'' He now knew all of the reasons and what they meant. That conniving little *witch*!

The banker clamped his hat on his head, shrugged into his coat, and looked hard at Elliot. Lowering his voice, he said, "Don't be too hard on Miss Polk, Elliot. When she needed the firewood, she probably didn't have the slightest idea she was using prime cypress." Glancing around, he shivered. "I imagine it takes a lot of fuel to heat this house, and with Mrs. Boone running off the way she did . . . You get my meaning?"

Oh, Elliot understood the banker's meaning, but he knew something the man didn't know; the cypress hadn't been used for firewood. He'd figured that out the moment he saw what remained of the upstairs walls.

"About those men, Elliot. Rest assured they won't get any information from me."

"Thanks." Elliot shook the banker's hand, wondering if the man could feel his simmering rage. But the banker didn't seem to notice anything unusual, much to Elliot's amazement.

"And if you need any more, um, help, you just come in and we'll talk. If you're half the man your grandfather was, then you're okay with me."

Elliot nodded, only half listening to the banker. He shut the door after him and slowly turned. "You can come on down now, Natalie." How in the world had he managed to say those words so calmly?

He wanted to *throttle* her.

He watched as her shadow grew on the stairwell wall. Finally, she came into view, head bowed, body tense. When she was halfway across the wide foyer, Elliot held up his hand. "That's far enough." She stopped, her nostrils flaring in alarm like some skittish mare sensing the lurking presence of a wolf. "I'm not sure I trust myself right now, so just keep your distance."

"Elliot, I—"

"No. No, let me speak. Then, I promise you, I'll expect you to try your damnedest to explain." He doubted she could manage such a miracle. Linking his hands behind his back to keep them from her pretty throat, he began softly, "You allowed me to carry around an enormous amount of guilt over something I could not avoid. You accused me of lying for my own gain when I attempted to explain why I had no choice but to sell Ivy House. You continuously reminded me of what a heartless bastard I was for wanting to secure the children's future.'' Elliot could feel his neck veins protruding and forced his anger down. There was time enough to explode after he put the puzzle together. ''And all the while, you were happily destroying Ivy House—the house you so desperately want to keep—to build *dollhouses*?'' His voice rose abruptly as his control slipped. ''Not only that, you didn't tell me when you had opportunity after opportunity. Instead, you *continued* to take Ivy House apart.''

She opened her mouth. He held up his hand for silence.

''You then allowed me to bring a potential buyer upstairs without any forewarning whatsoever. Have I got this straight?''

Natalie stood frozen, her face pale, her eyes dark and stunned as he dramatized the facts. Finally she nodded. ''Yes, you're right. But, Elliot—''

''Wait. I'm not finished.'' Elliot advanced several steps, a smile twisting his lips as she backed away, but he was far from amused. ''Smart girl. Very smart. So smart that you used your body to get what you wanted.'' He ignored her outraged gasp. ''But it backfired, didn't it, Natalie? I didn't give you Ivy House because I couldn't.'' His gaze swept her from head to toe. ''Believe me, it was worth it, if only Ivy House was mine to give.''

''Are you finished?'' Her chin angled out. There was a glitter in her eyes that warned Elliot, but he was beyond heeding.

''Am I? Is there anything else you're hiding from me, sweet Natalie? A tribe of Indians in the attic, perhaps? Or do we *have* an attic left?''

She ignored his mocking sarcasm, her voice matching his in temperature. "I'm not hiding anything else. You've said it all, but you're wrong. I didn't give myself to you in the hopes of getting Ivy House. You can think whatever you like. I'm sure you will, regardless, but it isn't true. I made love with you because I—" Her gaze faltered with her words. After a moment, she jerked her chin up again. "It doesn't matter. As for Ivy House, I tried to tell you about the lumber, but before I could, you mentioned how expensive the cypress was. I couldn't, after that." She shrugged, a hint of apology flickering in her eyes. "After a while, I justified what I was doing because I didn't believe you had to close Ivy House. I thought you were being selfish, greedy, that you just didn't want the responsibility."

"And now?" Oh, she was convincing, and oh-so-beautiful as she stood there in the foyer like a prisoner before the judge, Elliot thought. Ruthlessly, he braced himself against any and all weakness. Loving this woman had been his downfall, it seemed.

"And now . . . I heard what you said to Mr. McCormick, and I realize that you weren't lying about having to sell Ivy House."

"A little late for revelations, don't you think, Natalie?" Elliot snapped his teeth together in frustration. "I can't sell a house that isn't complete. When I realized you were responsible for the dollhouses, I should have figured it out."

Natalie took a step forward, then stopped. "I was going to replace the walls before you found out, but I didn't have time."

She came closer. Elliot stiffened. When she placed a tentative hand on his arm, he felt some of the anger seep out of him. She looked very sincere, but still—

"When Mrs. Boone left, I didn't know what else to do. The children needed food and clothing. We . . . we couldn't afford to buy the lumber. I had no choice." Her head tilted at a proud angle. "At first, it was just a silly idea, a pitiful hope. But when the first dollhouse sold, I couldn't believe our luck. Then we sold another, and another—"

"Then I came along, and with Marla's help, we managed to convince you there was even more hope," Elliot concluded. His gaze collided with hers as awareness hit him. She'd had no choice, just as he'd had no choice.

They were both responsible for transgressions beyond their control.

Natalie nodded. "So what do we do now?"

Rubbing his jaw, Elliot turned and began to pace, thinking. Yes, what did they do now? Evans was like a burr caught in a dog's fur; he wouldn't shake loose easily, but they had to do *something* to buy more time.

"I've got an idea, Elliot." When he speared her with a hard glance, she flushed and added, "That is, if you want my advice."

"Please." Elliot forced any lingering anger aside. He needed all the help he could get, and who knew better than he just how inventive Natalie could be? To his surprise and disgust, he nearly grinned at the thought.

"We could ask Cole and Brett to come home for a few days—I'm sure they would. If we all pitched in, we could have those walls back together in no time."

"And then?"

She paused a telling beat. "Then we put the house up for sale."

He saw that it cost her a great deal to say those words, and he felt a surge of admiration. Could he really blame her for what she had done? Wouldn't he have done the same in her place? Yes, he suspected he would have. "Your plan makes sense," he said. "But I don't know how long we have before Evans finds out."

Natalie shrugged, her eyes glinting in a mischievous way that made him chuckle. "If he does find out, I'm sure one of us will think of something."

Elliot was reminded of their first encounter and of how she'd fooled him into believing she was Nelda Boone. And what about all those times he'd attempted to go upstairs and she'd fabricated some convincing excuse? And, if not for Hickory's innocent slip of the tongue, he might still believe a hermit had made the dollhouses. Of course, that was Marla's doing. Or was it? And what did it matter now? He had more important things on his mind, such as how to avoid Evans—damn the man and his bloodhound ancestors, anyway! His blood heated up again just thinking about the bastard. He smacked his fist into his open palm. "If only whoever was responsible for scarring his face had finished him off, then we wouldn't have to worry about Evans—" He halted his vengeful tirade at the sound of Natalie's horrified gasp. "What? What is it?" he demanded.

She knew something—something momentous, but what?

When Elliot grasped her arms in a painful grip and shook her, Natalie remained silent. She was thinking, making absolutely certain of her suspicions. If she told Elliot her thoughts, he might go off in a rage and possibly get hurt or at the least, end up in jail. She couldn't bear the thought of either possibility.

Jo had described the man as having a funny scar that twisted his mouth into a grimace. She had been terrified of Evans, claiming he only reminded her of the man who killed her mother. Could it be . . . ? She licked her lips, staring into Elliot's expectant, impatient face. "What— what kind of scar, Elliot?"

"Why do you ask?"

She saw it then, realized that Elliot had already suspected and didn't want her to know. She jerked lose, the spark of anger igniting. "You suspected, didn't you? You suspected that Evans was the same man Jo remembers."

Nodding, he said, "I suspected, but I wasn't certain. Did she mention a scar, then? Is that what this questioning is all about?"

"Yes." Natalie thought about clamping her lips shut, but realized that not only would that be immature, it would be dangerous. "She described him to me, and he has a scar that twists his mouth like a—like a—"

"Snarl? Why didn't you tell me?" With a muffled oath, he shoved his hand in his pockets.

Natalie glared. "I didn't think it was important, and I wanted to make the story as short as possible so you'd leave." She caught a brief flash of hurt in his eyes, and it was enough to melt her heart. "That was before," she added. "Before I realized I had been wrong about you, and you weren't the greedy, selfish—"

"Bastard?" Elliot supplied, edging toward her. He stopped suddenly, out of reach, flinging his proud head back and closing his eyes as if to regain his control.

The action shot a quiver of desire right into her belly. Natalie pressed her hand there, silently berating her own lack of control. *It was over.* "I've said it once, and I'll say it again—I'm sorry, Elliot. I was wrong." She loved him, and because of that, she wanted him to believe that she fully intended to right the wrong she'd done him. "We'll fix the house, don't worry."

He opened his eyes. "I wasn't thinking about the house," he growled, then gave his head a wry shake before adding, "although I should have been. I was thinking about you . . . and me. How I wish things had been different—"

"We're wasting time." Natalie felt her throat burn with unshed tears. Did he have to keep reminding her? They weren't suited and never would be. She climbed mountains to accomplish what she believed in; he preferred to live in the flat lands where the going was easy and unencumbered.

It was perfectly clear that he wasn't the man for her,

and she wasn't the woman for him. There, she had admitted it.

Now that she had, would the hurting ever stop?

"Do I have your solemn promise you won't breathe a word of this to Natalie? I'd like to tell her myself." Elliot lounged against the counter, the letter from Warren tucked away in his coat pocket. The news was good, much better than he could have hoped. Warren needed a dozen dollhouses, and he had enclosed a substantial advance in the form of a bank draft. Now all he had to do was convince Marla to keep a secret for a few days.

He had a plan.

Rubbing her protruding stomach, Marla avoided his gaze and his question. "This baby's got to be a boy," she groaned. When Elliot continued to stare at her, she sighed. "All right, I won't tell her."

Satisfied, Elliot turned to leave.

"Where are you going?" When he quirked an eyebrow at her, she blushed and stammered, "I'm just asking because I thought you might like to have supper with us tonight."

A perfect opportunity to talk to Noah about his plan, Elliot thought. The sooner the better. "I'd be delighted," he said, grinning when Marla blushed again. He suspected she'd thought of the invitation at the spur of the moment to cover her impulsive question about his destination.

Natalie's friend was certainly one of a kind.

He whistled as he walked the short distance to the boardinghouse, shoving his bare hands into his pants pockets to ward off the cold. Snow, he thought, sniffing the wind. Snow was on its way, and snow always reminded him of Christmas. He suspected Chattanooga would be beautiful at Christmas, with snow covering the ground and the white-capped peaks of the mountains forming a picture-perfect background. Whether he would be here to see it depended on several things, one of which he was about to determine right now.

He found Evans in his room. Jules was nowhere in sight. Without waiting for an invitation, he pushed past a speechless Evans and took a seat at the small table near the window.

"I didn't invite you in," Evans snarled, slamming the door shut. "What are you doing here? Did you bring the money?"

Elliot was silent long enough to make the man nervous. Taking his time, he removed his hat and set it on the table. "I came to talk to you about our mutual little friend," he announced as if he spoke merely of the weather.

Evans froze in a half turn. "I don't know what you're talking about."

"Yes, you do," Elliot countered pleasantly, but Evans must have sensed the steel beneath his words, for he stiffened. "You did know the girl you accosted in the hall—and you knew her mother even better."

"You're crazy."

"In fact," Elliot continued as if the other man hadn't spoken, "you *killed* her mother."

With a gasp, Evans covered the few paces between them, visibly shaking. "That lying bitch! She's lying, Montgomery! She's the spawn of a whore—"

"She identified you, right down to that nasty-looking scar on your mouth." He paused, then added softly, "Don't suppose that's a coincidence, either. In fact, I know it isn't. Now, I've already talked to the sheriff, and he's of the opinion that you might be charged with murder, if Jo's willing to testify."

Evans made a strangling sound. "She can't prove anything, that lying little slut—"

Elliot shot out of his chair, his hand on the man's throat. He squeezed a warning before letting the man go. "Hasn't that ugly mouth of yours gotten you into enough trouble?'' he chided. Evans backed prudently away, massaging his throat. Elliot got down to business. ''I figure we could convince someone else who witnessed the murder to testify, with the right incentive.''

''What do you want?'' Evans croaked.

''I want you to leave.''

''Carnagie will send someone else.''

Elliot shrugged. ''All I need is time.'' He tapped his fingers on the table. ''Hm. Although I can't guarantee Jo won't testify, anyway. I hope she does.''

''They won't believe her,'' Evans blustered.

''Maybe. Maybe not. Question is, do you want to find out? There's bound to be a trial, at the very least—''

''I'll leave.''

Elliot smiled. ''Thought you would.'' Rising, he put his hat on and strode past the seething man. He turned before reaching the door. ''Oh, and tell Carnagie he'd better send someone without blood on his hands. As for you, don't ever come back to this town again. Next time, I'll make the threat good or kill you myself.''

Outside the boardinghouse, Elliot paused to take a deep breath. He'd lied about the sheriff's interest. The sheriff had told him it would be next to impossible to get the case reopened. Very few people would want to waste their time on a prostitute, the sheriff had stated bluntly, and they were unlikely to believe a child who had lived in a bawdy house most of her life.

With any luck, Evans would never speak to the sheriff. Elliot chuckled, suddenly very sure of it. Standing on the porch stoop absorbing his success, he reached for his pocket watch to check the time before remembering he'd sold it. But this time, he didn't mutter a curse at the loss.

He smiled without regret.

No, he was finished with regrets and useless wishes. He was ready to force fate to bend his way or exhaust himself trying. Getting rid of Evans had bought the time he desperately needed to put his plan in motion.

His next stop was the bank, and if his visit there went well, he would have a long, detailed conversation with Noah *without* Marla present. He was very fond of Marla, which was the reason he'd decided not to torture her with this particular secret.

Marla didn't need the added strain, he reasoned, grinning as he thought of her response should he tell her that. She'd probably forget her nice manners and tear into him as she did Noah when he took his smothering too far.

Elliot reached his hand inside his coat pocket and closed his fingers around the envelope. The contents would give his proposal more credibility, but right now, he felt as if he could convince anyone of anything.

Ah, the power of love.

Elliot's grin widened.

20

"$\mathcal{I}$'m serious, Natalie. They're keeping something from us." Marla had to nearly shout to be heard over the banging of the hammer. Elliot, Cole, and Brett were upstairs replacing the walls with new lumber. Not cypress, but good quality oak. Marla would have traded her eye teeth to know where Elliot had gotten the money for the lumber. She couldn't believe he would use the money from the dollhouses . . . No, he wouldn't.

But where . . . ?

"They might be keeping something from *you*," Natalie corrected with a disinterested shrug. She was going through Nelda Boone's things in the small sitting room that the housemother had converted to an office, packing the mountain of papers and books in boxes to be stored away in Marla's attic.

Marla huffed and crossed her arms, staring at Natalie in frustration. It seemed she couldn't get her friend interested in anything these days. She spent most of her time packing in preparation for the move. Marla didn't think it was healthy. "Natalie, a few weeks ago, I saw Elliot come out of the boardinghouse, then go into the bank."

"You've told me."

"And he and Noah have been cleaning out the store-room next door to the mercantile. Noah *says* he's planning to expand."

"Then I'm sure he is. Has Noah ever lied to you before?" Natalie wiped her dusty hands on her apron, then bent to retrieve a stack of papers from the bottom drawer of the desk.

"Well, no, but not more than two months ago, he was complaining about not having enough time at home with us. Now he's expanding the store? It doesn't make sense." This was driving Marla to distraction—almost as much as Natalie's disinterest was. "Oh—and last night, when I announced I was going to scrub the floors, he didn't stop me."

Natalie sniffed. "Maybe he's realizing that you won't break."

Marla ground her teeth. "Okay, how about this? They keep disappearing at night for hours, and when Noah comes home, he *says* they've been taking inventory at the store."

Natalie looked at Marla, her expression blank. She shook her head. "Noah takes inventory every year about this time, doesn't he?"

"For two weeks?" Marla squeaked.

"Why don't you follow them and satisfy your insatiable curiosity?"

"I did." Marla finally had Natalie's attention. She even got a smile out of her. Granted, it was a tiny one, a small victory.

"And what were they doing?"

"Taking inventory."

They burst out laughing. Grinning sheepishly, Marla said, "I'm still not convinced that's what they're always doing."

"Marla, Marla, give it up. There's nothing going on. Elliot's been working here during most afternoons with the boys, and when he's not here, he's helping Noah take inventory. What's so sinister about that?''

"Nothing," Marla admitted, then bit her lip. "But it's the way they both look at me—"

"You're imagining things. Stop worrying."

"Easy for you to say. You don't seem to care about anything these days," Marla muttered beneath her breath. But Natalie heard. She laid the stack of papers aside and took Marla's hand.

"I care, but I'm trying not to *think* about them."

"Are you all right"—Marla waved her hand at the boxes scattered around them on the floor, her eyes clouding with concern—"with all of this?"

Natalie squeezed her hand, then let it go. She sighed. "I have to be, don't I? Lori needs to feel secure, so I can't go around crying all the time."

"No, you save that for during the night, don't you?"

"So, you've noticed."

Marla grimaced. "It's hard not to. You've got dark circles beneath your eyes, you know. Still not sleeping?"

As if all of her courage suddenly left her, Natalie sank into the chair at the desk. Marla's heart gave a sharp wrench at the sight of her slumped shoulders and shadowed eyes.

"Not a lot. I'm scared, Marla. Scared of the future." She shrugged helplessly. "Ivy House is all I've ever known."

"Maybe Elliot—"

"I don't want his pity!" Natalie cried sharply. "And pity is what it would be. He doesn't love me, so get that through your thick head, Marla. He—he *pities* me, and he wants me in a physical way, but—"

"I think you're wrong." In fact, Marla was *certain* Natalie was wrong. She just couldn't figure out why Elliot was being so stubborn and slow about admitting it. This was the time Natalie needed him the most, right now while she packed away a lifetime of memories.

Perhaps in believing it herself, Natalie had convinced Elliot of the same. Or maybe Elliot couldn't get it through *Natalie's* thick head. Yes, that was probably it. Well, it was up to Elliot to convince her.

Marla gave Natalie's hand a sympathetic pat and left her alone with the painful task of packing. Another visit managed without telling Natalie about the letter from Warren, she thought proudly. She'd show those two men she *could* keep a secret. Oh, but she had wanted to, if only to cheer Natalie.

Outside in the cold air, she found Jo leaning against the porch post watching Jeb as he disappeared down the lane. Her expression was one of unmistakable yearning and a liberal dose of fear.

"Fine-looking young man," Marla offered, pausing near Jo. She could feel the tension radiating from the girl and wished she could help in some way.

Jo blushed, her gaze steady on Jeb's retreating form. "Yep, he is."

Marla hesitated, then decided she had nothing to lose by voicing her opinion. Jo was accustomed to it. "Don't let your past ruin your future, Jo," she told her quietly.

Jo was silent for a long moment. Finally, she looked at Marla as understanding dawned. "You mean like Natalie's doing?"

Marla nodded, making a disgusted sound in her throat. "Yes, like Natalie *and* Elliot are doing."

"Do you think they'll ever get together, Marla?"

"If we keep working on it, I believe they will." Marla flashed her a grin. "They won't have a choice. By the way, I've got an order that needs to be delivered tomorrow. Do you think Jeb would mind making that delivery for me? Y'all could take the buckboard and you could go along with him, show him the way."

"Well, I don't know . . ." Jo shoved her hands in her pants pockets, then gave herself away by glancing down at the boy's clothing she wore beneath a ragged man's coat. "I don't know, Marla—"

"Say, I think I've got a dress that would fit you nicely." Marla hooked her arm through Jo's before she could protest. They started down the lane. "What's Jeb's favorite color, do you know?"

"Green, I think. But, Marla—"

"Perfect." Marla gave an inward sigh of satisfaction. "It just so happens that the dress I'm talking about is green."

"Really?"

"Really," Marla lied without so much as blinking.

After Marla had gone, Natalie rubbed her tired eyes and rolled her stiff shoulders. She should heat the boys some milk and take Elliot a cup of strong coffee. Lori, who was comfortably settled in the warm parlor, away from the noise and mess, could probably use another cup of broth, too. Her cold was better, but it sometimes took her weeks before her full strength returned.

Natalie's overused muscles protested as she rose and went to the kitchen. Jo was nowhere in sight, which was unusual, Natalie thought with a frown. She shrugged and began preparing the coffee and heating the milk. In the meantime, she dipped a bowl of rich beef broth warming on the back burner and took it into the parlor.

Catching sight of her, Lori hastily dropped her sewing items in the basket beside the sofa and pasted an eager grin on her face. "Oh, is that broth? I'm starved!"

Natalie froze. Lori always complained about having to drink the broth. Proceeding more cautiously, Natalie cocked an eyebrow as she lowered the bowl to a table. "Lori? Are you all right?" Quickly she checked Lori's forehead. No fever. In fact, her normally pale cheeks were flushed. She looked healthy for a change—positively *glowing*.

Hmm. After adding more wood to the fire, Natalie

turned to study Lori again. The girl's eyes literally spar-
kled. Natalie's speculative gaze dipped to the basket of
sewing articles. "What are you working on? Can I see?"

"No!" Lori shoved the basket farther away and held
her hands over the opening. "I'm working on Christmas
presents, so you can't look."

"All right." Christmas presents, of course! She
should have guessed. "Eat your broth. I'll be upstairs
for a few minutes, taking the boys some warm milk and
Elliot a cup of coffee." She brushed her hands on her
apron and made her way to the parlor door.

"Yes, he needs lots of coffee," Lori blurted out, then
clamped her hand over her mouth. She looked stricken.

Natalie turned. "He does?"

Lori squirmed, her face turning bright red. "I mean,
he works an awful lot, don't you think? I'll bet he
doesn't get much sleep." Ducking her head, Lori started
to reach into her basket, waving Natalie away with her
other hand. "Go away—I've got work to do."

Despite her confusion and bone-deep weariness, Natalie smiled at Lori's bossy tone. Sometimes it was hard
to remember she was only eight years old, and other
times difficult to believe she was no longer that dainty
toddler who forever needed to be carried. This was one
of those times when she seemed far older than her years.

God bless her.

Arranging the tin cups of milk and coffee on a tray,
Natalie added a pile of Jo's sugar cookies, then made
for the stairs. Bells jingled overhead with every balanced
step she took. Natalie shook her head, smiling faintly.
Cole had insisted on decorating the stairs with cow bells,
and she hadn't the heart to refuse him. Jo had added
holly sprigs, and Lori had fashioned red bows to the
bells, turning a monstrosity into a festive, yet noisy and
unusual decoration.

Craning her neck to look at the bells, which Cole had
weaved along the bannister and draped overhead, Natalie

grimaced. He had positioned them too low. It was nearly impossible not to brush into them as she climbed the stairs.

She shrugged. At least they would know she was coming.

"Do you think it will snow soon, Natty?" Brett asked before she came into sight, confirming her thoughts about the bells.

"Possibly." She paused before the boys to let them grab a cookie and their milk. "Careful, it's hot." When she finally turned to Elliot, she slowly lifted her gaze to his face—and felt the usual stab of disappointment at his bland expression. He still hadn't forgiven her, it seemed.

As he reached for the coffee and murmured his thanks, Natalie snatched the opportunity to take in the signs of fatigue around his mouth and eyes, remembering what Lori had said. Yes, he did look tired. It appeared she wasn't the only one having trouble sleeping.

Perversely, the thought lifted her spirits.

"About finished?" she questioned softly, craving a smile, a flicker of interest, a look of the old passion that would weaken her knees and make her heart quicken with anticipation.

He shot her an absentminded glance, then quickly focused his attention on the wall in progress. "It's going slow. I want every piece to fit perfectly." His voice, like his expression, held little emotion.

With considerable effort, Natalie managed a bright smile before leaving. Normally perceptive to her feelings, the boys returned the smile with ease as if they sensed none of the cool tension between the adults.

Their apathy was the last straw.

When Natalie reached the kitchen, she flung the tray onto the table in a burst of pent-up emotion and stomped to the office. Once there, she slammed the door and indulged in rare tears of self-pity.

Everyone around her was cheerful and optimistic, while her world crumbled. The boys were happy with their new family and content to visit or help, Lori trusted the adults in her life to take care of her, and Jo was once more determined to set out on her own and start a new life as if the incident at the boardinghouse had never happened.

Elliot, obsessed with Ivy House and working with Noah, obviously had recovered from his infatuation with her—if he *had* been infatuated.

Natalie slumped in the chair and bent her head to her arms, weeping. She was ashamed of herself for envying her loved ones. Ashamed and horrified. Wasn't this what she wanted—for everyone to be happy? Of course it was! Then why this terrible feeling of worthlessness?

Slowly, she lifted her head, her eyes widening as the astonishing truth hit her squarely in the face.

She wasn't crying because she was losing Ivy House.

She wasn't crying because the children were going to be happy without her, although she had suffered shameful pangs of selfishness at first.

She was crying because without Elliot, *nothing* seemed to matter. Not Ivy House, not the potential success of the dollhouses, and not her own future, as dismal as it seemed.

Without Elliot, she felt empty, useless, hopeless. Alone. Keeping Ivy House and the children together wouldn't change that feeling, she suspected.

She feared nothing would.

Drained and weary, Natalie used her apron to dry her face. Her gaze fell on the thin stack of papers held together with a faded blue ribbon and now spotted with her tears. She hoped it wasn't anything important. She pulled the first page from the stack and moved the candle closer.

Natalie began to read, recognizing Nelda Boone's handwriting. Within a few sentences, she gasped. Nelda

Boone *had* written the letters—love letters to someone named—Natalie skimmed quickly down the page, her eyes freezing on the name.

Gill Montgomery? Mrs. Boone and Gill Montgomery, Elliot's grandfather?

Natalie was shocked. She held the letter, torn between guilt and curiosity. It would be wrong to read the letters, but Natalie desperately wanted to understand the woman who had raised her with such cold indifference. The same woman who had disappeared in the night without hesitation, leaving four helpless orphans behind.

Curiosity and need won. Her troubles momentarily forgotten, Natalie became engrossed in the letters Nelda Boone had apparently written but never gained the courage to mail.

A half hour later, Natalie sat in stunned silence, staring at the far wall. Incredible. The letters had revealed far more than Natalie had wanted to know about Nelda Boone, Gill Montgomery, and Elliot.

Nelda Boone was Elliot's natural mother.

Natalie rubbed an ache between her eyes as she tried to absorb this horrendous news. Elliot had spoken of his mother with unmistakable reverence, she recalled. But whenever Nelda Boone was mentioned, Elliot adopted a derisive tone flavored with outright contempt.

No, Elliot didn't know, Natalie concluded. She also doubted he knew about the brief affair between the un-wed Nelda Boone and his grandfather. It seemed Nelda had been Gill's housekeeper, and when Gill returned from the war to find his beloved wife dead and buried, he'd turned to Nelda for comfort.

Elliot had been very young at the time, fathered by a nameless soldier passing through. Nelda had managed to keep her young son a secret from the rest of the town. She must have been grieving as well, Natalie thought. But her grief hadn't lasted long. She had fallen in love with Gill, but he had loved his wife dearly and couldn't return Nelda's love.

Gill had converted Ivy House into an orphanage and had placed Nelda in charge. In return, she had given him the child she hadn't wanted: Elliot.

Natalie swallowed hard. Elliot would be not only furious and hurt because Gill had lied to him, but also he would be disgusted to learn that Nelda Boone was his mother. She fingered the edge of one of the letters, remembering how soft Elliot's voice became when he spoke of the great love between his grandparents. How would he feel to learn his grandfather had turned so quickly to another woman?

Her heart ached just thinking about how he would react, how he would feel. He would be devastated, then furious. After that would come the pain. Natalie winced. She loved him, and because she loved him, his pain was her own, even when he didn't know it.

Natalie eyed the flickering candle and drummed her fingers on the desk. Now she knew why Nelda Boone had locked herself in her room for days when someone left a baby on the doorstep.

Guilt.

Oh, she might have regretted giving her son away, and she might have grieved over the loss, but not enough, Natalie thought, squashing her rising sympathy, to fetch him back and raise him, despite the whispers and disapproval.

Nelda Boone had been weak, just like her own mother.

Now she knew why Nelda Boone had fled after finding out about Gill's death; she'd known Elliot would come to Ivy House. She had known and couldn't face him or didn't want to.

Natalie drew the candle closer, her lips firming with determination. Elliot need never know about the letters; they would only tear him apart and make him question

his own identity and destroy the deep respect he held
for his grandfather. Cherished memories would become
lies.

One by one, Natalie held the letters over the candle
flame.

Finding out about her father had been a comfort; in
Elliot's case, finding out about his mother would only
wound him.

She watched the paper flare and burn without regret,
her thoughts returning to the previous housemother.

Nelda Boone had spent her entire life clinging to the
past, allowing it to embitter the present. Natalie was determined not to follow in the housemother's footsteps.
She might love Elliot with all her heart, but she would
find a way to live with it without making those around
her suffer.

She *would*.

*This time Elliot knew which boards would creak. He
made it to Natalie's room without a whisper of sound,
a dark, silent shadow. Now, with his eyes having ample
time to adjust to the dark on his way upstairs, he stood
by her bed watching her sleep. There wasn't any moon,
but a strange, ethereal light seemed to surround her.*

*Her chest rose and fell, then hitched fitfully. With a
tiny moan, she flung her head back and forth on the
pillow. Elliot swallowed, watching her, wanting her.
What did she dream of? he wondered a little jealously.*

"Elliot . . ." she whispered.

*Desire slammed into him. He edged closer to the bed.
Reaching out, he ran his finger along the underside of
her arm, along the curve of her breast. She arched into
him, plunging her breast into his palm.*

*Elliot groaned and closed his hand around her soft-
ness.*

Her eyes flew open, and Elliot froze. He'd just wanted

to watch her, make sure she was all right—he hadn't meant to awaken her.

He shouldn't have touched her.

To his utter surprise and pleasure, she smiled at him, her eyelids drooping seductively. When she lifted her arms to him, he didn't hesitate.

It was heaven. She was warm, and her scent wrapped around him like a loving hand. She tugged on his head and brought their mouths together in a heated rush, kissing him with wild abandon, twining her hot tongue with his.

Elliot trembled, holding back, holding himself away from her, letting only his mouth plunder and enjoy. But she yanked him closer, wrapping her long, silken legs around him and pulling him tight against her heat.

"Natalie, I love you," he whispered, straining for control, realizing it was useless. Why did he hesitate? She was showing him that she wanted him.

"Love?" Her breathless, scornful laugh froze the hot blood in his veins. "What do I need with love when I have Ivy House? Ivy House is all I wanted, Elliot, and now that I have it—"

"What?"

The sound of his own harsh voice startled Elliot awake.

He trembled, lying sprawled against the mattress in his hotel room.

Not with Natalie. Not at Ivy House.

It had all been a dream, he realized, shivering as the sweat cooled against his skin. He shook his head, blinking to clear the fog of sleep that lingered and pulled at him.

No, he didn't want to go back to sleep, not if there was any chance he'd have that same dream again. Not that it was all bad, but the end didn't justify the beginning. With a muttered curse, Elliot rose from the bed and added wood to the glowing coals. Fire began to lick greedily at the dry wood, caught, and flamed to life.

He sat in the chair before the fire, fear gnawing at his insides despite his own self-assurances. There would be no more sleep tonight, he knew.

21

*I*t was a monster of a tree. By far the ugliest, most misshapen—

"Lovely, just lovely, boys. You did a wonderful job." Natalie shuddered inwardly as she moved slowly around the tree, her lips pursed contemplatively.

Hideous. The tree was too big, too tall, and so unruly she didn't think there was the slightest possibility of making it presentable.

As always, they would keep it.

"Jo, get the tinsel. Cole, you and Brett bring that basket of pinecones from the attic—the painted ones. There's also a box of ornaments Brett made last year. Bring those, too."

"What can I do?" Lori demanded, looking small and lost beside the monstrous tree.

Natalie chuckled. "Finish those beautiful garlands you were working on. I can't wait to see them on the tree." She took a deep breath and inhaled the sharp odor of pine and the nutmeg Jo had put in the eggnog. Christmas smells. Happy sounds. Smiling faces.

Their last holiday at Ivy House.

Natalie stiffened her spine. She would think nothing but happy thoughts. It was Christmas Eve, and she was going to make this a Christmas they would never forget.

The children seemed to have caught her determination, too. They were all happy and glowing, as if they had forgotten their lives would be forever changed after this holiday.

A rush of cold wind signaled an arrival. Natalie peered around the doorway to the parlor, smiling at Marla and Hickory. They looked like Eskimos, bundled against the cold. Marla had grown big with child, but she still moved with more grace than one would expect.

"Is it still snowing?" Natalie queried, waving them into the parlor. She took their hats and coats, answering her own question as she shook the fine white powder from the garments before hanging them. "I see that it is."

"Lots and lots!" Hickory shouted. "Papa and Mr. 'Gomery are bringin'—"

Natalie looked up, catching Marla in the act of clamping Hickory's mouth shut. She lifted a brow. "Keeping secrets?"

"It's a surprise, not a secret." Glaring at Hickory, she reminded him, "Remember, we're not supposed to tell."

Hickory's face fell. "Oh. I remember. Okay, I won't tell Natty that Papa and Mr.—"

Marla let out a frustrated breath and clamped her hand over his mouth again. She shot Natalie a rueful smile. "I told Noah he couldn't keep a secret. He didn't believe me."

Hickory clawed the hand away, his expression indignant. "I can to! See?" He folded his arms and pursed his lips tightly.

Natalie and Marla laughed.

Taking his hand, Natalie led him to the tree and gave him a handful of silver tinsel. "Throw this at the tree," she instructed.

His eyes rounded. "Really? I can *throw* it?"

Natalie nodded, watching him for a moment before linking her arm with Marla's. "Let's go sample Jo's eggnog. It smells delicious."

"You don't have to twist my arm," Marla groaned. "I don't turn anything away these days—if it can be eaten."

"Jo made these tiny little pastry puffs—"

"Stop!" Marla laughed helplessly. "I'm thinking about telling Noah we're having twins so he won't scold me for getting so fat!"

Natalie stopped dead. "You—you're *not* having twins, are you, Marla?"

"No, I don't think so." She shrugged. "We won't know until it's time, will we? By the way, I love the tree."

She sounded so sincere, Natalie burst out laughing. "Liar."

"No, no! I do. I hate perfect trees. Noah, on the other hand, won't stop looking until he finds the most perfect tree in the forest."

"What's that? Did I hear my name?"

Both women turned at the sound of Noah's jolly voice. The men had come in silently behind them, catching their conversation.

Natalie's gaze shot to Elliot's as if an invisible wire were stretched between them. Her heart slowed to a fierce, heavy pounding. He looked handsome and fit, smelling of snow and cold and pine. Snow sprinkled the shoulders of his dark coat and pooled on top of his hat. Natalie fancied she saw glimmers of snowflakes caught in his lashes as well.

"Elliot."

"Natalie."

"Oh, for heaven's sake, you two act as if you've only just met!" Marla grabbed her husband's arm and headed in the direction of the kitchen. "We'll get the eggnog.

You'd better see what Hickory's doing to your tree, Natalie.''

Natalie started to move, but Elliot's low command stopped her.

"Be still."

Her heart tripped. She froze, their gazes still locked. He came to her and gently cupped her face in his hands. They were cool, yet oh, so exciting.

"You're standing beneath the mistletoe," he murmured just before his mouth took hers in a slow, intimate exploration.

Natalie melted against him, sighing into his mouth. She had missed this, missed *him*. Oh, he'd been around plenty, but he hadn't spoken to her unless he was forced to and hadn't looked at her for more than a fleeting second. It was as if he agreed with her that it was all a mistake.

Now he kissed her as if they were alone, his mouth roaming over her lips, her jaw, and finally her throat.

"Are you going to bite Natty, Mr. 'Gomery?"

Her giggle was spontaneous. Elliot smiled into her laughing eyes before answering Hickory.

"I might. I'll bet she tastes good."

"Elliot!" Natalie blushed and moved around him, her knees weak and trembling. As she passed him, he bent close to her ear.

"In fact, I *know* you do," he whispered on a husky note.

"Hm." Natalie shivered and at the same time remained cautious. What game was Elliot playing? After weeks of cool looks and monosyllabic conversations, why was he suddenly looking at her as if she were a particularly tasty treat?

"Eggnog anyone? You were right, Natalie. Jo's eggnog is the best!"

Marla. Natalie closed her eyes in agony, humiliation flaming her cheeks. Of course. Marla had begged Elliot to be nice to her, to make her feel wanted. And he, being the gentleman that he was, had agreed. What other explanation for Elliot's sudden transformation could there be?

Hoping Hickory couldn't sense her inner turmoil, she bent to stuff more tinsel into his eager little hand. Her voice was a little hoarse as she said, "You're doing a great job, Hickory." She pushed him in the direction of the unfortunate-looking tree where Cole, Brett, Jo, and Lori had all gathered around to hang decorations.

"That is the ugliest tree I've ever seen," Elliot whispered in her ear, handing her a cup of spiced eggnog as he spoke.

Natalie stiffened, then forced herself to relax. She would not let anyone ruin her last holiday at Ivy House. Not even Elliot, who had the power to squeeze the last drop of blood from her heart. Nevertheless, she didn't do a very decent job of keeping the chill from her voice. "The children always pick the ugliest tree, probably because they realize no one else will want it. Amazing, isn't it, what our hearts will lead us to do out of pity."

His silence told her he'd picked up on her double entendre and decided to ignore it. "Didn't you like the kiss?"

She sucked in a breath, then let it out slowly. She wouldn't let him rile her—not tonight of all nights. Tonight was for the children. Shrugging, she took a sip of eggnog. "If I said no, would you believe me?" It was so *un*believable that Natalie nearly laughed herself. She fully expected that Elliot would.

"Liar."

Or call her a liar. Just as she formed her retort, Jo called out to Elliot, saving her. She breathed an inward sigh of relief. She didn't think she had the strength to fight with Elliot tonight.

"Mr. Montgomery! Will you put the angel on? Cole's still not tall enough."

Cole leveled a frown at Jo. "I am, but I thought Mr. Montgomery would like to do the honors."

Jo snorted, Brett brayed like a donkey, and Lori giggled. Hickory stood looking from one to the other, wearing a perplexed expression.

Elliot quickly took the angel and stepped forward before a fight broke out. Despite her anger and humiliation, Natalie was glad. She stepped back, watching him with tears burning the backs of her eyes.

He was tall, but the tree was taller.

Cole shot Jo a smug look before offering to help. "I'll pull the tree forward. That should do it." Overly eager, he grabbed a branch and pulled. The tree tilted, then began to fall in Elliot's direction. Elliot, in the act of stretching his arm skyward, had balanced himself against the tree.

He couldn't move fast enough.

The tree fell on top of him, knocking him to the floor.

Natalie gasped, adding her hands to the rest as they attempted to lift the tree from Elliot. She could hear Marla laughing helplessly behind her. What if he was hurt? What if one of the branches had pierced his chest or eye?

Her imagination made her frantic. She pulled at the tree, heaving and grunting along with the children while Marla and now Noah laughed uproariously. Finally, they managed to set the tree upright. Natalie dove to her knees beside Elliot, brushing aside tinsel and decorations until she uncovered Elliot's face.

He was laughing.

"Oh! You—" She smacked his shoulder, her face burning with embarrassment. He'd seen how concerned she was, and now he probably thought—"Oh, you!" she repeated, getting to her feet and resisting the urge to kick him.

Still laughing, Elliot lumbered to his feet. A silver strand of tinsel hung from his hair, and a pinecone rested in his pocket. When his laughter finally died away, he looked at Noah. "Is it time?"

Noah checked his pocket watch, grinned, and nodded. "Close enough. Let's go."

"Where are we going, Papa? Are we going to ride—" Hickory's eyes looked like round saucers above Noah's beefy hand. Prudently, Noah kept his hand over Hickory's mouth.

"Everyone get bundled up," Elliot ordered.

Natalie, who wasn't in the mood to be ordered, especially by Elliot, folded her arms and turned away. Elliot caught her before she reached the kitchen.

"Just where do you think you're going?"

"Away from you." Natalie felt like a petulant child, but she couldn't seem to stop. She'd had enough humiliation for one day at his expense.

"You were worried about me." It wasn't a question but a statement. He grabbed her chin and turned her face around.

Natalie obstinately kept her gaze lowered.

"Look at me." When she didn't comply, he tilted her chin until she had no choice. "I'm sorry I laughed. I didn't realize you thought I was hurt."

She opened her mouth to hotly deny his assumption, then snapped it closed. What was the use? He'd know she lied.

"Will you come with us, please?"

"Lori," she began.

"Lori is coming with us. We'll bundle her up tight."

"Then I guess I don't have a choice, do I?" Jerking free, Natalie went to get her cloak. She dashed the tears from her eyes before she joined the others gathered at the door, studiously avoiding Elliot's searching gaze. He was making it very difficult to keep her vow to remain cheerful for the children's sake. Each moment in his company jammed the arrow deeper into her heart.

It reminded her of how lonely it would be when he left.

"Ready?"

Everyone nodded at Noah, eyes glowing with anticipation as he threw open the door and ushered them outside.

They stopped as one on the porch. Rico stomped and snorted puffs of steam in greeting. He was attached to a long sleigh that would easily accommodate them all.

"A sleigh!" Lori cried, her voice muffled by several layers of scarves Marla had wrapped around her head.

There were ooohs and aaahs from the children. Jo grinned happily. Cole couldn't resist a smile. Brett rushed to look inside, exclaiming over the bench seats built into the sides of the sleigh.

"All aboard!" Elliot helped them in one by one, then took a seat beside Natalie. Noah commandeered the reins, and away they went, sliding easily over the freshly fallen snow.

"Where are we going?" Natalie asked over the rush of the wind and snow. She allowed Elliot to take her hand, thinking how bittersweet it was, sitting beside him on her first sleigh ride. Almost as if . . . Natalie shook the thought away.

"You'll find out," came his mysterious reply.

To Natalie's surprise, Noah pulled the sleigh to a stop in front of the mercantile. One glance at Marla sitting opposite her told Natalie that her friend was just as puzzled as she was.

Trying to catch Elliot's eye, Natalie stepped from the sleigh, her gaze drawn to a light in the window next to the mercantile. She frowned, looking once again at Marla, who shrugged.

"Close your eyes," Elliot commanded. When she did, he led her forward.

All around her, she could hear anxious giggles and shushed whispers. Finally, all was quiet. She knew she had stepped into a room because the wind and snow no longer stung her cheeks.

"You can open your eyes now."

It was Elliot again. Perversely Natalie didn't want to. She was deathly afraid of what she would find.

"Natalie . . ."

On a sigh, she lifted her damp lashes. Her mouth fell open.

The room, she realized immediately, was filled with toys. Elegant dolls dressed in the latest fashions, rocking horses she recognized as Brett's excellent work, and dollhouses, literally a dozen dollhouses in various forms of completion strategically placed around the room. One held center stage on a platform.

Natalie turned slowly, catching sight of Marla's amazed expression. So Marla hadn't known, but she could tell by their happy faces that the children had, even Lori. "What is all of this?" Because she suspected Elliot was responsible, she directed her shaky question at him.

"The shop belongs to you, Natalie. Of course, Noah here expects a small rent to be paid every month."

"I don't . . . understand. Why? How?"

"Warren requested a dozen more dollhouses and sent along a substantial advance." Elliot hesitated. "I invested the money instead of giving it to you. This way I had a solid plan to present to Mr. McCormick when I asked him to loan you the money to buy Ivy House."

Natalie's throat was dry. Everyone waited for her reaction, she realized, staring at their silent, expectant faces. "And did he? Loan you the money?"

"Yes." Elliot put his hands in his pockets and came closer. "I paid Carnagie and signed Ivy House over to you." He flashed a quick, anxious grin at her stunned expression. "Now *you're* the one in debt, as you have to pay the bank. Mr. McCormick and I worked out a fair payment plan we think you can handle."

She shook her head, many unanswered questions buzzing in her head. She gestured to the dollhouses. "But how did you . . . *when* did you . . ."

"I think I can answer that," Marla said tartly, but her eyes glowed with love and pride when she looked at her husband. "Remember I told you they'd been disappearing at night? They *weren't* doing inventory, just as I suspected. On the night I followed them, Hickory must have warned them I was coming."

Elliot nodded an affirmative. "And Cole and Brett didn't return to the Hacket farm at night," he added. "They bunked here. The twelve dollhouses Warren requested are finished—shipped, in fact. These are your inventory."

"We put up the cow bells so's we'd know you were comin' up the stairs," Brett said. "We didn't want you to catch us measurin' and cuttin' out the lumber." He jabbed a proud finger at his chest. "The bells was *my* idea."

"Oh." Natalie didn't know what to say. She knew she should be delirious, but she was numb at the moment. So much wonderful news to take in at one time.

She wasn't going to lose the orphanage, and the dollhouses had become the success she'd dreamed about.

Cole touched her sleeve, his young face earnest. "If you don't mind, Natty, we'll stay with the Hackets. They need us." He glanced at his brother, then back to her. "But they said we could work for you—that is, if you want us to."

"As long as we get home in time to do the chores at night," Brett added.

"I'd like to go ahead with my plans to work at the restaurant, too," Jo announced shyly. "But if you don't mind, I'd rather live at Ivy House."

Lori hurled her bundled form at Natalie. "Me, too."

Natalie's head whirled as everyone began to talk at once. Noah led Hickory to one of the rocking horses and settled him into the carved saddle. Elliot took Lori's hand and pointed to the dollhouse on display.

"It's yours. Merry Christmas, Lori."

Tears stung Natalie's eyes. She tore her gaze from the heartwarming sight of Elliot presenting Lori with the dollhouse. Lori's cries of joy and astonishment mingled with the laughter and good wishes.

She felt as if she would suffocate.

Natalie stumbled to the door and slipped outside, dragging in gulps of frigid, cleansing air.

It was all too much: the house, the shop, what they had all done for her. She didn't deserve any of it.

No, that wasn't what was bothering her. She didn't want it. What she wanted she couldn't have, and she was selfish, selfish, selfish. Sobs welled. Frantically, Natalie pushed away from the wall and stumbled through the snow, her skirts tangling around her legs.

She fell facedown in the powdery snow and lay there, gasping, the frigid air searing her lungs.

Elliot. She wanted Elliot. She wanted him more than she wanted Ivy House, more than she wanted her own successful business, and, God forgive her, more than she wanted the children.

Guilt racked her. Her tears mingled with the softly falling snow as she lay there. If only—

"Natalie."

She jumped, rising to her knees, then stumbling to her feet. Elliot stood watching her, his face cloaked by the night. If she couldn't see him, then he couldn't see her, she reasoned, swallowing a telltale hiccup. Wiping at her frozen face, she said, "I can't accept Ivy House."

"Why not?"

"I just can't. I—I don't want the responsibility—"

"Liar." Snow crunched beneath his boots. His hands were surprisingly warm on her face. "You're the most responsible person I know, Natalie. The most warm-hearted, generous, giving woman alive."

A sigh slipped through her lips at his words, but Natalie shored the weak spot. "I don't want your pity, Elliot."

"Pity?" Elliot laughed and pressed his warm lips to hers. When he finally lifted his head, she saw that his eyes gleamed not with pity but with desire.

"Try telling me the truth."

The truth? Natalie began shaking her head. Oh, no, she couldn't tell him the truth.

His mouth crushed onto hers again; his hands slipped beneath her cloak and stroked her chilled flesh until it burned.

"The truth, Natalie," he growled softly, nipping her bottom lip and nuzzling her cold nose. "I've got to know the truth."

She stilled as she caught the barest hint of desperation in his voice. "I'm so ashamed," she whispered. "The truth is . . . the truth is I'm selfish. Ivy House, the shop, the children being happy—it means nothing to me without you."

"Oh, God." His mouth took hers again, this time with unrestrained hunger. "I've missed you—needed you—loved you, and I've been going insane thinking—" He didn't finish, and Natalie didn't care, because when he wasn't talking he was making her very, very happy.

Her heart was singing, her mouth responding.

Elliot loved her.

Elliot *loved* her.

Suddenly, he tore his mouth away and pulled back, staring at her with such a solemn expression she felt a twist of fear.

"Natalie, I've been offered a job at the bank as an investment adviser. It doesn't pay outrageously, but it's a start."

"Elliot, that's wonderful!"

"So you'll marry me?"

Natalie stared at him, absorbing his love, her own

commitment shining in her eyes. "Yes. Yes!"

"Of course, we'll keep Ivy House open," he added.

"Yes."

"And the children will live with us, except for Brett and Cole, of their own choosing. They'll always have a home at Ivy House."

"Of—"

"Perfect, perfect, perfect!"

They whirled around at the sound of Marla's happy cry, followed by her vigorous clapping. She beamed at them as snow fell steadily all around them. "It's about time," she declared.

Elliot and Natalie exchanged an amused glance before succumbing to laughter.

Epilogue

"**O**pen your gift, Marla." Natalie grabbed Elliot's hand and squeezed, excitement turning her cheeks rosy and making her eyes sparkle. "Elliot, take your daughter so that Marla can open her gift."

But Marla wasn't interested in gifts; she was interested in the infant she held in her arms. Hard to imagine that a little less than a year ago, her own daughter had been this tiny. She glanced at the dainty toddler playing with Hickory on the rug before the fire. Lori sat nearby on the sofa, watching them with a relaxed but eagle eye.

In the corner of the parlor stood a huge, ugly Christmas tree decorated with a wild assortment of ornaments. Marla thought about their own perfect little tree and smiled.

Some things never changed.

"Okay. You can have the Ivy princess back, but only for a moment. I want to take advantage while Noel is distracted. She's so jealous of babies." When Elliot had taken his daughter, Marla took the package from Natalie and pulled the ribbon.

Inside lay the music box she had given Natalie many years ago.

Natalie spoke softly, her throat tight with tears. "You said to keep it until I found a home of my own." Her misty gaze lingered on Elliot and her daughter. "It took me a long time to realize that a house isn't a home until you share it with the ones you love."

Marla sniffed and wiped at her tears, meeting Natalie halfway in a fierce hug that made them both grunt. Pulling back, Marla grinned and spat on her hand.

Without hesitation, Natalie did the same.

They pressed their palms together and shook.

"Did you just—did I see—" Elliot sputtered, looking from one to the other as if he couldn't decide which one was more insane.

The women were saved from having to explain their little secret pact as someone knocked on the door.

"I'll get it." Jo sailed in from the kitchen, smoothing the folds of her new dress and moving with a confidence that never failed to make Natalie proud. Jeb followed close behind.

They were to be married in the spring, much to Marla's satisfaction.

A moment later, Jo entered the parlor with a young girl. The girl was dressed in an odd assortment of cast-off clothes and held a bundle protectively in her arms. The momentary silence was broken by a weak, pitiful squeak, followed by a thin squall.

Natalie felt a tingle in her breasts, the same feeling she got when Ivy cried in hunger. Following her instinct, she crossed the floor and took the bundle from the girl, swiftly unwrapping the filthy, damp material.

It was a baby, an infant, and it didn't look much bigger than Ivy. Tears sprang to her eyes as she gazed down at the wizened little face. Tiny arms thrashed as if to condemn the world for this neglect. His lips were nearly blue with cold.

"Your brother?"

The young girl nodded, her eyes full of weary resignation. "Be much obliged if you'll take him off my hands. Can't take proper care of a young'un, an' I heard you did that sort of thing." She stared at the baby as if she were reluctant to take her eyes from him. Her devotion was obvious. "Pa named him William. That was *his* name."

"What happened?" Natalie crooned and rocked the fussy baby in an automatic gesture. She thought her heart would break; the girl standing before her couldn't be more than twelve.

"My ma and pa got caught out in that last big snowstorm. They never came home, so I figured they froze to death." She nodded at the baby. "I fed him goat's milk until the goat died. Well, I'd best git goin'." She wiped her eyes as if embarrassed to be caught crying, oblivious to the streak of dirt she left behind. "You'll take good care of him, won't ya?"

Natalie nodded, the tears clogging her throat, preventing speech. The girl turned to leave, but Jo caught her arm. "You'll stay."

The girl drew herself up proudly. "That ain't necessary. I kin take care of myself."

Jo smiled. "So could I, but I stayed. It's a nice place to live." Before the girl could protest, she added, "Welcome to Ivy House. What name do you go by?"

Everyone held their collective breaths as the girl hesitated and glanced slowly around the room, pausing on each compassionate face. Even Noel and Hickory had stopped their play to stare at the stranger. When the girl spotted the refreshment table piled high with cakes and cookies, she licked her lips. "Dorothy. My name is Dorothy."

Natalie turned with the babe in her arms and met Elliot's gaze across the room. They exchanged a long, loving glance that needed no words. With a slight nod, Elliot placed Ivy into Marla's waiting arms.

"I'll get dry clothing," he said, his voice curiously gruff.

"I'll heat some water," Jo flung over her shoulder, taking charge. "Jeb, would you mind starting a fire in the boys' old bedroom? Lori, bring some extra blankets. Dorothy looks cold. Oh, and she might want a bite of something to eat."

" 'Bout froze my a—butt off out there," Dorothy agreed, turning her neck to take another look at her brother. He was sucking greedily at Natalie's milk-laden breast, his hands clutching her softness, his hungry grunts bringing fresh tears to Dorothy's eyes.

Letting out a long, shuddering sigh of relief, Dorothy turned away, satisfied that William was in capable hands. She followed Jo upstairs, gaping at the strange sight of the cow bells laced along the banister.

The painful tightness in her chest began to ease with each step she took.

Ivy House.

She rubbed at her eyes and savored the name.

Her prayers had been answered.